THE**SOMEDAY**GIRL

THE GIRL DUET

PART ONE

JULIE JOHNSON

To every girl who knows she's worth more than a Monday.

"I LOVED SOMETHING I MADE UP... I MADE A PRETTY SUIT OF CLOTHES AND I FELL IN LOVE WITH IT. AND WHEN HE CAME RIDING ALONG, SO HANDSOME, SO DIFFERENT, I PUT THAT SUIT ON HIM AND MADE HIM WEAR IT WHETHER IT FITTED HIM OR NOT.

AND I WOULDN'T SEE WHAT HE REALLY WAS.

I KEPT ON LOVING THE PRETTY CLOTHES —
AND NOT HIM AT ALL."

MARGARET MITCHELL, *Gone with the Wind*

PROLOGUE

Does my brokenness offend you?

Are my words too sharp? My shadows too deep? My pain too raw?

Are you haunted by my damage the same way I'm haunted by the memory of a man whose taste I can no longer conjure on my lips, whose handprints have long since faded from my skin? Does my misery make you uncomfortable, like a paper-cut on a knuckle that re-opens each time you flex your finger?

I'd apologize, but I really don't give a shit.

For a month, I have been trying. Trying to breathe. Trying to make it through the day without my chest aching with pain that will not end, without my eyes stinging with tears I refuse to let fall.

For four unrepentant weeks, I have attempted to piece myself slowly back together.

But there is no fixing me. Not really.

Putting my broken fragments back into place is like trying to reattach petals to a flower after you've ripped them off one-by-one and crushed them into pulp between your fingertips. A childhood game of chance gone horribly awry.

He loves me.
He loves me not.
He loves me.
He loves me not.

There is no returning to the girl I used to be. She is gone. Ended. Obliterated. She has faded out like a ghost. She has ceased to exist and become something entirely unrecognizable.

Because *she* is now a *we*.

I have never been more alone in my life than this past month. And yet, I am *never* alone. Not anymore. Much as I might like to deny it, I am altered on a molecular level. There is a tiny, unseen heartbeat pumping in tandem with mine, somewhere far below the surface of my skin where no one else can see. I cannot hear it, cannot feel it, but I know it's there. And no matter how often I press useless hands against my stomach, wishing to wake from a nightmare of my own making, I cannot change my reality. I cannot ignore the flutter of life growing ever stronger inside me. A war drum, thud-thud-thudding like a steadily-approaching line of enemy fighters on the battlefield.

Katharine Firestone: hot freaking mess.
...and... unfathomably, unpredictably... a mother?

Fear clenches me in a stranglehold at the mere thought.

I am unprepared.

I am unequipped.

A wreck of a girl, raised by a wretch of a woman. Reared with cold calculation in lieu of love.

How could I possibly carry a child? How could someone like me foster a human being into anything resembling normalcy or well-adjusted adolescence?

I will fail at this, just as I have failed at every other turn in my life.

I will break this child, just like I broke *him*.

After all, it's the only thing I know how to do with any kind of precision.

Smash. Wreck. Destroy.

Maple syrup leaking across a marble floor.
Ice in eyes made for heat and humor.
I am fire.

I am chaos.

I am a force of destruction, down to my marrow.

Please hear me when I tell you I am not intentionally heartless. I simply do not know my own heart. Do not recognize its true desires or understand its motivations. This senseless organ inside my chest is a stranger to me. I do not know which path it will lead me down, which star-chart it will steer me by. I haven't allowed myself to think that far ahead yet. Haven't allowed myself to feel anything except numb disbelief and clammy-palmed terror.

My hands find my stomach again. I press down hard enough to feel my lowest row of ribs jut through the skin like dull knives, carving me from within. Cleaving me in two. Tearing me to shreds of indecision.

A girl divided.

I am filled with contrary desires. Brimming over with conflicting interests. Torn, in every facet of life, in opposite directions between which I cannot choose.

I do not know if I want this child. But I do know one thing for certain.

This child will not want me.

CHAPTER ONE

"ARE YOU SURE YOU'RE READY FOR ME, HONEY?"
- The lady shaping my eyebrows with hot wax strips.

I stare at the dark red polish coating my fingernails as the SUV cuts a slow path through downtown Los Angeles. There is not a single chip marring their glossy surfaces. In this moment of undeniable anxiety, with my stomach clenched into a fist and my back rigid with tension, the girl I used to be two insufferable months ago would've picked at them until they lay like bloody petals on the sleek leather seat.

Now, even if I wanted to pick them off, I couldn't. The cheap, drugstore-brand polish of my past has been replaced by professional-grade lacquer, applied by a petite Vietnamese woman who came directly to my new house in the Palisades with a small cart of subtle shades in tow. My days of lukewarm pedicure baths and questionably-cleaned cuticle cutters are over... Along with almost every other recognizable facet of my existence.

Here lies Katharine Firestone, of the mussed hair and ripped cut-off shorts, of the day-old mascara and inappropriate drinking binges, who hurled headfirst through life hungover and heartbroken.

May she rest in peace.

The new Katharine Firestone is poised. Her hair is never messy. She never leaves the house still wearing makeup from the night before because she knows, beyond a shadow of a doubt, that the paparazzi's prying eyes are never far away. She is calm and collected. Her clothes bear designer labels. Her shoes cost more than the monthly rent of the crappy condo where she used to reside.

She is a stranger to me.

The weight of someone's stare makes me look up. My gaze finds the icy blue irises of my security detail and driver, Kent Masters, in the rearview mirror. I see his hands tighten ever-so-slightly on the steering wheel as he scans the deep shadows beneath my eyes, the haunted look in their depths that I can't quite mask, no matter how much expensive makeup coats my lids and lashes.

"Feeling all right today, Miss Firestone?"

I sigh. "Masters, how many times do I have to insist you call me Kat before you listen?"

"At least one more."

"You're dating my best friend," I point out. "Doesn't that make us friends by association?"

"Depends. You give all your other friends a three-figure salary and health benefits?"

My brows pull into a scowl.

"No," I mutter.

"Thought so."

His mouth twists as he merges left and turns onto a one-way street, heading toward Hollywood Boulevard. Traffic is even thicker than usual. It's the week before Christmas; shoppers are out in force, especially in this glitzy part of town. Tourists with time off for the holidays are pouring into the City of Angels — they crowd into double-decker buses and hang out the windows with cameras fixed permanently to their noses as they roll down famous palm-tree lined avenues, taking pictures of vibrant street art without ever stopping to look at it in person. Trading actual experiences for Instagram likes from followers they will never meet.

When they reach the movie studios, they will disembark and fork over a thick wad of hard-earned cash for the privilege of taking a mind-numbing tour of a vacant soundstage — likely led by an annoying guide who cracks corny jokes and speaks a bit too emphatically

5

into her microphone headset as she shows them a quote-unquote *genuine piece of Hollywood* before they shuffle back to their lives in some benign small town where nothing scandalous ever happens.

How was LA? their friends will ask.

It was okay, they'll reply. *But I don't see what all the fuss is about.*

I stare out my tinted window as we pass by a particularly vibrant strip of shops. The neon signs and congested sidewalks look more like something out of a Salvador Dali painting than a modern metropolis. If I crane my neck, I can see the looming shape of warehouses in the distance. I swallow to dislodge the growing lump in my throat. My perfectly painted fingernails dig small crescents into my kneecaps.

We're nearly there.

I refocus on Masters and try another tactic. "You know, I pay your salary — you're required to listen to me. That means you have to call me by my first name if I want you to."

"Actually, I'm required to protect you, not listen to you," he corrects in a bland tone. "And you're avoiding my question."

"Oh, did you ask something?" My voice is innocent.

"How are you feeling today?"

"Just fine."

His eyes find mine once more, holding my stare in a challenge.

"I'm fine, Masters." I swallow again, but it does nothing to clear the thick dollop of anxiety resting on the back of my tongue like peanut butter. "Really. You and Harper can't keep treating me like I'm made of glass. I won't fall apart when I see— when I see—"

Grayson.

Wyatt.

Together.

In the same room.

For the first time since...

6

I clear my throat so hard it hurts. "When I'm back on set," I finish weakly.

"Uh huh." Masters' eyes crinkle slightly. "Whatever you say, Miss Firestone."

I glance out the car window and feel my heart stutter inside my chest as I recognize the familiar sight of AXC Studios' wrought-iron gates.

We're here.

Masters hands over his identification to the man guarding the back gate and, before I have time to prepare myself, we're pulling into a reserved spot by Stage 13, where we filmed the first part of *Uncharted* six weeks ago, before flying to Hawaii to shoot the rest on-location. I stare at the imposing silhouette of the warehouse, looming in the bright midday sunshine, and try desperately to remember all the sensible advice Harper has given me over the past month.

It's useless. All her pragmatic suggestions and practical tips have vanished from my brain like vapor.

"Miss Firestone."

Masters' voice snaps me out of my stupor. I glance right and find he's already shut off the SUV and rounded to my side. He's holding open my door, waiting for me to climb out.

His eyes soften when they meet mine. "Just breathe. You'll be fine."

Nodding, I haul air into my lungs, steady my shoulders, and climb out. He closes the door behind me and comes to a stop at my side, a mountain of a man towering over me.

"Harper's doing makeup for that new teen werewolf show next door, so she's not far." His elbow grazes mine in a gentle nudge. "And if you need me, you know I'm just a call away. Harper programmed my number into your new phone as *Boy Toy* but I changed it back."

I snort. "Thanks, Masters."

"I mean it. Say the word and we'll leave. No questions asked."

"I can't just leave. It's my first day back. There's the photoshoot for the promotional posters, then later we're meeting at Sloan's place to go over the press tour itinerary for the next few weeks..."

"They need you more than you need them." His stare is unwavering. "If you can't handle this, there's no shame in admitting it. You're allowed to ask for help. Entitled to it, even."

"I'm not a quitter, Masters."

"Never said you were, Miss Firestone. But even badasses need to take a break, sometimes."

"I'm a badass, huh?"

He nods solemnly. "You are in my book."

My lips tug up into a smile he doesn't return. I take in his strong jawline, the aristocratic slope of his nose, the blond, short-buzzed crop of his hair. Six foot five, pure muscle in his ever-present black suit. If anyone here is a badass, it's Masters. And yet, after a month of him watching out for me — analyzing the security of my new home in the Palisades, organizing safety parameters for upcoming public appearances, making sure Harper and I are always completely protected every time we go farther than the terrace in my backyard — I know he definitely has a softer side. He just doesn't like to show it.

Ever.

"You're a big softie, you know that right, Masters?"

He still doesn't smile, but there's humor lurking in his eyes. "I don't know what you're talking about, Miss Firestone. Now, come on. You're already running late."

"Maybe if you didn't drive like such a geriatric..."

"Motor vehicle accidents are the fourth leading cause of death in the United States."

"Cheerful."

"Statistically accurate." He folds his arms across his chest. "Los Angeles was ranked sixth for traffic accidents last year, out of every major city in this country."

My eyes narrow. "Are you trying to bore me to death so I'll go inside?"

"Depends. Is it working?"

"Don't make me hurt you."

"That would be counterproductive, considering you're paying me to protect you," he deadpans.

I roll my eyes, straighten my spine, and stride toward the side door, trying not to trip over my low-heeled boots or tug on the hem of my dress or fidget with the cloth-wrapped buttons of the thin white blazer Harper picked out for me last night. Examining my reflection in the mirror, she assured me this outfit is *subtly sexy without trying too hard.* I nodded and thanked her and bit back the snappy retort on the tip of my tongue.

We both know the truth — no savvy outfit choice will make an iota of difference. Wearing a pretty power-blazer doesn't equate holding emotional sway over someone. Not even if that *someone* is you.

My pulse roars between my ears as I enter the hangar, Masters following close on my heels. It's a massive space — at least 10,000 square feet. The soaring ceilings remind me of a circus tent, crisscrossed by wires, lighting equipment, bird's eye cameras, and narrow black walkways where tech crew scramble around like acrobats during active filming. Today, the catwalks are abandoned, as is the remainder of the set. I walk by the space where we filmed the airport terminal scenes, hurry past the plane cabin where we shot the in-flight crash sequence, then wander around the shallow pool where Grayson and I spent two days treading water as a mid-sized jetliner smoked and shook and sank into the waves behind us at the prop-master's command.

It's unsettling to be back here — like returning to high school after you've graduated, seeing the halls empty, the teachers aged. It all looks somehow smaller, less intimidating than it was two months ago when I first walked through these doors.

Yet, the space isn't different; it's me, that's changed.

Still, I can't help the tiny embers of excitement that flare to life as I make my way across the warehouse.

It's the first emotion besides terror or guilt or regret I've felt in so long, I almost don't recognize it at first. But the closer I creep to the massive green screens across the lot where a small group of people are clustered, the more undeniable the sensation becomes.

My breath catches in my throat as my eyes scan the crowd. Searching. Seeking.

A blond Viking with eyes like the sky.

A messy-haired heartbreaker with forests for irises.

I don't see either of them as my gaze sweeps the dozen or so people gathered, setting up cameras and arranging a small-scale set for the photoshoot. My eyes flicker over Trey's familiar form, his blocky black glasses and smooth caramel skin recognizable even from a distance. They flit over Annabelle, her buxom build and popped hip unmistakable as she listens intently to the man gesticulating wildly — a slim, middle-aged figure with wire-rimmed glasses and an intensity that makes his production assistants lean in, rapt and ready for any instructions he might give.

Sloan Stanhope.

Three-time Academy Award winner. Yoga lover. Master cleanser. Legendary director.

As I approach, he turns and spots me.

"Kat! You're here!" He claps his hands together in a gesture of excitement that neither of his dour-faced PAs imitate. His hands land on my shoulders and his eyes grow concerned behind his lenses as he takes me in. "You're pale. And much too thin. Are you feeling all right?"

"Of course," I lie in as bright a tone as I can manage. "I'm just ready to get back to work."

"That's my girl!" He releases me and turns to stare at the green screen soaring behind us. The props are minimal: a few driftwood logs are scattered on a thin layer of white sand; a lone palm tree sits to the left, its branches swaying in simulated wind piped through giant, freestanding fans. Most of the background will be computer generated, just as most of my body will be photoshopped — made thinner, sleeker, sexier for the sake of selling movie tickets. By the time they're done, the lead actress in posters on the back of bathroom stalls and billboards advertising *Uncharted* won't look a damn thing like I do in reality.

"Great to be back, isn't it?" Sloan asks. "After we get you and Dunn into costume, we'll take a series of shots in different poses. We need to get these images to our marketing staff as soon as possible, now that the film is wrapped and ready to go."

"You've finished editing, then?" I ask. "You and Wy—" My words stammer into silence. I'm not sure why it's so hard to say his damn name. "You and— and— *Wyatt* are done in post-production?"

"Nearly." Sloan smiles, blissfully unaware of my unease. "It's coming together marvelously. I have some exciting news about the next few weeks — very exciting. I think you'll be pleased." He pumps his fist through the air, like a train conductor pulling an invisible horn. "Full steam ahead, Firestone!"

"Does that mean you've scheduled an official premiere date, then?"

He shrugs vaguely. "We'll talk more about it once everyone is together, at the meeting later. I don't want you getting distracted before the shoot. And I'd like Dunn and Hastings to be there, when I tell you — I've got a bottle of champagne set aside to toast the occasion."

Nerves shoot through me. "Where is he?"

"Who, Hastings?" Sloan asks, eyebrows raised. "Or Dunn?"

Isn't that the question of the year.

I evade a direct answer, shrugging nonchalantly. "Either. Both."

Sloan's mouth opens to answer me, but it's not his voice that reaches my ears.

"I'm here."

His words hit me hard. A punch to the back of the neck, rattling my spinal column, frying my nerve endings. I should be used to it by now, but I'm not. I don't think I'll ever get used to the effect of Grayson Dunn's smug, sultry tones on my body as long as I live.

"Dunn!" Sloan calls, looking past me with a grin. "Good to see you."

"You too, Sloan."

I feel him hovering behind me, waiting for me to turn and greet him. Waiting for me to acknowledge his arrival. But I cannot move. Cannot breathe. Cannot do anything except relive the memory of the last time I saw him, at three in the morning in the doorway of his Malibu mansion, with mussed hair and sleepy eyes and anguishing apathy toward my slow-breaking heart.

I can't be the guy you fell for in Hawaii. Maybe someday, I'll feel differently. Maybe someday, I'll be ready.

I bite my bottom lip, craving the distraction of physical pain as the conversation plays out in my head.

No, Grayson. Someday is an empty promise. Someday is a lie you tell girls you blow off, to make yourself feel a little better.

Futilely, I pull in a breath, hoping it might steady me.

Kat... Wait...

My hands curl into fists.

I can't wait for you, Grayson — I'll be waiting forever.

Sloan has turned away to scold Trey and Annabelle about something. There's only me and the man at my back — the man who built me up and then broke me into so many pieces I no longer recognized myself afterward.

Childhood crush. Co-star. Callous ex-lover.

Grayson Dunn defies definition.

"Kat."

One word.

It vibrates every hair on my neck until they each stand upright, then slithers down my spine like a living thing and pools inside my stomach.

I feel him take a step closer.

He cannot touch me, or I will come apart at the seams.

I turn, hands thrown out like a shield so he won't get any nearer. Five feet apart, frozen in place, our eyes lock instantly — green and blue colliding in a starburst. The air goes electric. The voices at my back go mute. We don't move or speak or do anything except stand there, searching for words we cannot fathom.

It hurts to see him. To see that he is just as beautiful as I remember — perhaps even more so. To feel the crippling ache of loss that's gnawed at my stomach like a canker since we left Hawaii. Since the day I realized I was mourning something that was never mine to begin with.

His mouth opens, closes, and opens again, but no sound escapes.

There is nothing to say.

There is everything to say.

I hate you.

I miss you.

I hate that I miss you.

Six weeks of distance. Six weeks of space. Six weeks of letting heartbreak run its course until he was out of my head, erased from my bloodstream... and yet, in this moment, without him ever touching me, I feel a sharp tug inside my chest, as though he's holding a thread wrapped directly around the valves of my heart and reeling me in, heedless of the damage he's doing to my most fragile organ.

Killing me for sport.

"It's good to see you," he says in an unreadable voice. "You— you look great, Kat."

Is that really the best you can come up with, Grayson?

My teeth sink into my lip again to keep from saying something I'll regret. I try to remember Harper's advice.

You are Katharine Motherfucking Firestone.

Don't let him see how much he hurt you.

Don't give him the satisfaction, honey.

He runs a hand through his hair in a familiar

13

gesture. "Listen, I should've— I was going to call you after— after—" He's uncharacteristically nervous. Two months ago, it would've made me cartwheel.

I have the power to make Grayson Dunn stutter, to leave the Sexiest Man Alive at a loss for words.

Now, I only feel numb as I watch him searching for excuses. Looking for a way to spin his absence into a pardonable offense. Always, always, always attempting to manipulate the situation to his best advantage with the least amount of effort.

"I don't— It just—" He sighs. Shrugs. Smiles endearingly. "I thought maybe you'd reach out to me."

Of course you did, Grayson.

I stare at him in silence.

His eyes scan my face, searching for a crack in my impenetrable indifference.

"*Kat,*" he murmurs, in that voice that used to incinerate all my careful defenses down to ash.

I am a stone. I will not move. I will not speak. I will not break.

"I should've called. I get that." His Adam's apple bobs. "The past few weeks have just been a nightmare of—"

"You know what?" I say brightly, smiling like I've just snorted a line of Prozac. "We don't have to do this."

He flinches. "Do what?"

"*This.* This polite, awkward, talking-around-each-other's-feelings thing." I shrug, as though his presence three feet away isn't slowly leeching all the strength from my bones. "In Hawaii... We had a moment. That moment is over. Let's just get through this press tour like professionals and then go our separate ways. No harm, no foul."

He blinks at me like I'm speaking another language.

"I'm going to change into costume," I inform him breezily. "Good to see you, Dunn."

With that, I turn on a heel and leave him in the dust, like he's no more than a stranger. An acquaintance.

14

Certainly not a man who has traced his fingertips over every secret part of me, who once fucked me senseless beneath a waterfall, and beat me at chess on a weatherbeaten board, and danced with me in solar-system socks around a hotel room until we were breathless with laughter.

No matter how much time passes, it's never easy to run into someone who once owned a piece of your heart. We put past loves into boxes in the dark, dusty corners of our memories, shove them out of sight and call ourselves *healed*, but that doesn't make it any simpler when they inevitably cross our paths again. When you're standing in their space, breathing their air, staring at features you once memorized in the dim light beneath bedsheets, wanting simultaneously to kiss their lips and kick them squarely between the legs... it's hard to keep the lid on that box firmly shut.

I take a deep breath and keep walking.

It's over.

I survived.

I saw him and I didn't fall apart.

I feel his eyes on me as I cross to the door that leads to the dressing rooms. The smile on my face is a forced, frozen grimace, but I must admit, it feels good to be the one walking away from him this time around. To let him watch *me* vanish for a change.

My feet move on autopilot as I make my way down the hall and slip inside my dressing room. Mechanically, I strip off my clothes and change into costume. Once a gauzy blue sundress, the garment has been altered to appear shipwrecked — stained by sun and sand, ripped at the bodice to reveal just enough cleavage to draw the eyes of male movie-goers. Someone in the costume department probably spent days calculating the optimal amount of side-boob to appeal to the masses.

I've just zipped the tattered dress closed when the door behind me swings inward. I suck in a startled breath, half-expecting to see Grayson standing there, but relax

15

when my eyes take in the sight of a familiar, feminine silhouette.

"Hiding out in here?" Harper asks, flipping a lock of lavender hair over her shoulder as she strides into the room, rolling a small cart of makeup and hair products behind her.

"No." My voice is defensive. "I'm just getting ready for the photoshoot."

She pins me with a skeptical look.

I plant my hands on my hips. "Don't look at me like that. I'm fine. Totally fine. Grayson Dunn has no effect on me anymore."

"You mean Giant Douchebag?"

"Harper."

"Just calling it like I see it, honey."

I roll my eyes and collapse into the chair in front of my vanity mirror with a huff. She grabs the curling iron out of her bag, plugs it in to heat up, then walks over to stand behind me. When her eyes meet mine in the reflection, I see a look of deep concern in their depths.

"Stop looking at me like that!"

"Like what?"

"Like you're about to break out the straight-jacket." My voice gets quiet. "It makes me feel pathetic."

"You aren't pathetic. But that doesn't mean I'm not worried about you."

"I'm not going to fall apart again. I'm *fine*."

"You've said the word *fine* so many times in the past two minutes, it doesn't even sound like a word anymore."

I scowl.

"Don't do that — you'll smudge your mascara." Her hands land on my shoulders. "It's okay, you know. If you aren't *fine* with all of this. With... him."

"But I am! He said hello. I said hello. It was... *civil*. Cordial, even." I swallow hard. "I can do this. I *will* do this. I will make it through this day."

"I know you will, honey." She extracts a hairbrush from the bottom of her bag. "I know you've been avoiding the tabloids, not going online to read the news, but I really think I should tell you about—"

"I don't want to know."

"But, Kat, they're saying Grayson and Helena—"

I grit my teeth. "I. Don't. Want. To. Know."

"You're going to find out eventually. Maybe if we talked about it now, you'd be more prepared to deal with it when—"

I cut her off. "Why do you insist on talking things to death? Can't you just be a normal human, who avoids discussing your feelings by pushing them deep under an emotional rug until you either explode or self-destruct by drinking your way to the bottom of a bottle of vodka?"

"Because that's worked out *so* well for you in the past, right?" she drawls sarcastically.

I'd laugh, but I don't think she intended it as a joke.

"Harper. Just let it go, okay?"

She brushes my hair in long strokes, saying nothing, but her lips are twisted in frustration. For weeks, she's been trying to prod me with information about my co-star and his ex-girlfriend, Helena Putnam — the gorgeous model-turned-actress who was originally supposed to play Violet in the movie, whose role I took over when she self-destructed. Once, I'd mocked her — I couldn't believe she'd be stupid enough to fall for Grayson and jeopardize her career. Couldn't believe she'd risk the role of a lifetime over a guy...

Let's just say, the fall from my high horse hurt like a bitch.

"Harper."

My best friend glances up at me, mouth pursed, and mutters a terse, "*What?*"

"You know the tabloids are full of crap. Almost everything they print is pure fiction. And... if Grayson has something to say to me, if he finally wants to offer some kind of explanation for his legendary douchebaggery... Well, he can tell me to my face. I'm not going to read about it in some gossip rag. Can't you understand that?"

She lets out a slow breath. "Yeah. I guess I can."

"He's taken up too much of my time, too much of my heart, too much of my headspace. I'm not going to give him any more pieces of myself — not when he gives nothing back in return except misery and self-doubt. *I can't.* I've given up too much already."

She nods, but says nothing. For a long while, we sit in silence and eventually I feel myself relax under her slow, methodical brush strokes. She's halfway through curling my hair into perfect beachy waves when she finally breaks the quiet.

"I haven't seen Wyatt in forever. Not since the night of the cast party."

My pulse kicks into overdrive at just the mention of his name. I say nothing, so Harper keeps talking.

"He hasn't even come to see your new house, right? Something must be going on with him. Do you think he's dating someone new?"

A dagger of pain shoots into my heart. Ignoring the ache, I fidget silently in my seat.

Harper sighs. "All I'm saying is, it's weird. We went from seeing him *every single day* in Hawaii to not seeing him at all. And that man *loves* to boss you around. He can't resist sticking his big, golden-haired head where it doesn't belong. He has a total savior complex. And yet... he hasn't been around in..." Her nose scrunches. "What, like, six weeks? It's weird. I think it's weird. Don't you?"

I make a noncommittal *mmmm* noise because I can't seem to form words. My throat is clogged with secrets I cannot voice.

About Wyatt.
About the night we shared.
About the stick I peed on last week.
About the prospect that I'm carrying a child.
About the reality that I'm not sure who fathered it....

18

Harper doesn't know I slept with Wyatt, or about the baby. No one does. Maybe because, if I say it out loud, I'll be forced to admit that it's really happening... and forced to make some decisions I'm not yet ready to face.

I'm not the kind of girl who keeps secrets from her best friend — or at least, I didn't used to be. Typically, I'm an open book. No filter. Over the years, Harper and I have discussed everything from politics to periods, from art to anal sex, and yet... this is different. The thought of telling her what I did... of admitting that I wrecked my relationship with the best man I've ever known... my Viking... my protector... my one source of sunlight in the midst of all the shadows I carry around like a cloak...

I can't do it.

I can barely stomach the memory of what I did, let alone say the words out loud. The shame of it is eating me alive.

"I just miss the big goon, that's all. I tried calling him a few days ago, but he didn't call me back." Harper shakes her head in frustration. "I know he's busy in post-production, and that we'll probably see him more often now, with the press tour starting up and the premiere approaching... but *still*. He could've at least called me back."

"Mmmm," I murmur.

"Have you heard from him? I'm sure he'd never ignore *you*..."

You might be surprised, Harper...

I think about the calls that have gone unanswered over the past month, the text messages I've sent sporadically in the small hours of the night, all with no reply.

Please call me back.

Please let me explain.

Please, Wyatt.

I remember the look in his blue eyes, usually so full of light, glittering instead with ice and furious incomprehension. I replay the last words he spoke to me, when he caught me sneaking out his front door, still stunned by the shocking intimacy of our drunken night together.

Just go. Just get out. I don't want to listen to you. Frankly, I can't even look at you.

He's made it pretty clear he doesn't want to see me. Doesn't want to hear from me.

And I don't blame him.

I offer nothing more than misery.

"You agree that it's weird, right?" Harper asks, curling the last section of my hair. "For him to just disappear on us with no reason..." She pauses, eyes narrowing. "Unless there *is* a reason..."

I blink innocently, keeping my expression blank.

"...nothing happened between you two, did it? You didn't have a fight, or something?"

I don't answer.

She tugs sharply on a strand of hair to get my attention. "Hello? Did you hear me?"

"Sorry. Maybe my coffee hasn't kicked in yet." I take a deep breath. "I haven't seen him in forever either. Anyway, is my hair done? It looks like it's done, and I should really be getting back on set, so..." Avoiding her gaze, I push to my feet.

She watches me with narrowed eyes. "What's wrong with you?"

"Nothing."

My bare toes press against the cold tile, grounding me.

"Katharine Firestone, are you lying to me right now?"

"Harper, I don't have time for this. They're waiting for me on set."

"Oh my god!" Her jaw drops open. "Something happened between you and Wyatt!"

"No."

"Something happened and you're *lying* about it!"

20

"I am not," I lie.

"You just did that weird head-tilt thing! You only do that when you're nervous that I'm about to catch you in a lie."

"Maybe I'm just nervous about spending the day pressed up-close-and-personal against the man who broke my heart."

She considers that for about a nanosecond. "Nope. That's not it."

"Harper." I start walking toward the door. "You're being a crazy person right now."

"I don't give a shit." She grabs my arm like a vise and halts me in my tracks. "What happened with Wyatt? And why are you so determined to hide it from me?"

Getting her to abandon this course of conversation is about as likely as convincing a junkyard dog to relinquish a raw filet mignon. I let out a sigh of surrender.

"I haven't been hiding it from you, Harper. I've been..." I press my eyes closed. When I speak, my voice is so soft it sounds like a stranger's — someone broken beyond repair. "It hurts me to talk about it this, okay? Even with you. It hurts just to *think* about it."

"But—"

"No. *No.* If I try to tell you what happened right now, I'll fall apart." My eyes crack open to meet hers. I hope she can recognize the sincerity in my gaze. "I cannot afford to fall apart today. It's taking all my strength just to hold myself together enough to make it through this photoshoot. So... please. Let me get through this. Afterward, I'll tell you everything. I promise."

I think she's going to bulldoze my excuses and demand answers, pushing me for more details despite my pleas, but apparently I don't know my best friend as well as I thought I did because she doesn't say another word. Before I can brace myself, she's hauled me into a hug so tight it makes my ribs ache.

"Harper—"

"Just shut up, okay?" she whispers into my hair. "Shut up and let me hug my best friend. Because, seriously, she needs a freaking hug right now. Even if she hates them."

I press my lips closed. My eyes are pricking with tears.

"And don't you dare start crying," she orders gruffly. "I just got your makeup perfect"

"Cow."

"Mule."

"Bitch."

"Priss."

We both laugh, still hugging tightly.

We stand like that for a long time. Too long. For once, I don't shrug off her affection or fight her embrace. I simply let her strength flow into me. And for the first time in over a month, I think that maybe, just maybe, I might not be entirely alone.

CHAPTER TWO

"Just fuck me up."
- *A caffeine-addict placing an order with the barista.*

"Come on, people! This is a romance, not a war drama. I need *passion*. I need *chemistry*. I need you to *move close enough together that we don't need a wide-angle lens to capture you both in the frame...*" Sloan's frustrated command is nearly drowned out by the mechanical whirr of the wind-machines.

I sigh and shuffle a step closer to Grayson. He quirks a sardonic brow, amused by my reluctance to get near to him.

"Kat—"

"Just shut up, okay?" I grit my teeth and take another step. "I know you're overly fond of the sound of your own voice, but this will be a whole lot easier if we don't speak."

His green eyes flash in challenge. "Fine by me."

"Great," I snap.

"I've always thought actions speak louder anyway, kitten."

I open my mouth to retort, but I don't get the chance.

His hands fly out and land on my hips. Before I can protest, he hauls me hard up against his bare-chested body. I squeak in surprise as the force of our collision causes the wind to whoosh from my lungs. My breasts flatten against his firm chest muscles. He doesn't wait for permission; he certainly doesn't ask for it. Without an ounce of hesitation, his hands slide from my hips around to the small of my back, his long fingers skimming the top of my ass through the thin dress, exerting enough pressure to plaster me against him. It's a carnal grip. Proprietary. Like he owns me, regardless of whether I want him to or not.

It pisses me off.

It turns me on.

Grayson, in a nutshell.

"Don't need words for this, do I?" he mutters, grinding his hips into mine. My cheeks heat when I feel the length of his erection through the thin, shredded costume shorts he's wearing. It calls to mind memories of waterfalls and solar systems and other things far better left forgotten.

"That's better!" Sloan calls. "But let's leave a *little* something to the imagination, shall we? We want them to actually pay to see the good stuff..."

"You heard him. Back off," I hiss, pushing at Grayson's shoulders until he eases up a bit. He chuckles lowly as his hands come unglued from cupping my ass cheeks, moving up to rest on my hips in a slightly less erotic position. "Don't do that again, Dunn."

"Why?" His voice is a sensual murmur. "Is it making you miss me?"

I snort. "Hardly."

"Reminding you how good we were together?"

"We were never together. And it was never good."

"You're right." His eyes find mine, an infinite emerald pool of lust. "We were fucking mind-blowing."

My throat is dry. My palms are sweating. I look away, because I can't look at him anymore, and find myself the subject of Annabelle's intense glare. Apparently, I wasn't the only one left heartsick over Grayson when we flew home from Hawaii. Her brown eyes are narrowed on our interlocked bodies in a stare so lethal, I'm surprised the clipboard in her hands doesn't burst into flames.

I quickly shift my gaze to the left, past Trey — who is trading flirtatious glances with one of the cameramen

— over Harper, who's hovering on the sidelines with a look of worry twisting her features, and finally to Sloan, who's making yet another adjustment to his camera lens. I try to ignore the Viking-shaped hole in the crowd. Try to pretend his absence doesn't make my stomach turn to lead inside my gut.

He didn't show.

"Can we get this over with?" I call, a touch of desperation in my tone.

Grayson chuckles again, the bastard.

Sloan is adjusting the camera's aperture. "Yes, yes, I'm almost ready... There, that should do it!" He glances up from behind the lens and cocks his head. "Okay, Kat, I want you to pivot your body slightly to the left. Yes, just like that. Now, reach your hand up and cradle it against Grayson's chest, just over his heart. Yes, that looks good." His eyes track the movement of my body as I follow his instructions, an unwilling marionette on strings I cannot control. "Now, Grayson, move your right hand down and rest it on Kat's hip. And widen your stance a bit. No, not like that — that makes you look constipated."

A giggle-snort pops from my mouth.

Grayson pinches the flesh of my hip in retaliation.

I flinch in sudden pain and stomp my bare heel onto the arch of his foot.

He only chuckles.

Where are my curb-stomping boots when I need them?

"Angle your right foot back slightly, Dunn," Sloan calls. "Right, that's better."

After nearly ten minutes of minuscule body adjustments, Sloan finally starts snapping photos. He switches lenses several times, barking orders at the tech staff whenever he needs the overhead lighting changed or the wind-fan speed adjusted. Harper and Cassie, the other on-set stylist, dart back and forth between takes, blotting our sweaty foreheads with white sponges, reapplying setting powder to keep our makeup from sliding off as we bake beneath the bright spotlights like buckets of fried chicken at a fast food restaurant.

The shoot takes a small eternity.

Changing positions every few moments, our hands and bodies brush constantly as we pose first one way, then another, my pulse pounding faster and faster as the minutes tick by in his arms. Much as I'd like to pretend otherwise, I'm not entirely immune to the fact that Grayson Dunn is insanely hot. My mind and my heart know that he's a total asshole; my hormones don't seem to give a shit.

"Dunn, can we try one with you holding Kat in your arms?" Sloan asks, because apparently he feels the need to take my torture to new heights. Literally.

Up I go — Grayson's hands beneath my knees, my arms around his neck, like a bride being carried across a threshold. I focus on the cameras, trying to channel Violet, my character, and tune out my own conflicting emotions. The problem is, I'm not sure I can discern the difference between acting and reality anymore.

Beck.

Grayson.

Violet.

Kat.

It's all tangled up inside my head.

I feel desire stirring in my veins, laced thick with a dose of self-loathing and a strong helping of anger. At him. At this situation. But mainly at myself.

Surely you are not this foolish.

Surely, you are not still vulnerable to him after everything he's done.

"That's great!" Sloan calls. "One more pose and we should be finished."

Grayson sets me back on my feet and I take a hurried step away from him, hauling a relieved breath into my lungs as soon as we break contact. I feel overheated, overwrought by this entire experience. Thankfully, before I can keel over, Harper appears and silently passes me a bottle of water. Her expression reveals she's more worried about my wellbeing than ever.

"Are you okay?" she whispers, voice hushed so no one else can hear.

"Nope," I clip shortly, chugging down the water.

"It's almost over." With a reassuring squeeze of my hand, she flies back to the sidelines so Sloan can capture our final pose. I glance at Grayson as I walk to the center of the set, skirting around a large driftwood log, my bare toes squishing against the warm sand. When I reach the middle, I find him studying me with a look I've never seen on his face before.

"What?" I snap, need and fury churning through me in tandem.

"Nothing," he murmurs. "Nothing at all."

There's no time to wonder about it, because then I'm in his arms again, and every ounce of energy is spent trying to keep myself in check.

It's infuriating that this man who put me through the emotional wringer still has the ability to make my heart beat a bit faster when his knuckles graze the hollow beneath my ear, when his callused fingertips stroke the fragile skin inside my wrist. It's downright alarming how good it feels to be back in his arms, his hands asking a lustful question my curves ache to answer.

I try to stay aloof and unaffected at his nearness, but after an hour of his hands on my skin, I'm flushed and having trouble focusing. Keeping my eyes trained solely on the camera, I shut out the set and the man wrapped around me as best I can.

Just part of the job.

I'm filled with desire, and there's absolutely nothing I can do to stop it. Our bodies recognize each other at a chemical level, down to our indivisible parts — we've done this dance before, too many times to act convincingly like strangers.

For our last pose, Sloan orders me to lean back slightly against Grayson's chest while he stands behind me with his hands on my hips. I try not to react as our bodies align, my ass nestling into his crotch where his cock pulses like a barely-caged animal. Grayson makes no such attempt at composure — he groans into my ear as his hips rub against me.

"You are fucking *killing me*, Kat."

His fingers dig a little too tightly into my hips. I make a breathy sound — half protest, half longing — as he presses harder against my curves while the shutter clicks down, again and again and again.

I am consumed by contradiction. Hate and want and hurt and longing. A tornado of masochism and misery, in his arms.

I feel him, long and hard, throbbing through the thin barrier of fabric between us. My body has betrayed me. My skin is burning up, every inch of me on fire, which makes no sense at all when the heart inside my chest is still a deadened block of ice.

How is it possible to be so equally consumed by passion and repugnance?

They are two vastly different animals, I suppose — lust and affection. I've heard the term *hate sex* and never really understood it until this moment. It's not simply sleeping with someone you can't stand; it's wanting someone so much, you'd let them strip you down to a shivering, self-abhorring mess just to feel their hands on your skin. It's desire so strong, it leaves you weak and whimpering and hating *yourself* almost as much as you hate them for wielding such indiscriminate power.

Just when I think I can't take another moment without combusting in front of the entire production crew, Sloan's voice calls out the blessed words I've been waiting for.

"All right, that should do it! Good work, you two."

I rocket away from Grayson. I need a cold shower and possibly a licensed shrink. My eyes search the crowd for Harper as I practically run off set, feet kicking up sand, arms wrapping around my body to hold the tumultuous emotions tightly in check. I don't want to look anyone in the eye, positive they can see straight through my flushed cheeks and rapid breaths to the emotional wreckage below.

"Kat! Wait—"

I pretend not to hear Grayson calling me as my gaze scans the perimeter for my best friend, flitting past a cluster of tech crew in all-black getups, a still-pouting Annabelle, a note-scribbling Trey. I don't see Harper anywhere, but abruptly my eyes halt on a heart-stopping figure in jeans and a fitted white v-neck, standing in the shadows like Hades waiting to drag Persephone down to hell. He's looking at me and I'm looking at him and there's nothing else. No air or time or other insignificant humans occupying space and sound around us.

Just *Wyatt*, looking over the set with an expression I'm not sure I want to name.

Just *me*, staring at a beautiful man who hates me almost as much as I adore him.

I stop short so suddenly, Grayson nearly barrels into my back. His hand curls around my shoulder, tugging me close. I don't notice much. I'm fully focused on Wyatt.

He looks incredible.

Biceps straining at the fabric of his sleeves, thick bronze hair pulled back into a bun with a distinct leather strap, chiseled features set in such a hard expression, he might as well be crafted out of marble. For a few breathless seconds, the whole world stops turning. My feet fail. My heart actually stops beating inside my chest, which should land me in the record books as the first twenty-two-year-old in history to die of heart failure from merely *looking* at a man.

I don't care in the slightest.

I would happily die, right here, just for the privilege of seeing him in the flesh.

My eyes drink him in. I had not realized, until this instant, how starved I was for his presence. How much I craved his steady composure, his stalwart guidance, his unfailing positivity. He's twenty feet away, but the distance seems insurmountable. I ache more than ever, as I stare across the space separating our bodies. I miss him like a plant misses sunlight.

Infinitely blue irises burn into mine with incongruous heat and steel-edged anger— the same irises that have haunted my dreams for weeks, since the night of the cast party when I stripped down to my skin and he grabbed me by the heart with those big hands, unfurling a relentless passion I was thoroughly unprepared for.

I do not notice my hand creeping up to lay across my stomach until it is already there, pressing firmly. I do not acknowledge Grayson, who collides to a stop at my back, full of petulant words I have no interest in. The passion I felt for him a moment ago is but a dim, flickering candlelight.

Wyatt is the sun.

My mouth opens. I need to say something. To fix this. To fix *us*, even though there is no such thing as *us*, because we never existed anywhere outside the realms of a drunken mistake.

No. It was not a mistake.

How could the most beautiful moments of my life be an error? How could I ever regret something so all-consuming?

"Wyatt," I whisper. My lips shape the word but the sound barely passes through them. He does not hear me, or chooses not to. Instead, his eyes break from mine to focus on the man behind me. So he does not see the sadness twisting my mouth, the regret pulling my brows together; all he sees is Grayson's hold on my arm, on my hip, his mouth poised by my ear, his poisonous words working through me like honey laced with arsenic.

I see something in those incredible blue eyes shutter. He calls something I cannot hear to Sloan, then turns away and heads for the side door.

He's *leaving.*

I feel my heart lurch.

"Wyatt!" I call, voice stronger this time.

He doesn't stop. I try to follow, but Grayson's grip on my arm holds me pinned. I struggle against him, watching my Viking fade into the shadows, helpless to stop it.

"Let go of me," I hiss at Grayson, tugging futilely.

He ignores me.

"Hey, Sloan," Grayson calls, still holding me captive. "I know I'm not the creative director here, but don't you need a few shots of us kissing for the promotional posters? After all, like you said... it's a romance, not a war drama."

Sloan pauses, midway through storing his camera lenses. His head tilts as he considers the thought. "Hmm... Well, we can't use anything with you two kissing in the marketing— a bit too heavy-handed for billboards. But maybe it wouldn't be a bad idea to take a few secondary shots, just in case we want—"

"No!" I yell, wrenching my arm out of Grayson's hold. I nearly rip my joint from the socket in the process, but at least I'm free. "No. I'm sorry, but I'm not doing any kissing scenes."

"Kat, be reasonable—" Grayson starts.

"I have to go."

Sloan jolts, startled, as I rush past him. His voice carries after me as I race for the side door Wyatt disappeared through.

"But, Kat, what about the meeting this afternoon at my place—"

"I'll be there!" I yell over my shoulder, not pausing as I barrel through the doorway and plow straight into Harper. She's so surprised by my sudden appearance in the hallway, she nearly upends her makeup cart all over the floor.

"Whoa! Where's the fire?"

"Can't talk," I pant, skirting around her, my eyes locked on the far door. "Explain later."

"Uhh, okay...?"

She clearly thinks I'm a crazy person. I don't care.

If I can just catch him.
Talk to him.
Explain...
I have no idea what I'll say, but I know I can't leave things like this between us. The loss of his friendship is slowly killing me. His absence in my life is like bleeding to death from a paper-cut — an insufferably drawn out process, rather than a quick, merciful strike to the heart.

My hands slam against the metal bar and the door swings open beneath my touch. I squint into the sunlight as I shuffle outside. My restless eyes scan the parking lot, searching for broad shoulders and blond hair and a black Audi convertible, but I don't see him anywhere. I take a few more steps, gaze moving up and down the distant rows of expensive automobiles, feeling hope disintegrate inside me.

He's already gone.

"If you're looking for Dunn, he's still inside."

The voice rumbles from directly behind me. I spin around, holding my breath, and see he's leaning against the warehouse wall, studying me with guarded eyes. I must've barreled right past him, in my desperate search. His arms are folded across his chest in a standoffish pose that effectively communicates just how unhappy he is to see me.

"I'm not looking for Grayson," I say quietly, trying to keep my breaths steady.

"Sloan's still inside, too."

I take a step nearer to him and watch his muscles go rigid, as if he's totally unsettled by the thought of me getting close enough to touch him. Seeing him react that way makes my eyes prick with tears. In all the time I've known him, from that very first day, he's never shied away from grabbing my hand, never hesitated to hug me when I needed it, to wrap his arms around me when I was cold or wet or tired after a long day of filming.

How quickly things change.

I blink rapidly to keep the tears at bay, but when I speak, my voice cracks with something that sounds a lot like grief.

"I'm not looking for Sloan, either." My eyes hold his for a long, suspended moment. He says nothing, but a muscle jumps in his cheek as we stare at each other. "I..." I clear my throat. "I was looking for you."

He shifts his pose against the wall and shoves his hands deep inside his pockets. "Well, I'm right here."

Except he's not. He's a million miles away, somewhere I can no longer reach.

"Right..." My eyes are stinging again. "I tried to call you a few times. I wanted to... to..." Words are failing me. I've spent a month thinking about what I might say when I finally saw him again, and now that the moment has arrived, I'm a bumbling idiot.

I stare at him leaning there against a stucco wall, but my eyes see ghosts — his head between my legs, my hands fisted in his hair, my back arched off the bed, his hands on my hips. A double-exposure of memory and reality, unquenchable passion blending with unbridled unwelcome.

"To what?" he asks impatiently, glancing at his phone.

"To fix it." My voice is helpless. "To make things right—"

"There's nothing to fix," he says, stunning me.

"What?"

"I knew what I was getting into, with you. I knew you were a mess. I knew you were a decade and a half younger than me. I knew you'd been drinking. I even knew you were still hung up on somebody else." He sighs heavily. "It's my own fault for treating you like someone you weren't, or expecting something you aren't capable of giving." He shrugs casually, but the look in his eyes is so cold, I could freeze to death right on the spot. "So, like I said... there's nothing to fix, Katharine. Holding you accountable for your actions would be like giving a child a priceless glass toy, and getting angry when they smash it to bits."

The blood drains from my face and I physically recoil, as though he's slapped me. I think I see a flash of something familiar in his eyes — something soft, something sad — but it's suppressed in an instant beneath this new, frozen facade. With utter horror, I realize his expression is one I recognize. One I know a little too well, because I've seen it on the faces of everyone else in my life at some point or another.

The shadowy expectation of disappointment.
The knowledge that counting on Kat Firestone, that inconsequential mess of a girl, will lead to nothing but ruin and regret.

I've seen that look from my mother, from my ex-boyfriends, from my stepfathers and old bosses and friends who fell by the wayside. Even occasionally from Harper.

But never from him. Not until now. He used to look at me like I was made of magic, down to my bones.

I mourn the sudden shift. The only person in my life who unfailingly saw the best in me, time after time, no matter how bad I messed up... is officially gone.

"Wyatt..." I try one final time, voice trembling. "Please, just—"

He glances back at his phone and types a rapid text message. "Listen, my ride is almost here. I have to go. If you have a problem concerning the movie that needs to be addressed, you can contact my assistant— you've got her direct number, right?"

I feel my mouth part on a whimper. No words escape; I've been stunned into silence.

He pushes off the wall and starts walking down the sidewalk. I trail after him helplessly, wondering if this can possibly be the same endlessly positive man I knew a month ago, who lifted me up whenever I was beaten down. Always there with a steady hand to correct my stumbles, a kind word to keep me going.

Every day, you have a choice about how you're going to live your life.

Choose sunshine, baby. Always choose sunshine.

You look so much prettier with light in your eyes.

That man is nothing but a memory. This man, walking away from me now, is a stranger.

And I'm the one responsible.

I did this.

I crashed into his life and poisoned him. A plague, spreading through his system, until every illuminated corner of his soul had been tarnished by the folly of my actions. And he won't even let me try to mend the damage I caused.

Anger spirals through me in a maelstrom as I watch him walk away.

"Wyatt Hastings!" I yell at his back, voice vibrating with authority. "Stop right there!"

He goes completely still. His shoulders are tense. His head turns halfway, so I see his face in profile, and his voice is emotionless when he clips out a reply.

"You bellowed?"

I stomp to his side, close enough to see the crystalline depths of his irises up close. If I were braver, I'd reach out and grab his hand.

I plant my hands on my hips to curtail the impulse.

"Well?" he prompts, jaw ticking again.

"I don't want things to be like this," I whisper recklessly.

"Like what, exactly?"

"You! You're..." I shift from foot to foot, bare toes pressing against the chilled asphalt. "You're so cold."

"Have I not been perfectly civil?"

"Civil? *Civil?*" I scoff. "Sure, I guess you've been civil. But I'd bet my ass a tour of Antarctica would be warmer than the shoulder you're giving me."

"I'm trying to be professional. You may not recognize it, because you careen through life like there aren't any rules, but this is what a professional working relationship looks like."

I pale at his words and feel my own evaporate.

His jaw clenches. Crossing his arms over his chest, he stares blankly down at me. "Katharine, I am not your friend. I'm certainly not your boyfriend. I'm your producer. I'm your *boss*."

"You've always been my boss." My protest is shaky. "You've never treated me like this."

"I'm treating you the way I'd treat any other actress on any other project."

"But I'm not just any actress. This isn't any project. Wyatt, even before things—" I break off.

His eyebrows lift.

"Before things got all messed up," I hurry on. "We were friends."

He stares at me impassively.

Emotional declarations come about as easy to me as climbing K2 in stilettos. There's a reason I'm an actress instead of a novelist or an artist — it's always been far simpler pretending to be someone else, borrowing their emotions rather than putting my own on display. If you've met my mother, it doesn't take a shrink to figure out why. Cynthia's words are never far from my mind.

Reckless, Katharine. Very reckless. You never listen to me.

How many times have I told you, always pick someone who loves you more than you love them? How many ways did I explain that caring more means you have less power?

Historically, whenever things get tough, I bolt. I let relationships die like grapes withering on a vine, rather than fight to make them work. I've done it with friends and boys and everyone who's ever gotten close enough to matter. So I know it's not a stretch to say that two months ago, I would've walked away without another word to Wyatt. I would've given up, moved on, and pretended not to feel the sting of loneliness radiating through me with each breath, like a punctured lung in my heartless chest.

36

Even now, in this moment, I am scared to fight. To make myself vulnerable. To let him see how much he matters.

But I'm even more terrified of the thought of walking away and never seeing Wyatt again except in passing at AXC events three, four, five years from now — our interactions reduced to a cool kiss on a cheek, casual conversation always within the safety of a group, the unfailing ache of regret eating me up inside as my eyes sweep the elegant woman by his side who wasn't stupid enough to let him slip away.

I stare into his eyes, steel my shoulders like I'm preparing for battle, and force myself to say the words that are eating me up inside.

"Wyatt. I... I *miss* you. I miss you so much."

His hands flex slightly and I swear he rocks back on his heels, like my words pack a physical punch. I think, just maybe, I'm starting to get through to him. To thaw the ice between us.

"I miss things the way they used to be," I say, taking a tiny step closer to him. "I know I messed it up. But you never even gave me a chance to explain—"

My words are cut off by the sharp honking of a car horn. We both jump, startled, and step back — we'd been leaning toward each other like two planets trapped in the same gravitational pull. A sleek, canary yellow convertible slides to a stop at the curb. A sunny blonde in her early thirties sits behind the wheel, beaming with far too many bleached white teeth for my taste. It's clear she knows Wyatt from the way he turns and smiles at her.

Something like dread settles inside my stomach.

"Hey there, good looking!" The blonde winks playfully. "Did you call for an Uber?"

Laughing, Wyatt steps off the curb and approaches the passenger door. "Yes, but I specifically asked for a fat bald man. I'd like to speak to your superiors. Very displeased by this."

"Shut up and get in." She rolls her eyes skyward. When they return back to earth, they settle on me. "Oh! Hi! I didn't even see you there."

Maybe because your eyes were glued to Wyatt's ass. I force a smile. "Hello."

Wyatt remembers his manners. Somewhat stiffly, he gestures from the woman in the car to me, where I'm hovering on the sidewalk like a discombobulated girl in gym class, waiting to be picked last for the volleyball teams.

"Caroline, this is Katharine Firestone — she's the lead in the *Uncharted* movie I told you about. Katharine, this is Caroline Foster."

I notice he doesn't offer an explanation as to how he knows her or clarify what they are to each other.

Caroline nods knowingly, sliding her Prada sunglasses down the bridge of her nose to examine me better. "Oh! That's the plane crash movie, right?"

I nod.

"That explains the costume, then!" Her laugh sounds like wind chimes — light and musical. Nothing like the wheezing snorts of mirth that so often escape my own mouth. She's wearing a chic tunic dress and there's a Birkin bag sitting on the seat beside her; I'm impossibly underdressed and outclassed, standing here in my tattered blue sundress and bare feet.

"I suppose that makes sense." She waggles her fingers at the torn fabric covering my midsection. "At first, I thought you were homeless or something!"

My smile feels stiffer than a piece of cardboard taped to my face. "And what are *you* supposed to be?"

Wyatt coughs sharply.

Caroline pretends she didn't hear my dig, but her eyes get sharp. "Well, Katie, it's been a pleasure to meet you! From what Wy tells me, it sounds like it'll be a fantastic film."

Wy?

My nose scrunches in distaste at the nickname.

Wyatt is being very careful not to look at me as he reaches for the door handle.

"Love to stay and chat," Caroline fibs easily. "But we have a lunch reservation at *Nirvana* in a half hour."

I might've corrected her for messing up my name if it hadn't been intentional. Might've asked where they knew each other from, if it wasn't taking all my energy to stand there exuding unfazed nonchalance instead of pulse-pounding nausea. Might've teased Wyatt about his newfound nickname, if I could muster up even an ounce of amusement about this hellish scenario.

I stand in silence and watch as he climbs into the passenger seat. Just before his door closes, he glances back at me. For the first time all day, his eyes are stripped of the careful barriers and cool distance. I see the hint of a smile on his lips.

"I'll see you around, Firestone."

I bite my lip so I won't cry, but it's useless. I feel my eyes flood with tears as I look at him. My heart is in my throat, thumping a mocking double-beat.

Thump-thump.

Too late.

Thump-thump.

Too late.

"Wyatt, I—"

His mouth opens to say something else, but the words are snatched away on the wind as Caroline floors the gas pedal and peels away from the curb, leaving me there alone, hands on my stomach, shaking like a leaf as silent tears track down my face.

CHAPTER THREE

"SHE ISN'T EVEN THAT PRETTY. SHE JUST HAS GOOD HAIR."
- *A girl stalking Facebook pictures of her
new boyfriend's ex-girlfriend.*

I'm not sure how long I sit there, crumpled on the curb in the shining afternoon sunshine like a forgotten rag doll, before Harper finds me. Seconds, minutes, years — time has lost all meaning. My tears have dried, but I am utterly numb inside.

She takes one look at my face and drags me straight to my dressing room. I let her undress me like a small child, not fighting her as she wipes the thick-caked foundation from my face and hangs my costume back up in its zippered bag. I hear her speaking into her phone in hushed tones, asking Masters to bring the car around.

I stare at my hands, at the perfect glossy manicure I have come to loathe for its perfection, so at odds with the rest of me. I chide myself for thinking things would go back to normal if I could just see Wyatt. It was delusional to hope that merely by looking at him and talking to him and maybe making him laugh, things would return to the way they were. That he'd tilt his head and call me *baby* and forgive me for being a human-shaped wrecking ball.

I never considered the fact that he has no *interest* in forgiving me.

That, when I finally got up the nerve to try and fight, he would want no part in it.

That he'd already moved on to someone else.

A sunshine girl, with a beaming smile and a bright

yellow car, far better suited for him than I've ever been.

Caroline is age appropriate.

Caroline probably doesn't have two decades' worth of damage and a tendency to self-destruct whenever times get tough.

Caroline is the kind of girl Wyatt belongs with.

He deserves someone stable.

He doesn't need me screwing up his life anymore.

"Come on," Harper says, heading for the door. "We have a few hours to get some food before you're due at Sloan's for the meeting."

"Grayson?" I ask quietly, as we walk down the hall.

"Already left," she confirms.

A relieved breath slips from my lungs. I can't deal with him right now, on top of the Wyatt situation. At least, not without some food in my system.

Twenty-five minutes later, I'm settled firmly in a low leather booth across from Harper and Masters, who is watching the door for any possible threats as though this sushi restaurant is full of genuine samurai about to slice us limb from limb, rather than perky waitresses bearing sashimi and sake cocktails. Harper orders a variety of food while I use the bathroom, and by the time I get back to the table, our server is setting down a wood tray garnished with an array of brightly colored dragon rolls. Two martinis follow suit.

I stare at the apple shavings floating on the surface of my drink, mesmerized. I haven't had a sip of alcohol in six weeks. It's barely two in the afternoon but, after the day I've had, I crave the soothing refuge of vodka sliding down my throat. I eye the untouched glass in front of me, hands itching to drain it in a single gulp. Even with the tiny heartbeat thumping double-time alongside my own — an ever-present reminder of my mistakes — the temptation is almost too strong to resist.

Eve had an apple...

...I have an appletini.

"Don't worry, they're mock-tails. Totally virgin,"

Harper assures me, misinterpreting the reluctant look on my face for responsibility. "I wouldn't derail your sobriety. You've been doing so well. I'm really proud of you."

She's doing her damnedest to keep me away from all forms of alcohol, the memory of my last bender still fresh in her mind. She doesn't know that, if not for the baby, I'd have crawled inside the bottom of a bottle and taken up full-time residence there.

I sigh — half regretful, half relieved.

I suppose I should be grateful I don't have to fabricate an entirely different reason that I'm abstaining from drinking the delicious green concoction in my glass. I grasp the stem and lift it to clink against hers.

"Cheers."

The tart liquid is refreshing, even without the bite of alcohol.

"Are you ready to tell me about it, now?" Harper asks softly. I can feel the impatience running through her like an electromagnetic charge. She's desperate for information, but too sweet to push me for it after witnessing my breakdown in the parking lot.

"Um..." My eyes dart to Masters.

"Oh, Kent won't say anything. He couldn't care less about anything that concerns other people." Harper elbows her boyfriend. "Isn't that right, honey?"

"It's true, I'm a total narcissist," he agrees dryly. "It's why she's so attracted to me."

"I meant *gossip*." She rolls her eyes. "You don't care about *gossip*."

His lips twitch in one of the rare smiles only Harper seems capable of coaxing out of him. It's gone by the time his eyes shift to meet mine. "Don't worry, Miss Firestone. You're paying me for my discretion as well as my protection. Anything you say is totally confidential."

"See!" Harper jerks her chin sharply. Her eyes narrow, patience wearing thin. "Feel free to start talking now."

I fidget in my seat and look around the restaurant. While we've missed the worst of the lunchtime rush, many of the tables are still full. Yet, our booth is in a private corner — a perk of my sudden A-list status — so it's doubtful anyone can overhear our muffled tones.

I take another sip of my drink and stare into my best friend's eyes. "Fine. But you can't freak out."

"I won't!"

"You can't react in any way."

"I said *I won't.*"

"You have to keep calm."

"*Kat!*" She tosses her hands up. "Honestly, you're starting to worry me. Just spill already."

I steady my shoulders and force the words out in as steady a voice as I can manage, considering it's the first time I've actually said them out loud.

"I slept with Wyatt."

"WHAT?!" Harper screams, loud enough to make every head in the restaurant turn our way. "ARE YOU— DID YOU JUST—BUT HOW—WHAT THE—*WHAT*?!"

Slinking down in the booth to avoid the sudden attention, I glance at Masters. "Good thing she didn't react."

"Really kept calm," he agrees, eyes crinkling. "Cool as a cucumber."

Harper's hands are pressed against her temples. "How in the mother-effing HELL did you keep this from me? *Why* did you keep this from me?"

"Oh, I don't know," I drawl. "Maybe because I knew you'd react like *this.*"

Her cheeks are flushed red. She sits in total silence, processing my words, then flags down the first waitress she sees walking by.

"Hi, yeah, I'm going to need another one of these." She lifts her appletini. "But this time, can you use alcohol? In fact, lose the apple. I'll just have a gin martini. Extra dry. Hold the olives. As fast as you can manage, and keep them coming. Thanks."

The waitress gives a startled nod and disappears.

Harper turns back to me. "Okay. Now that I've handled... *that*..." She shakes her head, still in shock. "Start at the beginning. I want to hear exactly what happened."

I take another sip of my fake cocktail, wishing more than ever that it was alcoholic, and begin my tale of woe.

"It was the night of the cast party..."

The sushi sits untouched between us as I walk her through the night.

Talking to Wyatt in the gazebo. Going upstairs to say goodbye to him. Walking down the hallway. Finding his bedroom. Seeing his silhouette on the edge of the bed. Taking off my dress. Letting him wreck me.

"Holy shit," Harper breathes, squirming a little as I describe him touching me. Even Masters, the epitome of composure, is looking a little red around the collar as I recall the way Wyatt's big hands gathered my wrists and pinned them to the bedsheets.

"That's so sexy." Harper sighs, but I can see her excitement is tempered by trepidation. There's already sadness in her eyes — that same foreboding that settles over you when you're reading Romeo and Juliet, wanting to root for the characters but knowing full-well that things are about to turn to shit. She sees the ending to this story will not be a happy one, no matter how much she hopes otherwise.

I somehow keep my voice from shaking as I recount waking in tangled sheets, totally alone. Deciding he regretted our rash, drunken fervor. Descending the staircase. Being confronted at the door with cool words and smashed plates and crumbling hopes. A ruined breakfast-in-bed, leaking across a tile floor.

Harper's eyes fill with tears.

And I find, when I reach this point in my story, that my composure cracks open like a fault line in the earth and I cannot go on. Cannot describe the rending heartbreak that scorched through me in those desperate moments, after Wyatt walked away, while I rode home in the back seat of a car service, barely able to articulate my own address to the driver.

"Oh, honey." Harper's hand finds mine, squeezing tightly. "Honey..."

I look away. Anywhere but into her eyes, because I can't bear to read the secondary heartbreak buried there. As all true best friends do, she adopts my emotions as her own, feels my heartbreak as hers. I can sense words poised on the tip of her tongue — useless things she wants to say to make me feel better, but can't because they simply aren't true. Things like *it'll be okay* and *it's not that bad.*

We both know it won't be okay.

We both know it truly *is* that bad.

"Well," she says after a while, for lack of anything better to say. "I guess that explains why he hasn't been calling me back."

I try out a smile. It wavers weakly on my lips, then falls away.

Her eyebrows pull together as she sips her martini. "So... today, when you saw him again....?"

I tell her about Caroline. Her frown deepens.

"Whoever she is, she won't last," Harper announces, wielding her chopsticks like weapons as she selects a piece of sushi from the board between us. "This *Caroline* girl is just..." She gestures vaguely. "An ego Band-Aid."

"Come again?" I scoff.

"A rebound. A safety screw. She's the girl you fuck to get over the one you love." Harper pops the sushi roll into her mouth and moans. "Damn, that's good."

"Wyatt doesn't love me." My voice is flat. "Or, maybe he did, maybe he *could've*, but he definitely doesn't anymore."

She rolls her eyes. "Uh huh."

"Did you not hear the part about him throwing the tray? About the month of total silence? About the cold shoulder he gave me when I tried to explain?"

"If anything, that's just evidence he still cares deeply about you." She grabs another piece of sushi. "Men don't waste perfectly good pancakes unless there's some serious emotion there. Furthermore, men don't make an elaborate breakfast-in-bed for women they have no feelings for. Sorry, it just doesn't happen."

"But—"

"Tell her I'm right, Kent."

When there's no response from my bodyguard, Harper elbows him sharply. "Hello! Earth to boy-toy!"

Masters glances back at us, brows raised. It's clear his attention has been elsewhere.

"What?"

"Tell Kat that boys don't make breakfast unless it's serious."

"Boys don't make breakfast unless it's serious," he intones. "Happy?"

"Yes," she announces, smiling. "Carry on with... whatever it is you're doing."

"I'm surveilling the area for possible threats."

"Right. Sure, honey." She pats him on the head fondly, like you would a delusional golden retriever who thinks he's an intimidating guard dog.

Masters' mouth twists. "Two paparazzi are parked outside in the blue sedan across the street. There's a girl taking Snapchat videos of Kat beneath the high-top near the bar. A teenage boy has walked past our booth three times, pretending to use the bathroom, but unless he's got IBS, my guess is he's trying to get a good look at Kat to store in his spank-bank for later. Gross, but harmless," he says, when he sees my grimace of disgust. "Also, our waitress has changed twice since we got here, so I'm guessing there's some kind of bidding war going on in the kitchen over who gets to snoop on our conversation while serving you your third martini." He stares at Harper, bemused, before turning back to watch the restaurant. "But, by all means, let me know if you need another vital opinion regarding your girl talk."

Harper and I both look at each other with wide eyes. *Oh my god*, I mouth at her.

So sexy, Harper mouths back, faking a swoon.

"Yeah, I am," Masters agrees without looking, somehow attuned to our wordless conversation despite the fact that we haven't spoken aloud.

I stare at my best friend for an incredulous moment. I don't know whether to laugh or applaud.

She's at a loss for words when it comes to her super-sleuth boyfriend. After another large gulp of martini, she swiftly shifts the course of conversation.

"Don't worry about Wyatt. We'll fix it."

"Whatever you say," I murmur doubtfully.

"The real question is, how do *you* feel about *him*?"

"I don't know."

"How did you feel while you were with him that night?"

"I don't know."

She huffs in frustration. "Okay, but how did you feel when—"

"Harper!" I snap.

"Fine, fine." Her face darkens into a scowl. "Apparently questions have been outlawed. Free speech is a thing of the past. *Excuse me*, I thought this was America."

"It is. Feel free to file a Freedom of Information Act request — your response should arrive in about six months." I smile sweetly.

"Yeah, you're a real patriot, Firestone." She shakes her head and sips her drink, muttering something that sounds like *obstinate idiot* under her breath between swallows.

"I'm not trying to be elusive, Harper." My voice gets quiet. "I haven't let myself think about it. It hurts me too much."

Her head tilts. "That should probably tell you something."

"What do you mean?"

"If you didn't care, it wouldn't hurt so bad."

I fall silent, considering that.

"What does this mean when it comes to you and Grayson? Does he know?" She shakes herself. "Oh, what am I saying, of course he doesn't know. *I* didn't even know... But do you think he'll find out? Do you think he'll freak? Do you—"

"Harper!"

"What?"

"You're doing it again."

"Sorry."

"It's fine." I lean back in the booth, resting against the leather. "Let's just stick to one catastrophe at a time, shall we?"

"Fair enough." She looks at my unused chopsticks. "You aren't eating."

Resignedly, I pick up the utensils and pluck a piece of sushi from the platter. It's nearly in my mouth when the smell of raw fish hits my nostrils — tuna, cold and slimy, glazed with some kind of wasabi mayonnaise. A few months ago, I would've swooned over each bite. Now, I feel bile rising quickly to the back of my throat. It's all I can do not to hurl right on the table.

"Excuse me— I have to— *Bathroom.*"

I shove to my feet, hands clutched over my mouth, and race to the back of the restaurant. Harper's startled calls of concern follow me all the way to the women's room. I rush inside the first free stall I see and throw the door shut behind me. I barely make it over the bowl before the dry heaves begin.

There's not much to come up — remnants of this morning's granola bar and a few sips of bright green appletini splash into the toilet. When my stomach is empty, the nausea subsides almost as quickly as it arose. I wipe my mouth with toilet tissue, flush twice, and walk to the bank of sinks. My reflection in the mirror looks sweaty and shaken as I swish water in my mouth to clear the awful aftertaste. I wipe at my damp, pale forehead with a paper towel and press a hand against my abdomen. *Not a fan of sushi, are you, you tiny dictator?*

The thought comes unbidden. I barely have time to steel myself against the alarming implications that I'm *talking to my damn stomach like a crazy person,* because the door swings inward and Harper strides into the bathroom.

"Honey, are you okay?" Her eyes are narrowed in suspicion.

"That appletini didn't agree with me. Too much syrup, maybe," I murmur, avoiding her eyes as I wash my hands. "I'll be fine in a minute."

"But we've had them before, you've never had that kind of reaction..."

I focus on the running water. "What's with the third degree?"

"I don't know, it's just strange. I've seen you eat burritos from seriously sketchy food trucks. I once watched you use the *five second rule* with a churro you dropped on the Santa Monica Pier. You're not exactly a weak-stomached kind of girl."

"Your point being..."

She shrugs. "Are you sure there's nothing—"

A stall door behind us swings open and a teenage girl walks out. Washing her hands at the sink beside mine, I see her peering from the corner of one eye with a curious expression on her face, likely trying to figure out where she recognizes me from.

"Are you sure it wasn't the sushi?" Harper pesters. "Because it seemed like—"

"*Harper.*" I cut her a deadly look that says *drop it or die.* I'm not about to discuss my sudden tendency to swoon in front of some Twitter-obsessed teen who'll tweet about it to TMZ faster than you can spell the words *accidental pregnancy.*

In the mirror, I watch as recognition lights up the girl's eyes. She turns to me, a question forming on her lips.

"Hey! Aren't you that actress from—"

"Nope," I cut her off, heading for the door without bothering to dry my hands.

"Nice." Harper scoffs, following me out. "Way to bond with your fan base."

"Whatever," I mumble as we walk back to the table where Masters is waiting. The sickening sushi has — blessedly — disappeared.

He gets to his feet, the keys to his SUV already in hand. "Miss Firestone, your meeting starts soon. We should leave shortly if you want to make it there on time."

"Okay. We'll pay. You bring the car around."

He nods and disappears as we climb back into the booth to settle the bill. I feel Harper staring at me silently as I calculate the tip.

My brows lift. "What?"

"Nothing," she says in a voice two octaves too high. "Absolutely nothing."

I snort. "Do us both a favor — leave the acting to me."

* * *

Sloan's house in the Hills is just as I remember it. A sprawling, modern monstrosity filled with contemporary, Asian-inspired accents that an unfathomably expensive interior designer shipped in from regions unknown to promote a "zen" atmosphere. I wave Masters and Harper off from the driveway, promising to call them for a ride when the meeting is finished. I can tell Harper is torn between wanting alone time with her man and accompanying me inside but, after multiple assurances that I'll be just fine on my own, she finally relents and drives away with him.

Walking past several ghastly lion statues lining the front walk, I ring the bell and wait, but there's no answer. After a few moments, I have no choice other than to grasp one ornate oriental handle and enter uninvited. Unlocked, it swings in easily.

"Hello?"

My own voice echoes back at me in the sparsely decorated atrium.

"Sloan?"

No answer.

I've only been here once before, the day I auditioned for my role in the movie, but the open floor plan is easy to navigate. I wander through the house, calling out for Sloan, but he's nowhere to be found — not in the kitchen or the living room or the music room or out on the deck by the pool. I'm on my way to check his yoga studio, feeling queasy again for the second time in as many hours at the prospect of seeing the spry director doing a downward facing dog pose, when a floorboard creaks behind me.

"He's downstairs," a disembodied voice says.

"AAH!" I jump about a foot into the air and whirl around, expecting a serial killer. It's far worse — Grayson is standing silhouetted in the pool of light at the end of the hallway.

"Someone's jumpy today." His laugh carries down to me. "Too much coffee?"

I wish — I haven't had coffee in so long, at this point I'd rob a Colombian bean farm for a cup, given half a chance. Pulse pounding, I plant my hands on my hips and glare at him.

"You snuck up on me!"

"Kat, if I was going to sneak up on you, you'd know it."

"That makes no sense. The point of *sneaking* is that your victim is unaware of said sneakiness. How would I possibly know?"

He laughs. "Because I'd be humming the soundtrack from *Jaws*. Obviously."

I blink at him blankly.

"You know..." Those green irises glitter with humor, even at this distance. He sticks one hand up behind his head like a fin. "*Da-dum...Daaaaa-dum.*" He swerves his body down the hall, like he's swimming toward me. It's a ridiculous sight.

"You're insane—"

"*Da-dum...*" He swivels again, both his chant and his steps speeding up. "*Da-dum!*"

"Dunn, you look like an idiot." I laugh, despite myself.

He keeps coming. "*Da-dum-da-dum DA-DUM-DA-DUM—*"

"Yes, okay! I get it, you're utterly terrifying," I exclaim, reeling backwards, but it's too late.

His teeth bared in a toothy grin, he throws out his arms like a monster and attacks me — roaring and seizing me into his arms, thrashing my body back and forth like a helpless seal in the grip of a great white.

"Grayson!" I slap at his arms fruitlessly. "Let me go, you enormous idiot!"

His arms lurch me sideways again.

"I'm serious!" My words are choked with undeniable laughter as I struggle against his grip. He doesn't listen — instead, he pretends to chomp on my neck. I feel the soft scrape of teeth against my flesh and scream again. "You're a lunatic!"

"And you're dead," he whispers against the column of my throat, stilling suddenly. I freeze, barely daring to move, and my laughter disappears on a nervous exhale.

His back presses a shade closer, and abruptly there's nothing playful about the way his arms feel around me. Nothing at all.

"Let me go," I whisper in a very different tone.

My heart is thumping so loud, I'm sure he can hear it.

His nose grazes the pulse-point near my carotid. "Nervous?"

Reason returns in a swift instant. The joy fades from my bloodstream as common sense overtakes me.

"No." I shrug out of his grip. "Come on. Let's find Sloan."

He doesn't fight me. His arms fall to his sides and he

follows me silently to the staircase at the end of the hall, which leads down to the basement studio. I don't want to feel it, but it's there; that magnetic charisma that first drew me to him, despite all my careful plans and well-rehearsed reasons to keep my distance.

Having fun with Grayson has never been the problem. The man was *made* for fun. For dancing in the middle of the night and drinking rum straight from the bottle beneath the stars, telling story after story until you're filled to the brim with belly-aching, eye-streaming hilarity.

The epitome of an extrovert, he's always at his absolute best when things are playful and lighthearted.

It's the *serious* stuff he seems to have a problem with.

Still, after a month of terror and worry and gut-churning heartache, that stolen moment of joy was like a sip of cool water on a ninety-degree day. I didn't realize how much I needed it until it bubbled up inside me and spilled out into the air. It's a relief to know I can still experience those emotions. Hell, it's almost enough to make me forget that Grayson is the reason for a large chunk of my sadness in the first place.

Almost.

Breathing deeply, I remind myself that it's impossible for the person who broke you to be the one who puts you back together.

He cannot be both poison and antidote.

"There you two are!" Sloan calls, looking up when we walk into his sub-level studio. The sound-proof wall panels and slew of camera equipment littering the space are top of the line — he could film a whole movie, without ever leaving his house.

He pushes back his desk chair, causing his hovering PAs to jump out of the way, and crosses to meet us. "I was just going over the photos from today. They came out beautifully — I've already sent them off to the marketing team to work their magic. We should have the first promo poster mockups back shortly. Plus, they're nearly finished with the sizzle reel."

"By the end of the day," Trey supplies, pecking furiously at his phone. "The full-length trailer will take a bit more time. Though we've finally finalized the official soundtrack, at least."

"Tell me you got Woods on board?" Sloan asks.

Glancing up, Trey adjusts his glasses on the bridge of his nose and smiles fleetingly. "Of course I did."

Sloan claps. "Trey, remind me to give you a raise."

"Will do, sir."

Not to be outdone, Annabelle leans toward her boss. "Sloan, you asked me to remind you that your personal trainer will be here in ninety minutes. Also, here's your smoothie."

"Right! No time to waste, then." Our director claps his hands together and gestures at the massive black sectional on the other side of the room before grabbing the glass out of Annabelle's hands. "Sit, sit! We've got a lot to discuss."

We settle in. Thankfully the couch is large enough to seat about fifteen people, so I'm careful to leave a cushion of distance between Grayson and me. He smirks, as if he knows exactly what I'm trying to do, but doesn't close the gap.

"Trey, get the schedules, will you?" Sloan smiles as he takes a seat, propping his bare feet up on the coffee table. He's wearing loose-fitted yoga pants and sipping his disgusting looking green smoothie. He catches me eyeing it. "Kale, spinach, and unsweetened almond milk. It's a power blend. Loads of electrolytes. You want one? I can have Annabelle whip one up for you."

Even setting aside the odds that Annabelle would spit into my smoothie, there is literally nothing in the world that could entice me to drink that foul mixture. I don't care how healthy it is. The only blender drink I'm interested in contains eighty percent Patrón and comes garnished with salt and lime.

"Thanks, I'm good."

"Anything else?" he prompts. "Water? Kombucha? Black tea?"

Grayson asks for a bottle of water and I do the same, thinking it's probably safest to consume something with a factory seal as I watch Annabelle stomping off to the mini-fridge on the far side of the studio, more than a little miffed that she's been demoted to a glorified waitress. If she didn't hate me before, she definitely hates me now.

Trey passes me a sheet of paper and I scan the list of dates. It's a rigorous schedule — and a surprising one. Over the next month, we have several radio program sitdowns, in addition to multiple talk show appearances and advanced-screening film festival events, all leading up to the premiere just before Valentine's Day. My eyes widen.

"Valentine's Day?" I ask, startled.

"Yes!" Sloan is smiling. "A bit sooner than we'd planned, perhaps, but it's an ideal launch date for a romantic drama — sure to draw big bucks from millions of couples in need of a post-dinner flick. The only better option would be a summer release, but frankly then we'd run the risk of our little love story getting lost in the shuffle between the big action-hero blockbusters."

Annabelle returns with our bottles of water. She shoots me a dark look as she passes one my way, *accidentally* dropping it before I've got a firm grip. It rolls beneath the coffee table. I sigh at her pettiness, but her plan backfires — before I can hunt for it, Grayson bends and retrieves it for me.

He winks as he hands it over, warm fingers grazing mine.

"Thanks," I murmur, jerking my hand away from his. I unscrew the cap and take a long swig.

He chuckles, then turns to Sloan. There's a note of concern in his voice. "Valentine's Day is only six weeks away. Will the film be ready to premiere, by then?"

"It'll have to be." Sloan is placid as ever. "Don't worry, Wyatt has been working on this round the clock.

Uncharted is his baby. His passion project. He'll make sure it's ready to fly before we send it into the wild." He blinks, as if just realizing the man in question isn't present, and glances at Annabelle. "Where is Hastings, anyway? He should be here."

"His assistant emailed and said he has another commitment—"

Sloan waves away her words. "Call him. Get him over here, now."

Annabelle huffs and disappears, already dialing.

"We're letting AXC handle the distribution and they've given us the go-ahead for a wide release." Sloan sounds thrilled by the news. "We'll be in every theater in the country, come Valentine's Day."

"Christ," Grayson says, echoing my thoughts. "I'm surprised the executives gave a green light so soon. Then again, when your producer's father owns the company..." He snorts.

"Wyatt's connections there certainly haven't hurt us," Sloan agrees. "But that's not their only motivation. Their last three romances underperformed, so they're desperate for a hit. Plus, they think *Uncharted* could be a smash — there's potential it'll stick around in theaters all spring, until the summer blockbusters come out."

"Assuming the critics don't pan us," Grayson murmurs.

"Positivity, Dunn! It's the key to success." Sloan peers at me from behind his wire-rimmed glasses. "You're being very quiet, Katharine."

"Sorry..." I clear my throat. "I'm just...still processing the news."

Truthfully, I'm stunned by the quick turnaround. I'd assumed the studio would favor a summer release... that there'd be time to figure my life out, before being thrust fully into the spotlight. Apparently, I couldn't have been more wrong.

Sloan's smile widens. "Well, you'd better process quickly, because your first interview is tomorrow."

56

CHAPTER FOUR

"DEAR GOD, THAT'S HOT."
- Someone pulling a baked potato from the oven.

By the time Wyatt gets to Sloan's house, we've moved upstairs to the kitchen and are clustered around the marble island munching on snacks put out by a begrudging Annabelle, before she vanished back downstairs to work. Ravenous after the sushi failure earlier this afternoon, I shove crackers into my mouth with gusto while Sloan doles out a game plan for the press tour. Grayson looks bored to tears — he's done this before, too many times to count — but I soak up as many tips as possible. If anyone messes up an interview, it's not going to be me.

"We'll give all the hosts a list of pre-approved questions, but don't be surprised if some of them attempt to ambush you with unexpected topics and throw you off your game. Nothing makes for better news than a celebrity putting their foot in their mouth." Sloan sighs heavily. "I'd prefer it if we could get through this without either of you needing to issue a series of deeply apologetic tweets for saying something vaguely offensive that gets blown out of proportion by internet trolls."

"I don't even have a Twitter," I point out.

"Well, get one, Firestone. For god's sake, we're living in a millennial age. Even the goddamned President tweets — no matter how much we might wish otherwise."

Grayson snorts.

"Now, there's one more thing I wanted to discuss with you before we pop that bottle." Sloan gestures at the expensive champagne chilling in a nearby ice bucket. "Trey, do you have them?"

"What? Oh, the tabloids. Yes, they're right here." Trey looks up from his phone long enough to locate a thick stack of magazines on the countertop behind him. He transfers them onto the kitchen island, so they're on full display for me, Grayson, and Sloan to peruse.

I've been avoiding this very moment for more than a month, much to Harper's chagrin. There's no avoiding it, anymore — Sloan has forced my hand. My eyes scan the headlines. As expected, almost every one of them features a story about Grayson and his ex-girlfriend.

HELENA HOSPITALIZED! HER DOWNWARD SPIRAL OF DRUGS AND DEPRESSION...
GRAYSON'S GONE: INSIDERS DISCUSS THE DOOMED LOVE AFFAIR
GOODBYE BABY — DID HELENA MISCARRY? EXCLUSIVE!
"HE COULDN'T SAVE HER" — DUNN'S CLOSEST FRIENDS TELL ALL

My mouth gets dry, my spine stiffens. I sense Grayson looking at me, but I keep my eyes on the glossy covers. So, *this* is what Harper's been trying to tell me.

Whatever Grayson and Helena had is officially over. From the looks of it, it's been over for a while now.

"Sloan, why are we looking at this bullshit?" Grayson asks, pushing away a particularly offensive headline about drugs and drama.

"Because, my boy, this *bullshit* is exactly the kind of press we are trying to avoid. What do you see here?" Sloan jabs a finger from one cover to the next. "Grayson and Helena. Grayson and Helena. Grayson and Helena. *Helena, Helena, Helena.*"

"Your point?" Grayson sounds bored, as though he's seen it all before. "I'm not dating her — I was never dating her. All I did was try to be the good guy for once when she hit a rough patch a few weeks back, and as an added thank you for my chivalry, I got lambasted as a villain by the press."

Questions bubble up inside me; I shove them to the back of my mind.

Grayson sighs heavily. "The truth is, it doesn't matter what I do. They still print this shit every week. I can't control what they say and neither can you, Sloan."

"True enough," the director concedes, expression animated. "We can't stop them from writing about you. But we *can* change the narrative."

Grayson's eyes narrow. "I don't know what you mean."

"They're focused on the wrong love story, don't you see?" Sloan's eyes dart from me to Grayson and back again. "We don't want them talking about you and Helena. We want them talking about you and *Kat*."

"W-what?" I stutter. "I don't have anything to do with this. Leave me out of it."

"I'm sorry, Kat, that's simply not an option." Sloan sounds entirely serious. "We have a movie to promote. And no one will want to see a movie about Grayson's character falling in love with yours if they think he's a rotten bastard who's sent his potentially pregnant ex-girlfriend to rehab — no offense, Dunn."

"None taken," Grayson says dryly. "I still don't see what you mean, though."

"The press are like children. If you want them to relinquish one toy, you have to give them something else to play with. Something better."

I'm not sure I like the sound of that — not at all.

"Elaborate," I suggest through clenched teeth.

"It's like this..." Sloan walks to the cabinet and pulls out several champagne flutes, setting them against the countertop with a gentle clink. "The public loves to root for co-stars falling in love off-screen as well as onscreen. So, if we're going to successfully sell you two as Violet and Beck in *Uncharted*..." He cocks his head at me. "Well, we're also going to have to sell you as an item when the cameras *aren't* rolling."

"What?" I hiss, blood pressure leaping. "You mean... pretend to be together? Me and Grayson, fake being a couple for the cameras?"

"Yes, that's exactly what I mean."

I scoff. "You cannot be serious."

Sloan ignores the slightly manic tone of my voice. "As a heart attack, my girl."

Grayson is oddly silent. I can't look at him — I can't do anything except stare at Sloan, waiting for him to say, *Gotcha! Only messing with you, Kat!*

But he doesn't.

He just watches me with that infuriatingly calm manner, waiting for me to process this insane idea.

"Think about it," he says after a few seconds of silence. His free hand sweeps through the air, tracing invisible headlines. "*Childhood co-stars fall head-over-heels in paradise! Star-crossed couple films romance of the decade!* The fans will eat it up. They'll be clamoring for more. They'll watch every interview. They'll read every news story. They'll tweet and re-gram and write fan fiction and take selfies with you two every time you appear in public. It'll be a frenzy. And it'll make the movie a smash, I guarantee it."

"Absolutely not." My voice is resolute. "That's not happening."

"Kat, just think about it—" Sloan starts.

Grayson still isn't saying anything.

"Why are you so quiet?" I ask incredulously, turning to him. "You cannot possibly think this is a good idea."

He shrugs, expression unreadable. "It's not the worst idea I've ever heard."

"What?" I practically scream the word. "Am I the only one around here who hasn't gone insane? Am I the only one who sees what a total fucking disaster it would be for the two of us to fake a relationship for the entire world?"

"I for one think it's a *great* idea," a dispassionate male voice interjects from the doorway.

Chills race down my spine even as anger flashes through me.

"Hastings!" Sloan calls, turning to greet the new arrival. "You finally made it!"

My eyes latch onto Wyatt as he steps into the room. I could be imagining things, but it seems like he's being very careful not to look at me.

He won't look at me, won't talk to me, won't forgive me... but he'll tell me to date another man for show?

For the first time in weeks, I feel a little of my namesake fire creep back into my veins.

"Apparently you're just as delusional as these two, then," I snap at Wyatt.

His eyes finally move to meet mine. They're heavily guarded — I can't read a single emotion in their bright blue depths.

"I don't see what the big deal is," he says in a deadly soft voice. "It's not like it'll be much of a stretch to act like you're in love with—" In lieu of saying Grayson's name, he just jerks his head in his direction.

I grind my teeth together to keep from yelling. I don't risk saying a word, because I have a feeling anything that escapes my lips at this moment will come out at the top of my lungs.

"After all," Wyatt continues softly. "No one can resist the *Sexiest Man Alive.*"

His words are teasing, but his tone is lethal.

Grayson shifts on the stool beside mine, clearly pissed, and I can almost feel the ice of his glare as he stares across the room at Wyatt. They're on the same side in this argument, but you'd never know it. There's a new bite to the chill frosting the air between them. The temperature in here has dropped so much, I'll soon be able to see my breath.

I'm in no mood to mend fences. I'm too pissed off.

I hop off my stool, plant my hands on my hips, and

whirl from Wyatt to Grayson to Sloan.

"Listen up boys, and make sure you hear me, because I'm only going to say this once. *I am not a trading card to be played whenever it's convenient for you.* I am a grown woman. I am an actress. I am a professional. I agreed to film this movie, to do everything in my power to help you promote it. But I draw the line at being your— your *puppet.* I'm not going to be used as a pawn to make up for Grayson's emotional shortcomings and messy romantic entanglements." I drop my tone to an indignant growl and resist the urge to stomp my foot. "You may have a say in my career, but you do not have a say in my personal life. *Got it?*"

There's a long moment of absolute silence as the three of them stare at me, startled by my outburst. I'm panting as I look around the room from man to man. Even Trey, loitering in the far corner, looks a little stunned; for once, his fingers have stopped pecking at his cellphone screen.

"No need to get all worked up, Kat. It was just a suggestion." Sloan's voice is soothing. "Have you ever considered yoga? I really think you might benefit from a relaxation tool. Personally, I've found it to be..."

He's still speaking, but I've stopped paying attention. I'm looking at Wyatt, at the almost-smile tugging up the corner of his mouth, and find that my brain has gone utterly mute, like a television set with a faulty audio cord. All picture, no sound.

When he sees me looking at him, the smile vanishes almost as soon as it appeared. I notice the air grows slightly less frigid, though.

A sharp pop makes me jump — sound rushes back and I turn to find Grayson has opened the bottle of champagne. Before I can protest, he's shoved an overflowing flute into my hands.

"Cheers!" Grayson grins.

"To a successful premiere," Sloan toasts, raising his own glass.

Even Wyatt joins in, his big hand looking ridiculous as it holds the delicate stem of a flute. "To *Uncharted*," he echoes.

They're all looking me, waiting for me to say something eloquent. I'm fresh out of eloquence, so I go for honesty instead.

"To making it through this alive," I murmur.

We all clink. I watch the three of them draining their glasses and, without thinking, lift mine to my lips. The bubbles fill my mouth before I remember a certain surgeon general's warning. I try to be discrete as I spit the mouthful back into my glass, but there's really no way to casually regurgitate champagne. Choking, I cough it back up and gasp for air.

"Kat!" Sloan exclaims. "Are you all right?"

Wyatt lurches forward, an involuntary instinct, concern etched on his features. He stops himself almost instantly, no doubt remembering that he hates me, now.

"I'm fine," I wheeze, hauling in air.

"What happened?" Grayson asks. "First time drinking Dom?"

"Hilarious," I mutter.

Wyatt is staring at me intently. His curious eyes move from the glass to my face.

"The sip just went down the wrong way, that's all." My pulse is pounding. I look down at my hands, to avoid those eyes that see far too much. "I'm fine, now."

Grayson claps me on the back. "Need me to give you mouth to mouth?"

I roll my eyes. "I'm all set, thanks."

He clinks his glass against mine again. "Your loss. Drink up."

"Oh," I hedge, staring at my untouched glass. "I spit in it, so I don't really want to—"

"I'll get you a fresh glass," Sloan offers, walking toward the cabinet.

"No!" I yell a bit too hastily.

He stills, arm extended toward the glasses.

"No," I repeat in a more composed tone. "Thanks anyway. I'm fine."

"If you're sure…"

"I'm sure." I glance at Wyatt and find his eyes are still narrowed on my face. My heart starts beating faster. It's silly, but part of me thinks he can sense I'm trying to hide something. He was always eerily attuned to my every hidden facet, my innermost workings, all the darkest truths I never wanted to reveal. From day one, he could see straight through me.

The last thing I need is for him to detect the newest skeleton in my closet…

"You know what, I should be going anyway." I yank my phone from my purse and dial Masters. "Tomorrow is going to be a long day."

"Kat's right. We should all be resting up," Sloan says sagely. "My nightly yoga session starts in a half hour, when my trainer arrives— you are all welcome to join me. It might be beneficial to balance your inner selves before…"

I tune him out again as I lift the phone to my ear and listen to it ring.

Wyatt is still watching me from across the room — seeing far too much as his eyes scan my face. His arms are folded across his chest and there's an aura of skepticism around him that makes me nervous. All my worry and fear and guilt are swarming just below the surface of my skin, plain for him to witness.

I swallow down my panic.

"You need a ride?" Grayson offers. "My car is here. I can drive you home."

I shake my head. "My driver is just around the corner. I'll wait outside. See you tomorrow."

I don't wait for Grayson to say goodbye. I don't even look at Wyatt as I walk out of the room and head for the exit, phone pressed tight to my ear as I order Masters to break several traffic laws, so long as he gets here in the next two minutes.

I've got to get out of here.

I can barely breathe, with those too-blue eyes staring through me, unearthing all the secrets I fear I'll never be ready to tell.

* * *

The sun is setting as we drop Harper off at her place. When I first moved into my new house in the Palisades, it was full of shadows and blank walls and empty rooms. I didn't want to be there alone, so Harper stayed over almost every night — helping me settle in, rearranging furniture with me, making sure I didn't go off the rails again. But now that the house is mostly decorated and I'm able to get through the day without dissolving into an emotional puddle, she's gone back to her own space.

Not that I can blame her — a straight month of sleepovers here was a serious cock-block for her and Masters' sex life. Still, the house feels vastly too large for just me. Sometimes, I almost miss my crappy little condo — neighbors screaming through too-thin walls, appliances that barely functioned, a pink-tiled bathroom too dilapidated to be considered *vintage.*

Okay, I take it back. I don't miss that place at all.

Masters and I drive in comfortable silence, neither feeling the need to chatter. Harper is generally the one who fills the empty air — she spent the entire ride home from Sloan's telling me all about Helena Putnam. A month's worth of gossip, crammed into a thirty-minute car ride.

This is what I've been dying to tell you! Don't you understand? There was never *a baby! She had a hysterical pregnancy and had to be committed. At least, that's what I've heard from the other girls who do makeup at AXC... Grayson came back from Hawaii to try and talk her out of hurting herself... Apparently, he's the one who took her to rehab... He's still the only one she'll talk to...*

I ache to forget her words. I don't want to know that Grayson Dunn might be a good guy disguised as an asshole. It's much safer to keep him in strict shades of black and white. Saint or sinner. Good or evil. Selfish or selfless. But people rarely stay so easily confined to a single category. And the more I learn about Grayson Dunn, the more I realize he is a man made exclusively of grayscale hues.

He does monstrous things.

...But he is not a monster.

I make foolish choices.

...But I am not a fool.

Is it any wonder we were such a disaster together?

An already-broken girl who let a boy break her a bit more, just for the hell of it.

It's strange — I once saw my own weakness as a character flaw. But I think perhaps when I first met Grayson, I was like a bone that snapped long ago and never healed correctly. Perhaps I had to be broken worse and then reset to ever have a chance of supporting my own weight.

Perhaps loving Grayson Dunn, letting him break me, was the only way to make myself whole again.

When I met him, the break was already there, built from twenty-two years of hating the reflection I saw in the mirror, hating the ugly girl inside who wore beauty like a mask to hide her true nature. The damage was already so severe it crippled me, after two decades of hearing I wasn't good enough, that I'd never make my mother proud, that I didn't deserve good things like happiness or commitment or basic human decency....

The fault line was always there. Grayson simply applied enough pressure to set off the quake.

By the time we reach my neighborhood, I'm falling asleep with my cheek pressed up against the back window, exhausted in every way a human can be — emotionally, physically, spiritually. It's already been what feels like the longest day of my life... and, as we approach my house at the end of the one-way lane and I see the bright green car parked outside my security gates, I realize it's not yet over.

"Is that—"

"My mother," I finish, groaning.

I should've known she'd track me down eventually. Cynthia is like a mythological hydra — you can cut off her head, but eventually she'll crawl back out of whatever hole she burrowed into, with two more grown in its place. I fired her last month, but that doesn't mean she's ready to stop messing with my life. Especially now, when I'm on the cusp of the stardom she spent so many years pushing me towards.

"Do you want me to keep driving?" Masters asks. "We can do a lap, come back in an hour or so..."

"She'll just keep showing up," I say, voice resigned. "Let me out. I'll talk to her here. But I'm not inviting her inside — they say, once you let a cockroach in, it'll lay eggs and cause an infestation."

Masters pulls the car to the side of the road. It's a quiet dead-end, lined by massive hedges and security gates to maintain the privacy of the wealthy residents. My house is the last on the cul-de-sac, separated from my neighbors by a generous slice of greenery on either side. There's no one around. No witnesses, if I decide to murder Cynthia right there on the beautifully manicured sidewalk.

Kidding.

Mostly.

She climbs out as I approach her monstrous Cadillac. She looks the same as she has since I was a little girl — blonde hair swept into a beehive, nails chiseled into acrylic talons, a crisp white blazer and tailored slacks that taper into stiletto-heeled boots. Either she's found the best plastic surgeon in Beverly Hills, or time really doesn't touch immortal monsters.

We stare at each other for a moment in silence. I don't ask how she tracked down my new address; she doesn't ask why I didn't inform her I was moving.

"I'd have thought you had better sense than to buy a house so high up in the Palisades," she says finally, crossing her arms over her chest and leveling me with a condescending look. "Waterfront is a much better investment. I could've gotten you a great deal in Manhattan Beach, if you'd bothered to consult me. You always were rather shortsighted, though."

No water view is worth being your neighbor, mother.

"Hello, Cynthia," I say tiredly. "Don't worry, you won't be invited to the housewarming — you won't have to *suffer* through an evening at this altitude."

Her eyes narrow. "I wasn't expecting an invitation, given our last conversation. I had hoped you'd have regained some of your common sense and called me by now, though. Thankfully, I'm used to disappointments where you're concerned."

There was a time those words would've reduced me to tears.

That time is long gone.

"I've got sense in spades, mother dearest — that's exactly why I *haven't* called."

A dark look contorts her features — she's always been so quick to anger, the fury boiling just below her skin easily provoked to the surface with a few pointed words or a carefully-timed quip.

"Katharine, when will this little stint of independence end? It was cute, at first, but now it's threatening your career."

"And how is that, exactly?"

"You need me," she snaps icily, striding closer. An acrylic nail points directly at my face. "You may've forgotten, but I'm the one who's gotten things done for you since the time you were crapping your Cheerios into diapers. Without me to manage things, you'll fall to pieces."

"I'm doing just fine without you."

"Oh, really? Who's managing your public appearances? Who's negotiating new deals for you? You won't be able to ride on the success of *Uncharted* forever. Have you thought about what you'll do in six months, or a year, when you've blown through most of your money and the residuals slow down? Have you given a single thought to your future?"

I swallow hard and say nothing.

"I thought as much." Her smile turns taunting. "You should already be making calls, auditioning for other roles, lining up new work before they forget who you are and you're back to begging for two-bit parts on teenage vampire shows."

I grit my teeth. "We've only just stopped filming."

"You stopped filming over a month ago."

"I have a press tour to get through!"

"You can juggle the promo and still hunt for new work."

"*Stop*. Just stop." My hands curl into fists. "I'm entitled to a break."

"A break? Do you think Katharine Hepburn took breaks? Do you think Vivien Leigh became a star sitting home on her ass?" She scoffs coldly. "They worked and they pushed and they never, ever stopped, not even for a moment."

"Cynthia—"

"You're on the cusp of success, but you're not done yet. Don't you see? You could have everything! And you're letting it slip away!"

"I'm not letting anything slip away," I protest. "It's Christmas in a few days — there are no auditions happening right now. People want to spend the holidays with their families." I pause. "Unless they're related to you, that is."

"Well." Her lip curls in contempt. "Perhaps Santa Claus will bring you another acting role. Apparently that's the only way you're going to land one."

"Let it go, will you? I'm not going to cold-call random producers, hunting for roles I don't want. When the right part comes along, I'll know it."

"You foolish, foolish girl." She's trembling with outrage. "I raised you to become someone extraordinary.

Imagine my surprise to find, when you finally get the chance, you'd rather remain utterly unremarkable."

I flinch.

Coldness settles over my heart as I stare at the woman who raised me.

You are worth more than this, a voice whispers from the back of my mind. It's frail and faint, barely audible over the roar of self-doubt, but it's there. *You deserve better than a mother who lacks the capacity for love. Her failings are not yours.*

I straighten to my full height, thinking about everything she's done to me over the years. The harsh words. The constant criticism. And, above all, the toxic inability to love me, even in those undeniable moments when a girl simply needs a mother — *any* mother. Even a bad one.

First crush, first kiss, first period, first breakup.

Cynthia wanted no part in any of that. Her interests were far more aligned with practical things.

How many pirouettes did you do today?

Stand in front of the mirror and do fifty more.

How did your audition go?

Next time, wear the shirt that shows more cleavage.

It's no wonder I'm so fucked up. Irreparably damaged. Unfixable.

She poisoned me from the first breath. She made me feel like I was worthless long before I even realized there might be an alternative theory.

But... My hands creep up to my stomach as an inexplicable protective feeling swells inside me. *She will never do that to my child. She will not come near this fragile little life inside me, inflicting a fresh horror story on a blank slate.*

I swear on it with my every thumping heartbeat.

"Leave," I say softly. "Get away — from my house, from my life. I don't want you here."

"I'm not going anywhere. I'm your family. You don't get to just cut me out when it's convenient for you. I'm your mother—"

"No, you aren't. As of this moment, we are officially done. If you come near me again, I'll tell a judge you threatened my welfare and take out a restraining order against you."

Surprise flashes in her eyes. "You cannot be serious."

"Oh, but I am."

She shakes off my words. "Katharine, this is absurd. I'm not leaving until we've—"

"Masters!" I call.

He steps out of the shadows by the car and appears at my side in an instant. "Miss Firestone?"

"I'm going inside." My voice is small but stubborn. "Please make sure Cynthia doesn't follow me."

"Yes, ma'am."

"Katharine! Don't you walk away from me!" My mother calls, furious.

My feet never falter as I walk to the security gate.

"This isn't over! Do you hear me, Katharine! This is *not* over."

I hear her struggling with Masters as I punch in the code and walk slowly up my driveway.

"Get your hands off me, you oaf! Don't you dare touch me! That's my daughter! I have every right to talk to her. Katharine! KATHARINE, GET BACK HERE! You'll regret this! I swear you will!"

I smile as I slide my key into the front door and step inside my new house, shutting out the toxic tone of her voice with a definitive click.

Goodbye, mother.

* * *

The lights beat down so bright I can barely make out the shapes of the audience as they chat and wave and whisper excitedly under their breath, only half paying attention as a PA doles out the standard pre-show instructions — no photographs, no leaving your seat, no loud noises or cellphone use while taping is in progress. Harper and Masters are sitting out there somewhere, but I can't find them in the crowd.

I try not to fidget as the cameras flicker to life and the crew members start counting down the minutes until the broadcast begins. Grayson sneaks a glance at me from behind the opaque wall where we're standing, waiting in the wings.

"*Breathe*, Kat."

I smile blandly. "I'm fine. I'm great, in fact."

I hear a snort from Wyatt and shoot a glare in his direction. "Do you have something to say, Hastings?"

"Nope. Nothing at all." He grins broadly, a flash of white in the dark backstage shadows, and the sight makes the breath catch in my throat. I haven't seen his smile in so long, part of me worried I'd never see it again. True, it's a byproduct of him mocking me, but that doesn't diminish the warmth that spreads through me as I watch joy dawn across his features.

I didn't think I'd see him at all today; producers don't usually make it a habit to show up at press events, unless they're the ones being interviewed. I doubt he'd be here at all, if we weren't about to sit down for a taping of *The Eileen Show*, which happens to permanently occupy Stage 1 on the AXC lot. It's not exactly a big commute for him; his office is about fifty yards away.

I have a feeling he and Sloan selected this as our first public appearance for exactly that reason. It doesn't get much more strategic than having an AXC talkshow host interview the stars of an AXC-backed movie. A textbook case of one hand scratching the other — boosting daytime ratings with a big star appearance, simultaneously cross-promoting the upcoming *Uncharted* premiere. Everyone wins.

Except perhaps the audience.

They actually think they're here to watch their favorite talk show. *How adorable.* They have no idea they're essentially watching an hour-long advertisement for our movie.

Maybe it's sleazy, but that's how Hollywood functions. Virtually everything that makes it onto a TV or movie screen these days is controlled by one of four competing media conglomerates. Objectivity went out the window ages ago.

How did Wyatt once describe it?

Nepotism. And a blatant disregard for moral scruples.

I'd laugh, if I weren't so nervous.

The sound of high heels clicking across the tile draws my attention. A petite, impeccably dressed African American woman approaches, examining Grayson and me with shrewd intelligence. It's jarring to see one of the most recognizable faces on the planet in person for the first time. Most people only ever witness Eileen Dillan through a television screen.

Her dark mocha skin is luminescent under the overhead track lights, her hair is elegantly coiffed in a French twist. She looks perfectly at ease despite the fact that we're about to do a live studio broadcast — which, I suppose, shouldn't come as such a shock, given that she's been hosting this gig for nearly a decade now. *The Eileen Show* is an American institution. If daytime television had a hierarchy, Eileen would undoubtedly reign as queen.

Her smile is brilliant. "Grayson Dunn, as I live and breathe."

"Hello, gorgeous." Grayson gives her a one-armed hug.

"Don't flirt with me, I'm old enough to be your mother."

He winks. "As if that would stop me."

She laughs. "What's it been, a year since you came for a visit?"

"Two, at least," he says. "I haven't been here since the first Starkiller movie premiered."

"You're overdue for an appearance, then. Don't keep that handsome mug away so long next time, you hear me?" She turns to me, still smiling. "And you must be Katharine. It's wonderful to meet you."

I attempt to smile back, but I'm still feeling rather queasy. "It's great to meet you too, Eileen. Thanks for having us."

Her head cocks sideways. "First time doing a TV interview?"

I nod.

"Oh, goodie!" Her voice drops to a conspiratorial whisper. "I love virgins."

A startled giggle bursts from my mouth. I feel more at ease already.

"Don't worry, we'll take good care of you." Eileen squeezes my hand. "I'll do a quick intro before we launch in. Grayson first, then you following. Just remember — no profanity. This segment airs nationwide in about an hour, so we don't have time to edit much out."

I gulp.

She smiles kindly. "Relax. Be natural. Be yourself. Don't overthink it too much."

"Thanks."

"Plus, you've got Grayson here to keep you on course." She pinches his cheek playfully.

He swats her hand away.

Eileen adjusts the wired microphone inside her blouse as she peers out at the set. A producer is waving wildly at her.

"That's my cue! I'll see you out there, kids."

With that, she walks out on stage, waving at the crowd. They roar and rise to their feet, applauding like mad as she makes her way over to her trademark white chair. There's a matching settee, big enough for Grayson and me to sit on, set up beside it. If not for the crowd and the three enormous cameras zooming in on Eileen to capture her every angle, it would look like a posh living room in a Pottery Barn catalogue.

"Welcome to *The Eileen Show!*" Eileen settles in on her chair, perfectly at ease as three hundred people chant her name. She ignores them, speaking directly into the center camera. "We've got a fantastic show lined up for you today and some great prizes to give away later." The cheers swell to a roar. "But first, I'd like you to put your hands together and give a very warm welcome to our first guest. You'll recognize him from the famous *Starkiller* franchise — as well as the shirtless poster of him hanging over your teenage sister's bed —" Grayson snorts. "That's right, folks! We've got Grayson Dunn here today to talk about his new movie! Grayson... get your toned butt out here!"

The screaming crescendoes so loud that the air seems to vibrate as Grayson walks onto the stage, his demeanor shifting subtly with each stride. His eyes adopt a seductive glint, his mouth purses in his trademark bad-boy pout. He always exudes raw sexual energy but as he steps in front of the crowd now, it's like someone has reached inside his chest and turned a knob from simmer to boil. He's magnetic. Every eye is on him as he swaggers to the settee like a god.

Confronted with the object of all their fantasies, the frenzied women in the crowd scream his name and dissolve into a mob of estrogen-fueled madness. I see their red cheeks and streaming eyes, their hyperventilation and hysteria, and it kindles an uncomfortable sensation inside me. There's something alarming about that level of devotion from people you've never actually met.

It takes a long time for them to settle down. Eventually, Eileen has to rise to her feet and motion for silence.

"So, do you think they're excited to see you?" she asks dryly, staring at Grayson.

He gives his best *you-know-you-love-me* grin as the crowd cheers again.

Eileen giggles girlishly. "I have another surprise guest to introduce in a few moments, but first let me tell you all a little story about the first time I met Grayson..."

Shifting back and forth on numb feet, I tune out the anecdote the crowd is licking up like ice cream off a spoon. Nausea grips me tightly.

How the hell am I going to follow *that* thunderous introduction? Most of these women in the crowd either don't have any idea who I am, or they hate me for supposedly breaking up Grayson and Helena, thanks to the slew of unflattering tabloid stories that ran while we were filming in Hawaii.

Visions of them staring blankly — or worse, booing — as I step from the wings flit through my mind. I can feel myself starting to spiral into panic as I watch Eileen and Grayson conversing easily on the stage, knowing that this recording will be broadcast into every house in the nation in a matter of minutes.

It's almost unbelievable that, after all my time in front of the cameras, all my experience at auditions and call backs, I'd be suffering from stage fright *now*, in this moment. And yet, undeniably, that's what I'm experiencing — the shallow breaths, rapid heartbeat, aching temples, and foggy thoughts are a dead giveaway.

Perhaps my sudden panic is because, until this point, it's never mattered much what I said to the press. I was nobody. Four months ago, I could've stood naked on top of Warner Brothers' studio doing the flamenco and no one would've blinked twice.

But now... nothing I do goes unnoticed. There's a very good chance I could, in fact, fuck things up beyond repair — not just for my own career, but for the movie.

If I'm stiff and awkward and charmless... Who would pay to see me on the big screen? Who would care about my chemistry with Grayson?

Don't go out there.

You'll screw it up.

Cynthia was right.

Bail. Run. Bolt.

"Hey." A voice pulls me out of the dark place I've slipped into. I feel a warm palm on my shoulder, a solid presence at my side. "Hey. Don't look at them. Look at me."

My wide, desperate eyes dart up to lock on a steady sea of blue.

"You're okay," Wyatt says, pivoting my body toward his, so the stage is at my back.

"I can't go out there, Wyatt." I gulp. "I can't do this. I'm sorry, I thought I could, but I think—"

"Katharine." He gives me a light shake. I feel the press of his fingertips against my skin and try to focus on that instead of the fear and the panic churning through me. "Take a deep breath. That's it — in through your nose, out through your mouth. Good. Do it again. One more time."

He breathes with me, applying firm pressure on my shoulders as I stare up at him.

Saving me, even when he hates me.

Eventually I feel my jagged breaths even out into something remotely normal. The panic is still there, swirling through me, but it's walled off behind a barrier of calm, built brick by brick out of Wyatt's steady hands and soothing words.

I hear Eileen winding down her Grayson story, starting to make my introduction. "I've got another surprise for you today — no, it's not Ryan Gosling, there's a law in Los Angeles that he and Grayson aren't allowed to be in the same room, it causes riots," she jokes, but it all sounds somewhat distant as I look into Wyatt's eyes. He doesn't pull away.

"We've got the exclusive first look at *Uncharted*, Grayson's new movie!" she says, making the crowd roar again. "But, that's not all..."

I suck in another deep breath.

"We've also got his new co-star Katharine Firestone in the house! It's her first time on the show, so let's make some noise for her!"

The cheers build to an undulating wave of sound.

"You can do this, Katharine." Wyatt pivots my body toward the stage again. His mouth hits my ear. "You hear me? *You can do this.* I know you can."

"Okay," I whisper, staring at the stage, but the word is lost in the clamor of the crowd.

Wyatt gives me a small push between the shoulder blades and I stagger out of the wings, blinking at the bright lights overhead. The rumble of hundreds of voices hits me like a punch to the stomach.

I can do this.

I smile and wave as I walk to the settee, trying to take in the sight of the crowd, but I barely see it. My mind is fully focused on the memory of two bottomless blue irises, an ocean where I'd happily drown... and a warm set of hands stroking the bare skin of my biceps... and the gruff, steady sound of a voice pulling me back from the brink.

Out of the shadows.

Into the sunshine.

CHAPTER FIVE

"Baby, you turn me on."
- A lamp.

The crowd goes wild for the footage of *Uncharted*.
It's the first glimpse the world has ever seen of
Violet and Beck's epic love story — barely more than
thirty seconds of clips roughly cut into a teaser. And yet,
their excitement is palpable. They gasp at all the right
places, elbowing each other and squealing when the giant
screen behind us flashes with a shot of Grayson emerging
from the waves, shirtless and dripping. Sighing when the
screen fades out to a montage of us kissing on the beach
at sunset.

It's surreal to see myself, larger than life, on the
screen, being watched by strangers. An out of body
experience that sets my heart galloping in my chest and
makes my palms grow clammy with sweat. I'm thankful
for the audience's long applause when the sizzle reel ends
— I find I need the time to recover. My days as a child
star on *Busy Bees* did not adequately prepare me for this
moment.

So far, the interview has gone better than I dared
to hope. Eileen truly is a pro at making her guests feel
at ease, and Grayson is well-practiced after years in the
public eye. Between the two of them, the conversation
flows easily — trading jokes and anecdotes, keeping
things light and fun, avoiding the landmine topic of
relationships; a stipulation we agreed to before the
interview. The attention is rarely on me, for which I'm
grateful, and when it does stray my way, somehow Eileen

manages to make me sound charming and composed, instead of mulish and tongue-tied.

"Whew!" She makes a show of fanning herself with both hands, looking out over the audience. "I don't know about y'all, but I think I need a moment to compose myself! How sexy was that sizzle reel?"

Whistles and cheers echo back from the audience.

Eileen turns to look at Grayson and me. "I think I speak for everyone here when I ask... where the heck do I buy my ticket?"

We both grin.

The rest of the interview passes easily, talking about the film and our time shooting in Hawaii, getting the audience excited for the premiere in a few weeks. By the end, I'm almost giddy with relief — I couldn't have asked for a better first appearance. There's a buoyant sort of joy bubbling inside me when Eileen's face twists into a mischievous grin that tells me she's about to throw a curve ball my way.

The buoyancy dissipates in an instant.

"We're just about out of time, but I'd be remiss if I let you go without asking one final question that's just *killing* me."

My eyebrows lift.

Eileen leans in, like we're friends gossiping over margaritas. "How on earth did you spend two weeks on a tropical island with this guy and not fall in love with him?"

"Um, I... I..." I stammer, feeling my cheeks heat. My mouth goes dry. My tongue feels swollen to twice its normal size as the seconds tick on and I try desperately to think of something — *anything* — to say besides the truth.

I did fall in love with him.

There's a swell of anticipation from the audience. They want the answer to this question, too.

Grayson scoots a fraction closer to me on the settee, sensing my panic.

80

"Oh, come on. Give us the dirt, won't you Kat?" Eileen prompts. "Just a few juicy details."

"Well, we... we..."

There's a glint in Eileen's eyes. She's a shark, smelling blood in the water. Sensing a good story.

"I *must* know..." She jerks her thumb at the screen behind us. "Was any of that chemistry real? Or was it all for the cameras?"

You're not supposed to ask me that! I want to yell. *This is none of your business!*

I feel anger rise up inside me. Eileen's bright smile and light laughter were a well-laid trap. A parlor trick, designed to loosen me up so I'd easily spill my secrets... and boost her ratings.

I open my mouth to say something I'll likely regret, but Grayson beats me to it. Before I can get out a single word, his hand lands on top of mine, stilling me to silence.

"Actually, Eileen, the truth is... we've been trying to keep this quiet. Kat didn't want to tell anyone yet, because it's new and, well, we're still figuring things out." His booming voice carries across the set. Every member of the audience is listening intently, leaning forward in their seats to catch his words.

"Figuring what out, Grayson?" Eileen sounds breathy with excitement.

He squeezes my hand. "Our relationship. *Us.*"

My mouth gapes. I shoot him a look of disbelief and find he's staring at me with an indecipherable expression.

"Grayson!" Eileen gasps. "I'm sorry, are you saying what I think you're saying? Are you two... are you and Kat... *together?*"

He doesn't hesitate. "Yes. That's exactly what I'm saying."

There's a collective gasp from the crowd.

I try to speak, try to force out the words to counteract his lies, but nothing escapes my lips except a squeak of distress.

Grayson scoots over until our shoulders press together. "I'm sorry, sweetheart, I just couldn't keep it a secret anymore. Don't be mad at me." His warm fingers twine with my limp ones as he pulls my hand up to his mouth and presses a soft kiss to my skin. He slides his other arm around my shoulders and pulls me in close. "I want the world to know how I feel about you."

I cannot breathe.

"My goodness!" Eileen's eyes are welling with fake tears. "If that isn't just the sweetest thing I've ever seen!"

Several women in the crowd are weeping audibly. I feel like joining them, though my own tears will not be joyful.

"What do you say, Kat? Do you forgive him for letting the *cat* out of the bag?" Eileen asks me. "How could you not, right?"

The cameras push in on my face. I look out at the audience and see they're all buzzing with delight about my new relationship. And I know, beyond a shadow of a doubt, that I have no choice. I have been neatly boxed into a corner.

I glance over my shoulder, almost involuntarily. It's silly — I can't see into the stage wings, from here. And, even if I could spot Wyatt, I'm not sure it would matter.

It won't change a thing.

Grayson's hand squeezes mine almost to the point of pain, and I realize I haven't responded.

"Ow!" I yelp. He squeezes again, warningly. "I mean, *Oh*. Yes, of course I forgive him," I lie, hoping my extreme anger isn't too noticeable as I smile like a lovesick idiot.

"Thanks, sweetheart." Grayson's voice is silky sweet — like honey, sliding down the back of my throat. I could choke to death on it. "I'm still getting the hang of this... this *boyfriend* thing." Grayson drawls, full of false modesty. "I'm sure you know — I've never exactly done it before."

"Oh, we know!" Eileen looks happier than a kid in a candy shop. "I just can't believe it. It seems impossible that Grayson Dunn, serial bachelor, breaker of hearts, is in a committed relationship!"

"Eileen, two months ago, before we filmed this movie, before I fell for this incredible girl, I would've agreed with you," he says solemnly. "Now, I know that *nothing* is impossible when it comes to love. My darling Kat taught me that."

Pretending to nuzzle into his side, I dig a sharp elbow into his gut. I hear him wheeze softly in pain. He soon gets his revenge, though — grabbing my chin, he turns my face and plants a soft kiss on my lips that makes every woman in the building sigh.

When he pulls back, Grayson makes a tender show of tucking a loose strand of hair behind my ear. I resist the urge to bite his fingers off when they come within an inch of my mouth. My grin says *I love you, darling.* My eyes scream *I am going to murder you with my bare hands.*

"My goodness! You two are just *adorable!*" Eileen dabs an invisible tear with a tissue. "Aren't they adorable?"

The audience cheers.

"Color me shocked. Flabbergasted!" She glances at her watch. "Oh, would you look at that! We're officially out of time for the day! But remember, folks — you heard it here first! The Sexiest Man Alive is officially off the market!"

"Yes, I am. And frankly, I couldn't be happier." Grayson laces his fingers with mine again. "Sorry. I mean *we* couldn't be happier."

* * *

"She still hasn't said anything?" Harper sounds concerned.

"Nope," Grayson confirms cheerfully.

"Not a word?"

"Not one."

"Nothing?"

"Silent as the grave." Grayson's head tilts as he examines me. "Though, the constant pacing is communicating quite a lot. Nonverbally, that is."

I stop pacing. I open my mouth to speak, but nothing comes out, so I start pacing again.

"Really thought she was going to say something, that time," Masters murmurs.

I take a few more strides back and forth across the small conference room in the AXC executive suites where I've been making tracks in the carpet for twenty full minutes. My breaths are ragged with fury. Each time I catch a glimpse of Grayson, sprawled across a nearby sofa looking more goddamned pleased with himself than Michael Phelps at the Olympics, my hands itch to wrap around his throat. And not in a sexy, semi-erotic way; in an *asphyxiate-you-until-you-die* kind of way.

After the interview, as soon as the cameras stopped rolling I sidestepped out of Grayson's arms, said an entirely insincere *thank you* to Eileen, and escaped offstage. I reached the wings in a flash, my eyes roaming every dark corner for a glimpse of bronze hair and broad shoulders, but there was nothing. No one.

No *Wyatt*.

I scared a meek PA half to death when I grabbed her in a vise-grip and shook her until she squeaked out that he'd left a few minutes before the interview ended.

"When, exactly?" I pressed, needing specifics.

"I—I don't remember. I'm sorry, Miss Firestone." She shrugged helplessly. "I was watching the show..." Her cheeks flush. "I got distracted when Grayson kissed you, only for a minute, and when I turned around I noticed that Mr. Hastings was gone. He must've left right around then."

Of course he did.

I relinquished my hold, feeling somewhat guilty for taking my rage at Grayson out on her. In penance, I only scowled a little when she followed up with a request to take a selfie with me.

"What's it like, being Grayson Dunn's girlfriend?" she asked, clicking the shutter button of her camera phone.

"Swell," I bit out through clenched teeth, heading for the exit.

"Kat!" Grayson called. "Kat, where are you going?"

His voice was like a gunshot at a track meet — faster than a sprinter off the blocks, I bolted out the door and across the parking lot, weaving through parked cars and golf carts zipping between stages, dodging the bustling crowds of tourists and audience members pouring out the warehouse doors. I ducked down to avoid detection and practically crawled my way to the executive offices... only to find, when I arrived with scraped knees and wild eyes and loose hair, that Wyatt had already left for the day, according to his unenthused personal secretary, Jane, who passed me a water bottle and led me to a conference room to cool off out of sight.

Grayson, Harper, and Masters tracked me down a few moments later. By that point, the pacing had started; now, a half hour later, I can't seem to make it stop.

"Should I slap her?" Harper asks, sounding a bit too intrigued by the idea for my liking. "They're always slapping people out of stupors, in the movies."

"She's not in a stupor." Masters sighs. "She's just processing. Let her process."

"I don't know what she needs to process." Grayson stretches like a cat in the sunshine. "It's not like this is a death sentence. She's dating me, not dying of cholera."

Harper snorts.

My feet freeze. My head spins around and I laser-in on his face with the most lethal look I can conjure.

"Don't look at me like that, kitten." He winks. "This is going to be fun. I promise."

I suck in a breath.

That's it.

That. Is. *It.*

"ARE YOU OUT OF YOUR GODDAMNED MIND?"
I scream at the top of my lungs, throwing my hands up
in the air. "I mean it! Of all the asinine, awful, idiotic,
infuriating, short-sighted, selfish things you've ever done,
Grayson Dunn, THIS ONE TAKES THE GRAND FUCKING
PRIZE!"

"So... I gather you're a bit peeved." He grins again.

"*PEEVED?*" I roar.

"A tad upset?"

"No, I'm not upset. Upset is too tame a word for
what I'm feeling. I'm... I'm... I'm *seething*. I'm *furious*. I'm
infuriated."

"Huh." He has the nerve to laugh. "And here I was
thinking that murderous look in your eyes was all for
show."

I scream incoherently. Distantly, I hear the door
click closed — Masters and Harper have fled to give us
some privacy — but I don't pay it any attention. I'm too
busy glaring at my co-star.

"Honestly, I don't see what the big deal is."
Grayson's face is carefully blank as he pushes to his feet.
Even if I gave a damn what he was feeling right now —
which I do *not* — I wouldn't be able to read his expression.
"You were floundering. Eileen's question threw you off
balance. The way I see it, I did you a favor."

"You didn't do me a favor!" I growl. "You fabricated
a relationship!"

"I did what needed to be done for the movie. For
both our careers. And I'd do it again in a heartbeat. I don't
regret my choice."

"But it wasn't just your choice to make! This affects
me, too." I grab my hair at the roots, tempted to pull it
out. "I know you're allergic to commitment and have
never been in a relationship, so maybe you don't realize
this, but you can't just *say* we're a couple and expect the
public to buy it. Now, we actually have to act like a couple.
Go places together. Engage in PDA for the paparazzi. Post
photos on social media." I scream again at the thought.

"This isn't some little white lie you tell to make yourself more endearing. *I walk shelter dogs on Sundays and read to orphans whenever I have free time.* No! This is a life-altering ruse that's going to mess with every single part of both our lives. Don't you understand that?"

He shrugs, looking totally unconcerned. "So, we act like a committed couple for the cameras. Still don't see why you're freaking out."

My eyes widen. "You... I... *Grayson*," I plead. "Think about this for a second. You won't get to sleep around. You can't go to clubs to hook up with slutty girls. You can't stumble home to your Malibu mansion with a Victoria's Secret model on each arm at four in the morning."

"I know that." His face twists into a scowl. "I'm not a complete idiot."

"Could've fooled me!"

"Stop with the flattery, you'll make me blush."

I ignore him. "It doesn't bother you that you've essentially just condemned yourself to a life without sex, then?"

"Isn't that kind of a given, in a committed relationship?" He smirks. "Once you settle down, hot sex pretty much goes out the window."

I glare in lieu of a response.

"So... since we agree it's necessary to be seen in public together... how about I pick you up tomorrow, for the radio interviews? I'll be there around noon. Just need your new address."

"No."

"Fine, I'll get it from Sloan."

"You think this is a joke," I say, stunned at his self-absorption. "But this isn't a joke to me. This is my life. And you've already reached your quota for fucking it up, all right?"

He goes still. I watch his face darken like a storm.

"It's not a joke to me." He takes a step toward me, his ever-playful demeanor dropping away like a mask. The man I suddenly glimpse below the surface is a strange, unfamiliar creature, filled with slow-burning anger. Something long-felt and well-hidden. Something I've never seen before, in all my time knowing him.

This is not the man-child, incapable of real emotion.

His voice cracks with intensity. "It was the right call, and you know it. I'm not sorry, Kat. Not even a little bit."

"You're *never* sorry, are you Grayson?" I snap, too pissed to curtail my mean-spirited words.

"Oh, we're back to that then, are we? Back to Hawaii?"

"No," I mutter. "This isn't about Hawaii."

"Bullshit." He takes another step toward me, eyes flashing. "You expect me to believe you're over it? That you're not still pissed off at me for leaving? That this anger, right here, this fight, isn't at least partially about the way things ended between us?"

"Things didn't end; they never even started."

"Nice dodge." He rolls his eyes. "You keep pretending we can be cordial co-stars, that none of this affects you, but we both know that's a load of shit. You're still pissed at me, and it's not about some bullshit interview answer. It's about what I did to you when I walked away. When I let *you* walk away, without fighting to make things work. You might not want to face that because it's painful... but it's the truth."

I consider his words for a second.

"Good try, but *no*. This actually *is* about your stunt during the interview. Because, once again, Grayson Dunn makes unilateral decisions that affect someone else, without ever stopping to consider their opinion on the matter. That behavior doesn't make you cute or charming — it makes you an asshole."

He scoffs. "Tell me again how you're *not* mad?"

"Oh, I'm mad. I'm mad about your behavior *today* and the fact that I'm going to have to deal with the fallout of that behavior for the next six weeks. I'm mad that you've made a decision that affects both of us, when I specifically said I wanted no part of it at Sloan's yesterday. I'm mad for a whole slew of reasons, but hear me when I say this..." I jerk my head, furious. "I'm not pissed off about Hawaii anymore, so you can get that out of your head. I'm not pining. I'm not heartbroken. I'm not crying into my pillow or drinking myself into oblivion or waiting around for your call. I'm *fine*. I'm me again. I'm over Hawaii. Over *you*."

I didn't mean it as a challenge.

He takes it as one anyway.

With two long-legged strides, he closes the distance between us. Before I can move, he's yanked me into his arms and crushed his mouth against mine. He kisses me with fury and frustration, pouring all the heat from our argument into each scrape of his teeth, each stroke of his tongue. Ravaging my mouth, as if he's burning alive and wants me to burn with him.

Kissing me into submission, like he's done a thousand times before.

Stealing my fire with seduction.

Lulling me into complacency with lust.

He is a silver-tongued manipulator, using the best weapons in his arsenal against me.

Except, this time, I know better.

I don't return his kiss. I struggle in his arms, thrashing like a wild creature caught in a net, until my lip is bleeding and he's cursing from a sharp kick to the shin. Swearing, he releases his hold. My arms are free for less than a second when I reel back and slap him full across the face.

The crack of my hand against his skin makes us both go still.

He doesn't move to block my strike. He doesn't even react. He stands there, staring at my swollen lips, his gorgeous face marred by a stark red handprint on his cheekbone.

He's stunned I hit him; frankly, so am I.

I'm panting hard. The emotions swirling inside me

are pressing at my ribs, filling my chest cavity to capacity. It's only a matter of time before I crack wide open, unable to contain them.

You cannot sway me with a few lustful kisses.

My opinions will not be swallowed with a few swipes of your lips against mine.

I already learned that lesson — learned it the hard way, clawing my way up from the bottom of a bottle, hating myself for my own weakness every inch of the way.

My voice is eerily hollow when I speak.

"You treat people like pawns on your chessboard, always calculating how to bend the pieces to your will, always seeking to overthrow the balance of power so you're in control of the game. But you've never seemed to realize that, when you win at chess, you end up all alone on the battlefield. A sad, crooked king, with nothing to show for his victory except a crown no one is even left to admire." I brush my bleeding lip with the back of my hand and stare at the bright smear of red against my skin for a long moment before my eyes drift up to his. "I'm so tired of fighting with you. So tired of being mad all the time. So... I'm *done*. Done caring. As far as I'm concerned, when the cameras are off, we have nothing more to say to each other. For the sake of the movie, I'll keep up appearances during the rest of this press tour. But, when it's over, I never want to see you again. I mean it."

"Kat—"

"Don't you get it? I don't want to play your game anymore, Grayson. I can't." My voice is empty. "You *win*. Checkmate. Consider this my forfeit."

His eyes go flat. I watch his Adam's apple bobbing up and down as his throat works, and wonder if he'll say anything to contradict my words. He doesn't... because I think, deep down, he knows there's nothing he can say. He's made our bed — now we both have to lie in it, at least until the premiere.

Six weeks.

I will survive this.

90

I will survive him.

I look at Grayson, really look at him — allowing my eyes linger on his perfect face, feeling my heart slow its rapid patter inside my chest. I search for the anger, for the outrage I felt just moments ago, but it's gone.

I have no more fight in me. I have waded waist-deep through the sea of grief and reached the far-flung shores of acceptance.

Denial was a duffle bag on a sandy beach.

Anger was a kiss ankle-deep in salty waves.

Bargaining was a doorbell ring at 2AM.

Depression was the bottom of a bottle

Acceptance was a slap across the face.

Five recognized stages of grief: I've cycled through them all in the past few weeks. The unbearable heights and intolerable lows of loving Grayson Dunn have filled me with more emotion than I was ever equipped to handle, then wrung me out like a wet paper towel — the cheap, store brand kind that disintegrates after a single use.

And finally, *finally*, I find myself here — shredded, but still standing. Ready to relinquish him for good. Because, with one final strike of a hand across a cheek, the fury has finally burned out.

I am a girl of ashes and embers.

And now... I will rise.

A phoenix, reborn into something better. Perhaps a little sadder, but definitely a lot stronger.

I look at the beautiful boy who made me see stars, the almost-man who offered me something he wasn't ready to give, and realize the weight of this heartbreak is a boulder on my chest, keeping me pinned against the earth. Holding me down, when what I really want to do is fly.

Fly like the birds I once watched spiral into the sunset as he held me in his arms beneath a waterfall.

Fly like that phoenix from the ashes, to a distant horizon where far, far better things await me.

He opens his mouth to say something — maybe to keep fighting, maybe to apologize.

I don't know.

I don't care.

I don't hesitate.

I turn on wings of self-determination and fly away, leaving my selfish stardust boy behind on the ground.

I will not keep waiting for him to grow wings of his own. Not for another instant.

* * *

I step outside into the crisp December day. It's overcast and unnaturally cold, by LA standards. I'm not paying attention as I dig through my purse in search of my cellphone; in truth, my thoughts are back with Grayson, in the conference room, which is probably why I don't see the figure stepping into my path before it's too late.

"Hey."

"Jesus Christ!" My hand flies up to cover my heart. "Trey, you scared me half to death."

"Sorry." The PA doesn't look sorry at all as he shifts from foot to foot impatiently. "Sloan asked me to track you down after the Eileen interview, but you ran out so fast I didn't have a chance."

"Has there been a change in the tour schedule?"

He shakes his head and pulls a gilded silver envelope from his ever-present clipboard. "I'm afraid Sloan has gotten it into his head to host a New Year's Eve party. Your attendance is requested."

I take the envelope from him and run a fingertip over my name, hand printed in fancy calligraphy across the front.

"Of course, I've told him a million times, it's dreadfully late to send out invitations *now*, with barely a week's notice, but does he listen? No." Trey throws up his hands, as if his boss is a lost cause. "Not only does this mean I have to give up my own plans, the sad fact is that everyone with even an iota of social capital already has an invitation somewhere. At best, we'll end up with a group of losers who don't have better things to do. *Pop the champagne!* I can hardly wait."

It's the most words I've ever heard Trey string together all at once. I'm so stunned I can't think of a thing to do except blink at him, baffled, and say, "Actually... I don't have any plans."

"Oh! Well. That doesn't mean you're a loser." His nose wrinkles, as if he doesn't quite believe his own assurances. "Anyway, I'm off — I have caterers to yell at, decor to coordinate, and guests to harangue into attending. *Ciao!*"

He pivots on a glossy Prada dress shoe and vanishes.

Shaking myself, I watch him disappear down the sidewalk. I'm about to start digging for my phone again when Masters' SUV pulls to a stop by the curb. A darkly-tinted window rolls down, revealing Harper's worried face.

"Did you kill him?"

"Tempting as it was, I really don't feel like serving a thirty-year sentence just for the pleasure of permanently removing Grayson Dunn from my life." I climb into the backseat and sigh heavily as I relax against the leather. "God, I need someone to take me out."

"On a dinner date?" Harper asks.

"Or with a sniper rifle. Either one."

Masters laughs.

I'm stunned; I didn't think he knew how to do that. When he realizes we're both staring at him open-mouthed, the laugh morphs into a cough and his lips press into a stern line.

"Don't look so shocked. I know how to laugh."

Harper snorts. "Babe. We've been together a month. I've never heard so much as a chuckle from your general direction."

"Just because I don't cackle like a hyena at every little thing, as the two of you are prone to..."

"Hyenas?" I wrinkle my nose.

"Definitely not hyenas," Harper concurs.

"What's wrong with hyenas?" Masters asks.

"Besides the fact that they're the ugliest creatures on the planet?" I grimace. "Nothing at all."

"We're much cuter than hyenas," Harper murmurs. "Meerkats, maybe. *Oh*! Or otters. Otters are adorable. Did you know they hold hands to keep from floating apart while they nap?"

Masters merges the car left, taking the turn toward my neighborhood. "Don't care what you see yourself as, so long as you can acknowledge you're also *crazy*."

"Rude," Harper says.

"True," he mutters.

We reach my house fifteen minutes later. I'm barely out of the car when Harper spots the silver envelope in my hands and swipes it from me.

"What's this?"

"See for yourself, you've already stolen it."

She pulls the thick card-stock out and reads aloud. "*A masked affair...* Sloan's having a New Year's Eve masquerade party? Am I invited?"

"Does it say I get a plus one?"

"Yes."

"Then consider yourself invited."

"Excellent." Her eyes glitter. "I have an Olympic gold medal in coordinating cute New Year's Eve outfits."

"Didn't know they gave those out," Masters says dryly.

She waves his words away. "You're just jealous because you aren't invited."

He glances at me. "Assuming you'll need a designated driver?"

I nod.

He glances at his girlfriend. "Apparently, I'm invited."

I laugh as she narrows her eyes at him, then stomps inside. Alone with Masters, I pause before following her in.

He looks at me questioningly.

"You're good for her," I inform him.

His brows go up. "But?"

"Who says there's a but?"

He just waits.

I sigh. "*But*... if you screw it up... you know I'll have to kill you, right?"

"Appreciate the sentiment." His lips twitch. "Not planning to screw it up."

"Glad to hear it."

"You okay?" he asks. "The Dunn situation. Not ideal."

I let a gust of air out from between my lips. "No. Definitely not ideal."

"You gonna tell him?"

"About?"

He waits a beat, eyes flickering down to my stomach and back.

I feel my heart lurch. "You know."

He nods.

"*How* do you know?"

I don't know why I bother asking — Masters is the most observant person I've ever met. He knows *everything*. Still, he humors me.

"No alcohol in weeks. Running to the bathroom at the sushi place. Keeping saltine crackers in your purse everywhere you go to stave off nausea — figured you're either seasick or pregnant, and you don't strike me as the nautical type."

"Shit. Apparently, I'll have to be more careful. Still... No one else has figured it out. Even Harper..." I blanch. "Wait... you didn't tell her, did you?"

"Not my place to tell her, Miss Firestone." His eyes are steady on mine. "But, for the record, I think *you* should."

"I can't. Not yet. She'll freak."

He nods. "Yeah. She does that. But, when she's done freaking, she'll help. And, right now, I'm thinking you could use some help."

"You aren't wrong," I admit softly.

"Plus," he says quietly. "Secret like this... there's only so long you can keep it."

His eyes drop to my stomach again. I haven't started showing — it's still too early for that. But it's only a matter of time.

"Wait too long, you won't have to tell," he murmurs. "It'll be plain for everyone to see. Even someone as self-absorbed as Grayson Dunn."

I bite the inside of my cheek.

...And especially someone as observant as Wyatt Hastings.

CHAPTER SIX

"**I** NEED YOU RIGHT NOW."
- A girl waiting at the window for the pizza delivery guy.

After the way we left things, I wasn't sure Grayson
would actually show up to drive me to the radio interview
the following day, but at noon on the dot there's a short
beep at the gates outside my house. I push a button to
open them and watch as his Bugatti glides to a soundless
stop by my walkway.

He doesn't get out to greet me as I lock my front
door and approach.

I don't say anything as I climb inside and strap on
my seatbelt, replaying the last words I spoke to him over
and over in my head.

*As far as I'm concerned, when the cameras are off, we
have nothing more to say to each other.*

A frozen silence descends over us and doesn't thaw
for the entirety of our trip from the Palisades to the
LA-FM building downtown, a sleek glass tower home to
five of the biggest West Coast radio stations, where we're
scheduled to record multiple interviews with different
entertainment news shows.

There's a mob scene of paparazzi waiting for us
when we pull up to the valet. They go wild when they
recognize the car. Grayson's security team, following at a
discreet distance in their dark SUV, climb out and do their
best to keep the crowd under control. Even with their
solemn expressions and steel-forged shoulders clearing a
path for us to the doors, I'd feel safer with Masters by my
side.

"Showtime," Grayson mutters.

They're eager for photographs of Hollywood's newest couple; we do our damnedest not to disappoint them.

Grayson holds my door open like a gentleman, making a show for the camera-wielding men lining the curb. I lean into his chest and let him kiss my forehead like a smitten idiot, all for the sake of his fans, who live-stream our images to various social media platforms with cutesy hashtags that make me die a little inside.

#GrayKat

Outside, I'm smiling.

Inside, I'm screaming.

Moving between several different recording rooms, we do three radio interviews back to back — joking and giggling while the microphones are live, holding hands to keep up the appearance of a loving couple as we enter the recording studio and greet each host. They've all heard the news, by now. Clips from our interview with Eileen have been playing on a loop on every entertainment site, trending worldwide on every social media platform, and freeze-framed on the front of every gossip magazine.

The radio personalities want to know about everything — all our firsts. First kiss, first date, first moment he knew I was *the one* finally worth giving up his man-whorish ways for.

The saddest thing is, we don't have to fabricate much. It sounds, to the unknowing ear, like a fairy tale: two childhood co-stars, reunited after a decade of distance, starring in the most epic romance of the year. A love tailor-made for movie screens.

Unless, of course, you know the truth.

That the hero wouldn't stay.

That the heroine couldn't change his mind.

That it wasn't really love at all — just the potential for something wonderful, wasted on two people who were never meant to be.

I smile as I listen to Grayson talking about our waterfall hikes on the shores of Oahu, I laugh as I hear him describing our moments drinking rum beneath the stars. I'm the perfect impersonation of a happy, star-crossed girl, chiming in with careful details here and there, to flesh out the tale. But, all the while, inside me something is unraveling. The last shred of attachment, cut clean through with the sharp blade of his calculation, for I cannot fathom how he could so casually lay bare all our secrets for strangers, or use our story as fodder for the masses.

All for what?

Soundbites and ticket sales.

I sit beside him, listening to him talk about our love affair as if it happened to someone else, and know that he is not the man I thought he was, nor the man I wished he could be. The Grayson Dunn in my head has always been an embellished version of his true self — kinder, more compassionate, infinitely more caring.

I have been loving and hating and mourning an illusion.

When we reach the car, he holds open my door like a gentleman, but there's anger in his eyes. I rip my hand from his grip as soon as we're out of the paparazzi's line of sight. He slams my door with a bit more force than necessary. I smash the buckles of my seatbelt together with a harsh click, then stare pointedly out the window as he climbs into the driver's seat and starts the engine.

Neither of us speaks. We have used up all our falsely bright words and unfailingly happy smiles on strangers. The only thing left to simmer in the air between us is resentment and rage.

The drive home is slow and silent. It calls to mind another car ride with him, back before everything got so sad and twisted and broken between us, when he dropped me off after playing chess in my favorite park. It seems far longer than two months have passed, since then. I was a different girl entirely. Someone I don't even recognize.

We pull up to my security gate and I murmur the code under my breath. He punches it in with aggressive jabs and pulls silently up to my front walkway. The car has barely pulled to a stop but I'm already reaching for the door handle, eager to escape him.

"See you tomorrow, *sweetheart*," he snaps as I step outside.

"Can't wait, *darling*," I drawl, voice thick with sarcasm.

I slam the door and disappear inside.

The next day follows a similar pattern as the *Uncharted* press junket continues — we do two more talk show sit-downs in front of a studio audience, then make an appearance at AXC to take photos with fans who've paid for a VIP studio tour package. I spend hours smiling until my cheeks ache, laughing at things I find humorless, letting Grayson run his hands over my body and leaning into his touch instead of smacking his hands away.

It's painful… but it's part of the job.

For days, I barely see anyone except Grayson. Harper comes over in the mornings to do my makeup and Masters checks in on me at night, but the majority of my waking hours are spent alone with my co-star, either grinning at each other for the cameras or glaring at each other in private. We don't discuss the hostility burning bright between us. There's nothing left to say. Rehashing the same old arguments would be a waste of breath, and we're both too stubborn to apologize — him for his hasty actions, me for my antagonistic words.

By the third day, the tension has reached a breaking point. It's Christmas Eve, and everyone around us is practically overflowing with holiday spirit… which only seems to make our silent war of wills more strained by comparison. There's something physically draining about being surrounded by happy people when you're acutely miserable. Perhaps that's why suicide rates skyrocket this time of year. Depression in the face of all that god-awful cheer makes you wonder if something is wrong with you, down to your DNA.

We're walking back to Grayson's car after a particularly mundane interview with a panel of popular teenage internet bloggers who Sloan assures us are *influencers*, when a paparazzo slips through the security perimeter on the sidewalk, camera shoved close to our faces.

"Grayson! Kat! Can I get a picture of the two of you?"

His voice is piercing, and his question is less request than confirmation — I can hear his shutter clicking down rapidly as we try to skirt around him. The security guards are occupied, holding back a swarm of teenage girls desperate to get close enough to touch the legendary Grayson Dunn.

"Hey!" I snap, pushing the telephoto lens away when it practically smacks me in the nose. "Watch it!"

"Kat, how do you feel about Grayson's past conquests?" the man yells from my left. "Do you really believe he'll stay faithful?"

"Back off." Grayson grabs my hand and tugs me behind him with an indelicate jerk. "Or I'll make you back off."

"So you don't care about the other women?" the pap yells, ignoring Grayson's warnings. "Even after what he did to Helena Putnam?"

Grayson stops short. I see his shoulders tense.

"Grayson," I mutter, tugging at his hand. "Ignore him."

But the paparazzo isn't about to drop it. "Do you feel at all responsible for her current situation?"

Grayson's voice is a furious growl. "*That's not your business.*"

"We have no comment," I insist, tugging at Grayson again. He doesn't budge.

"Do you know anything about her rumored hospitalization or current mental state? Have you even been to see her?"

"No comment!" I yell, stepping in front of Grayson when he whirls, hands clenched, to face the man with the camera. I glance over my shoulder in warning. "Seriously, drop it."

But he doesn't.

The shutter clicks down again. "Do either of you have a comment regarding her apparent hysterical pregnancy?"

"Sure. *Here's* my comment." Grayson reaches out and grabs the long lens of the camera. With a vicious tug, he rips it from the man's hands. Before I can stop him, he reels back and hurls the expensive equipment with all his might. It sails through the air and lands in the middle of the street, the impact shattering it into several pieces.

The paparazzo screams bloody murder as a car runs the camera over, obliterating it beyond recognition.

"My camera! You broke my camera!" He's wailing incredulously, staring at Grayson with furious eyes. "That's a thousand-dollar lens! You're insane! I'm calling the police!"

"SHUT UP!" I yell at him, before he antagonizes a still-fuming Grayson further. It's taking all my strength to hold him in check. "Unless you want him to break *you* next."

The man wisely falls silent, and I don't wait around for him to reconsider. I grab Grayson's hand in mine and drag him to the car. A stunned valet hands me the keys to the Bugatti and vanishes, no doubt terrified by the dark look on Grayson's face. I don't trust him behind the wheel at the moment, so I push him toward the passenger side and round the hood. It says something about his mental state that he doesn't fight me on my decision to drive.

I can hear the paparazzo getting worked up again on the sidewalk behind us, screaming at Grayson's security team, who have finally stepped in; I don't spare them so much as a glance. Sliding into the low leather seat, I stare at the complex dashboard. It looks like a damn rocket ship — all glowing panels and indecipherable buttons. I find the ignition and start the engine, but my feet are so far from the pedals, I'd need stilts to successfully operate it.

"How the hell do I adjust the seat?" I mutter to myself, searching for the controls. I finally locate them and, after a cursory adjustment of the rearview mirror, I jam my foot against the gas.

Mistake.

Big mistake.

This beast of an engine does not drive like my crappy old Honda or even the sporty little convertible I purchased with my *Uncharted* check. The Bugatti was built for speed and acceleration. The tiniest pressure of my foot on the pedal sends us lurching forward at light speed.

Later, after a curiosity-fueled Google session, I'd learn the technical specs are zero to sixty in 2.46 seconds.

But now, in this moment, all I feel is terror. My stomach slams back into my spine. My heart stutters inside my chest as the world blurs around us.

"Christ, are you trying to kill us?" Grayson shouts.

I've never been a particularly religious person, but someone up there is definitely looking out for me, because the stretch of street ahead of us is empty. If not for that, we'd most definitely be dead — flattened like a pancake against the back bumper of another car.

I ease up on the gas, but we're still careening far too fast.

"Kat, the *brakes*! Use the fucking brakes!"

"Sorry, sorry!" I yell, pounding my foot onto the other pedal. We stop so short, Grayson's head slams against the dashboard with a resounding thud.

"FUCK!"

"I'm sorry!" I yell again, readjusting my foot pressure. "I think I've got it now."

"You *think*?"

"I've got it! I swear, I've got it."

And I do. The car glides along smoothly, practically purring beneath me, and for the first time I actually understand the allure of a well-crafted engine. I drive for a while, lost in appreciation for the automobile. I might as well enjoy it while it lasts; no doubt Grayson will never allow me within a five-foot radius of it ever again.

I glance over at him and see he's rubbing at a large red lump in the center of his forehead. It's not funny — really, it's *not* — but a laugh pops out from between my lips anyway.

His eyes narrow. "First she tries to kill me, then she laughs at my pain..."

"I'm sorry!" I say, gasping for air as mirth overtakes me. "It's not funny. I'm not laughing. Really."

"*Convincing.*"

Another snort escapes. "I really am sorry."

"For the attempted vehicular homicide, or the shameless amusement at the goose egg on my forehead?"

"Both." I grin at him, the first real grin I've had in days. His eyes watch my mouth stretch with an intensity that makes me nervous.

"Kat—"

I press my lips together to quash the smile. "Yeah?"

"I—" He cuts himself off. "Just... watch the damn road, please."

Flushing, I turn my attention forward and focus on getting home alive. I hear him sigh, deeply relieved, when I punch in my security code and we pull into my driveway a few moments later. The air is unnaturally silent with the engine off.

"I should've said this before, when I first found out — I'm sorry about Helena," I blurt, cheeks flushing. I glance at him. "I don't know what happened exactly, but I'm sure it wasn't an easy situation for you. I'm really sorry."

"It's not your fault." He runs a hand through his hair. "It wasn't anyone's fault, really. She just... *broke.* Sometimes this life, the pressure... Not everyone can handle it."

We're both quiet. The air is so heavy I can barely breathe.

"I've heard it makes some people go on crazy camera-smashing rampages," I say carefully.

He smirks. "That guy had it coming."

"So long as you realize he's going to sue you for damages…"

"I have a fleet of overpriced lawyers for exactly this kind of bullshit." He shrugs. "They'll take care of it."

"Ah." A massive yawn cracks my face in two. "Damn, I'm beat. Thank god we have the next few days off."

His mouth flattens. "We do? Why?"

"Don't you read your schedule?"

"That's what assistants are for."

I roll my eyes. "Typical."

"Really though — why don't I see you tomorrow?"

"Dunn, tomorrow is Christmas. We've got the next week off."

"*Oh*. Right. Still, I'm surprised Sloan is giving us a break."

"He might be a hard-ass, but even he takes this time of year off." My eyebrows lift. "Aren't you doing anything with your family?"

"Parents always spend the holidays in Florida, and I'm an only child." He shrugs. "Never been big on it, as holidays go. Fourth of July is much more my speed."

"Fireworks, beer, BBQ, and bikinis — I wonder why."

His eyebrows waggle, a flash of his old mischief. The man is incorrigible.

"Enjoy your time off while it lasts — I'll see you after the holidays, Dunn. Are you going to Sloan's New Year's Eve party?"

"I may make an appearance. I may go out with Ryder." He shrugs. "I don't like to commit to any one thing."

I know he's talking about parties, not relationships, but I have to bite my tongue to keep from snapping, *Yes, I figured that one out on my own, thanks.* I'm not sure what else to say, so I just undo my seatbelt and reach for the door handle.

"Kat."

I pause, arm midair, taken aback by the emotion suddenly infused in his voice. I'm afraid to look at him, so I stare at my hand, stuck in limbo, shaking slightly as I hold it aloft.

"I know you think I'm an asshole. I know I'm the bad guy in your story. Trust me, I know." He swallows audibly. "If I was a better guy, I'd go on being the villain you seem to need me to be. I wouldn't apologize or ask for your forgiveness, because I know I don't deserve it after all the shit I've put you through." He pauses. "But I'm not a better guy. So I'm asking."

I inhale sharply.

"Forgive me. Stop hating me," he pleads softly. "Not because I deserve it. But because I won't survive if you keep thinking I'm scum."

"Why now?" I ask, almost inaudibly. "What's changed? You didn't seem to care what I thought of you a month ago. You didn't seem to give a shit about making me angry yesterday, or a week ago, or the decade before that, for that matter."

He expels a sharp breath. "I don't have an easy answer for you. I wish I did. All I can tell you is... I hate this. I hate you hating me. I hate waking up in the morning, knowing you're going to spend the day wishing you were somewhere else. With someone else."

"So you want me to forgive you because my anger is an inconvenience?" I shake my head. "Sorry, that's not good enough."

"No! *No.* I want you to forgive me because it's killing me to be this fucking close to you and not be able to touch you or talk to you or laugh with you. I want you to forgive me because it's Christmas and at Christmas, you're supposed to put aside all the miserable shit that makes your life hell for three hundred and sixty-four days out of the year, and be thankful for the rare things that make you happy."

I look back at him, at the pleading look in his eyes, and for a fleeting instant I want to break down and give him everything he's asking for. A crazy, delusional part of my brain sees the shadowed parts of this broken boy, and recognizes them as the match for my own terrible darkness.

Maybe it's only fitting for someone like me, stitched together with damage and destruction, to wind up with someone like him. Maybe, if I stretch my arms out in the darkness, I can grab hold of him, because he lives there too. Maybe choosing shadows won't be so bad, if we're stuck inside them together.

"You make me happy," he finishes in a whisper. "Even if I've done a shitty job at showing it. And I don't know what the future holds. I don't know if this — *us* — has a shot in hell at working. But I promise, I'm going to do better. Whether it's just as friends or something more... I promise, Kat, if you'll just give me a chance to make this right, I'll prove it..."

I reach out and put my hand over his mouth, stopping his words.

"*Don't.* Okay? Just... Please don't. Don't say something you don't mean just because you're lonely and sad and it's the holidays. Don't tell me you miss me because it's tough to be alone." My eyes hold his. "The thing I'm learning is, it's okay to be alone, Grayson. Good, even. It helps you figure out who you are and what you want, without other people's influence."

"But—" The word is muffled against my palm.

"You're searching for something missing in your life. You think that something might be me, but it's not." I pull my hand away. "You're not looking for me; you're looking for *you*. You're lost. And that's okay — everyone is a little lost. Look who you're talking to." I sigh. "I don't know much, but I do know you can't find yourself by getting lost in someone else."

Indecipherable thoughts are swimming in that set of infinite eyes.

My voice is cautious. "You know what I want for you, more than anything?"

He shakes his head.

"I want you to figure out who you are — without the cameras or the press or the drama. I want you to look in the mirror and like the man you see looking back. Not because he's rich or famous or good in bed. Not because women lust after him or men want to be him." I smile softly. "Because he respects himself. Because he knows who he is and what he wants, *truly* wants, out of life. *That's* a man I'd be interested in getting to know."

His face flickers through so many emotions in such a short span, I can't keep track of them all. Nor do I want to.

"Merry Christmas, Grayson," I whisper, my eyes holding his for a long moment. I reach for the door handle. I'm halfway out, when his voice stops me again.

"Kat?"

"Yeah?"

"You told me what you want for me." His jaw clenches tightly. "But what do you want *from* me?"

My breath catches in my throat. I can't give him the answer; I don't know it, myself.

With a head shake and a sad smile, I turn and flee into the house.

* * *

Christmas has never been my favorite holiday. Cynthia wasn't big on giving gifts to others, and my revolving door of stepfathers were unpredictable when it came to leaving presents under the tree. Still, when I wake this year and walk downstairs, there's an immutable feeling of loneliness stirring in my veins. I fix myself a cup of decaf coffee and walk out onto my terrace, the slight chill in the early morning air seeping through my thin sweater and fuzzy white knee-socks.

All over the world, families are huddled around trees, tearing paper and singing carols, hugging each other close and celebrating together. And I am totally alone, staring out over the hillside toward the Pacific, where early morning light stains the expanse of ocean a steely gray shade.

Harper will come over later, of course, probably dragging Kent in her wake. We'll exchange gifts and drink disgusting eggnog and sing off-key Bing Crosby, and I'll tell myself that everything in my life is perfect, even though it's a lie.

I set my coffee cup on the deck railing and wrap my arms around my body for warmth. In a moment of weakness, I allow myself to wonder what Wyatt is doing this Christmas. Will he be with the all-powerful Hastings clan, talking business over bourbon and smoking cigars at a lavish family gathering? Or curled up somewhere with Caroline, celebrating their first holiday together by a dazzling tree beneath that massive chandelier in his front room, making love in front of a fireplace until the sun fades from the sky?

My eyes are stinging precariously.

He's not mine to miss, but I miss him anyway. I miss his laugh and his smile and that undeniable sense of safety I always feel inside his arms.

What would he say, if I called him right now? Would he even answer?

My hands itch to find out.

I've put him out of my mind over the past few days. The press junket has been a grueling parade of smiling bright and saying all the right things at all the right moments. At the end of each day I've collapsed into bed without even bothering to eat dinner, falling into a dreamless sleep before my head hits the pillow, jerking awake to the blaring sound of my alarm only moments before Harper arrives to make me beautiful so it can start all over again. Nonstop. There's been no time to think of Wyatt.

But in this brief lull, my feelings catch up to me with the force of a freight train. I pull my phone from the back pocket of my sleep shorts and scroll down to his name.

The sight makes me smile.

Wyatt Albus Percival Wulfric Brian Dumbledore Hastings

If I close my eyes, I can almost still hear his laughter the day he programmed it in, on our way to Hawaii. Memories slide over me — salty waves and warm sand, his arms dunking me beneath the surface but keeping me tethered. Always, always, always keeping me safe.

My smile fades.

I click a button to power off my phone.

No.

I will not call him. I will not inflict myself on him again. I will not drag him back into the wreckage of my world, not when he is so much better off without me.

No matter the personal cost.

Even if it kills me.

Seeking his forgiveness would be a selfish act, not a selfless one: I'd feel better but he'd feel worse. Like a terminally ill patient who infects the person unfortunate enough to take up the bed beside theirs with a deadly virus.

Sorry for killing you, but at least now I don't have to die alone.

A snapping sound cuts through the sinister web of misery inside my head. I whip around in time to see a man dressed fully in black, perched on the bough of a tree in my backyard. There's a massive camera clutched in his hands and a slender tree branch cracked in two beneath his heavily booted feet.

"What the hell..." I murmur, watching in disbelief as he lifts the camera to his face and starts clicking.

Shit!

Heart pounding, I flee inside, slam the sliding door shut behind me, and dive onto the floor by my sofa, out of sight. I lie there in a pile of limbs, waiting for my sluggish thoughts to start making sense.

There is a man in my tree, risking criminal charges for a photograph of me drinking coffee in fuzzy socks.

He must've scaled the fence, desperate for a few pictures to sell to the gossip rags. I can almost see the headlines he was so hopeful for: *Kat and Grayson's First Christmas! See the exclusive photos on page 12...*

Joke's on him.

I'd laugh at the ludicrous situation, but it's not remotely funny. Belatedly, I realize I should probably call the police. Somehow that feels like an overreaction, so I call Masters instead. He answers on the first ring.

"Are you okay?"

"Yes, I'm—"

"Are you inside?"

"Yes, I'm—"

"Good. I'm pulling into your driveway. Don't come outside."

"But, Masters—"

He's already hung up. I army-crawl like a damned idiot across my hardwood floors, all the way from my kitchen to the front room. Twitching the curtains aside, I peer out and see — sure enough — there's a familiar black SUV parked behind my red convertible. The engine's off; the driver's seat is empty.

Where the hell is Masters?

I've barely had a chance to wonder that when he emerges from the side yard, muscles straining against the confines of his white button down as the man in his arms thrashes to get free. It's no use — Masters is a giant. I'm pretty sure he could dead-lift a baby elephant without breaking a sweat.

The flashing lights of a police cruiser appear at the end of my driveway. In less than ten minutes, Masters has deposited the trespasser into the officers' custody and given them a brief statement. He glances back at the window I'm watching from, my face pressed against the glass with the same intensity I use to peruse cupcakes at Magnolia Bakery. He gives a slight head-shake as if to say *stay inside, idiot.*

I decide not to argue with him.

The police drive off with the paparazzo bolted firmly in the backseat of their cruiser; Masters vanishes around the side of the house, presumably to check for other intruders. He's back a few moments later, standing at my front door with his hands shoved casually into the pockets of his jeans. I let him in, eyes fixed on the shocking garment.

"*You* own *jeans?*" I ask, stunned. "And here I thought you were born wearing that badass looking security-dude suit."

"Security-dude suit?" He snorts and locks the deadbolt firmly. "Trust me, I wouldn't be here in jeans if it hadn't been an emergency."

"How did you know he was here?"

"Remember when you first moved in, and I spent several days rigging all manner of cameras and security sensors around the perimeter of your house, while you and Harper laughed at me and called me *paranoid in the extreme?*"

My cheeks heat. "I might... possibly... recall saying something along those lines..."

"Right." His eyes crinkle in amusement. "Long story short: motion sensor went off, sent a ping to my phone, I got in the car and came straight here."

"You could've called me."

"I assumed you'd still be asleep. And I was worried you'd do something stupid, like confront the bastard by yourself."

"When have I ever done something stupid?"

He just looks at me.

"Second thought, don't answer that," I murmur. "I'm too fragile to handle the truth."

Masters walks to the kitchen and pours himself a cup of coffee.

"That's decaf," I warn.

He grimaces, but takes a sip anyway. "Caffeine's effects are mostly mental, anyway."

"Says the man who can consume it any time he wants."

"Jonesing for a jolt?"

"You have no idea." I hop up on a kitchen island stool, swinging my legs. "What will happen to the pap?"

Masters shrugs. "They can charge him with criminal trespassing. Stalking would be a stretch — this guy doesn't seem like a repeat offender. You haven't noticed him lurking before, have you?"

I shake my head. "There's always a swarm of them, like flies on a carcass." I pause. "The carcass being Grayson, of course."

"And you." Masters sounds serious. "You're big time now."

I snort.

"Miss Firestone, there was a man camped out in your eucalyptus tree twenty minutes ago. Believe it or not, that's not a normal occurrence for regular people. You need to accept that your reality has changed, and start acting accordingly when it comes to protecting yourself."

A groan rumbles from my throat. "I know. It's just hard to see myself that way."

Masters shrugs. "We've all got crosses to bear."

The sharp ring of my doorbell makes my eyebrows shoot up to my hairline. I wonder if it's the police, back to take another statement, but somehow I doubt officers of the law make it a habit to jam their finger repeatedly into the doorbell despite me calling, "Just a minute!" on five second intervals as I race for the front room.

I undo the deadbolt and she storms inside, a messy cloud of magenta hair sticking out in all directions. There's not a lick of makeup on her face. I blink slowly, stunned. I haven't seen Harper Kline without eyeliner since... ever. I was beginning to think she was born with twin birthmarks in the shape of perfectly winged cat-eyes.

"Oh good," she says stormily. "You're not dead. That means I can KILL YOU MYSELF!"

I wince. "Merry Christmas to you too?"

Still scowling, she yanks me into her arms and squeezes the wind out of my lungs.

"Paparazzo in my tree," I wheeze. "I'm fine."

"I thought something terrible happened. Kent sat straight up in bed, grabbed his phone, and bolted so fast I could barely get a word out of him. And since neither of you had the courtesy to answer your damn cellphones... here I am." She pulls away, eyes watering. "I didn't even brush my hair or swipe on a single coat of mascara."

"I love you too," I whisper, recognizing a declaration of affection when I see one.

She pins her boyfriend with a lethal stare. "You! *Mr. We-Don't-Need-Secrets-Babe.* Ha! Next time you race out of the house without a word to save my best friend, you're taking me with you."

"I'm not," he says, swallowing a slow sip of coffee.

"Come again?" Harper hisses.

"Not taking you with me."

Her face flushes with fury. "You're an ass."

He shrugs. "Maybe. But I'm an ass who likes his girlfriend's *very fine ass* safe in bed, not chasing down bad guys in backyards at six in the morning on Christmas."

Damn, he's good.

I turn my head to hide my smile.

Harper huffs, but I can tell she's losing grip on her anger. "Well, *fine.* You're going to keep secrets, then so am I."

He laughs, and it's even better than the first time around. A stunningly rare sound that makes the whole room go silent in appreciation.

"What's so funny?" Harper snaps, but her eyes are gooey with warmth.

"Babe." He shakes his head, amused. "I already know all your secrets."

"We've been dating a month! You don't know anything. You can't possibly."

The laughter disappears. His eyes get alarmingly serious. "Maybe I don't know them all, but I know enough."

Harper rolls her eyes dismissively. "Uh huh. Whatever you say."

She starts walking toward the kitchen, but he blocks her path.

"Already know I have to order double bacon on the side of breakfast, otherwise you'll steal mine. Already know you spend almost as much money buying new makeup products as you make applying them to people's faces. I know that when you say you're going to yoga on Sunday mornings, you're actually at church because your mom back home in Iowa would worry if you didn't go, but religion isn't considered *cool* in LA. I know there's a thirty percent chance your hair will be a different color every time I see you. Also know, no matter what color it is, it'll look good on you. I know that even though you insist you want to stay in your tiny ass city apartment forever, you really want a big house in the suburbs with four bedrooms you can fill with kids, because you've got two Pinterest boards filled with fixer-upper Victorians and Tudors set as your damn computer homepage." He pauses. "Know that I'd like to help you fill those rooms, too."

Harper's mouth is hanging open and her eyes are wet with tears.

Mine are suspiciously wet, as well.

Masters smirks, pleased with himself. Walking over to Harper, he plants a quick kiss on her forehead, then turns and heads for the kitchen.

"Got any eggs, Miss Firestone? I'll make breakfast."

When he's gone, Harper looks at me, weeping steadily, and I stare back at her with watery eyes.

"So... I totally love him," she says miserably.

"I know." I grin at her.

"You realize what this means, don't you?"

"What?"

"I'll never have a secret again! Our whole lives together, he'll know everything about me! That's... that's just wrong! It's disgusting!"

"Disgustingly *cute*, maybe," I correct, smiling faintly.

She scoffs. "Whatever. I need eyeliner. And a hairbrush. And coffee. In that order." She scoffs. "But everyone probably already knows that, because apparently I have no secrets anymore."

I lay a hand over my stomach as I watch her stalk upstairs to my master bathroom. My smile dims a few watts.

"Secrets are overrated," I whisper to the empty room.

CHAPTER SEVEN

"I THINK WE SHOULD PROBABLY SEE OTHER PEOPLE."
- A guy who is already seeing other people.

The rest of the day is remarkably unremarkable. We eat a massive breakfast prepared by Masters because apparently there is nothing in the world he does poorly, and that includes cooking a feast of pancakes, bacon, and Eggs Benedict. I'm careful about what I put on my plate, wary of setting off another untimely bout of morning sickness by angering the tiny dictator growing inside me.

I consider it a Christmas gift that I make it through the entire morning without hurling once.

Thoroughly stuffed, we collapse on my couch and watch old, black and white holiday movies for hours, until the late afternoon shadows slant long and low across the hardwood floor.

We're all drowsy and half-sleeping when the security gate buzzer goes off.

"It's busier than LAX here today," I mutter, heading for the front door with Masters tight on my heels. Harper isn't far behind.

I reach blindly for the button to open the gate, but Masters stares pointedly at the video-com panel on the wall.

"That monitor? Not just decorative. It's there for a reason. *Use* it."

I sigh and press a button to pull up the video feed. A sleek black Mercedes, driven by an unfamiliar, middle-aged woman, is loitering at the entrance. Between the gleaming Rolex on her wrist and the leather briefcase on the seat beside her, I'm guessing she's not here to rob me at gunpoint.

I push a button to open the gate and watch as her car rolls down the drive. She steps out in a tailored suit and walks to my door, wearing impatience like some women wear perfume — in a cloud, saturating the very air around her.

"Can I help you?" I ask, cracking open the door.

"Katharine Firestone?"

"Yes."

She snaps open her briefcase, whips out a thick manila envelope, and thrusts it into my arms. "You've been served."

With that, she pivots and heads back to her car. Halfway there, she hesitates.

"Merry Christmas," she calls back, an afterthought.

"Merry Christmas," I echo dully, clutching the papers in my hands until my fingertips turn white. Harper leads me back inside while Masters ensures the gate closes properly behind the Mercedes. I grab a knife from the block on the countertop, filet the envelope like a fresh fish, and lay the papers flat against the shining granite of my kitchen island.

I start to read.

Then, I start to laugh.

And laugh. And laugh some more, until I'm gasping for air. Until tears are streaming from my eyes and snot is leaking from my nose and the whole world goes slightly static around the edges.

"What is it?" Masters asks. "What's going on?"

Harper is scanning the documents. I hear her gasp.

"It's her... her..."

"My mother," I croak, laugh-crying.

"Your mother?" Masters sounds confused. "What about your mother? Is she okay?"

"*Okay*?! Oh, I'm sure she's great. Never better, in fact." My voice is laced with a hysterical edge. "She's suing me."

"Your *mother* is suing you?"

"Me, the AXC Network, Wyatt..." I shake my head. "Basically, everyone she could think of who might possibly be exploited for cash in a quick settlement."

"On what grounds?" he asks, shocked.

"Unlawful termination. Failure to compensate. Breach of contract. And about ten other ridiculous charges she pulled out of her ass, just for a thrill."

"What a bitch," Harper hisses.

Masters looks concerned. "Does she have a case?"

"I don't know."

"Did you ever sign a contract?"

I think back. "No. But I was a minor when she started representing me. She's my *mother*; I didn't think I needed a contract. Besides, until a few years ago, she had the legal authority to make decisions on my behalf. I'm not sure if she could've signed something that grants her rights over me now, as an adult... I've never seen the paperwork. I'm not even sure there *is* any paperwork."

Masters is looking graver than ever.

"Don't worry," Harper assures me thinly. "We'll figure it out. You just need to get a lawyer. Talk to the network, see if they have a strategy for this kind of thing. And... talk to Wyatt. He's tied up in this too. I bet he'll know how to handle it."

I was worried she'd suggest that.

With a grunt of disbelief, I drop my forehead onto the cool granite.

Harper strokes my hair and murmurs under her breath.

"And to think, I complained one year when my mother got me *socks* for Christmas..."

* * *

My hands shake the whole drive across town. I tighten my grip on the steering wheel to keep them steady and attempt to distract myself with a glance at the odometer. I'm stunned to see my new convertible has traveled less than fifty miles total, since I drove it out of the dealership last month with Harper riding shotgun.

That's what happens when you spend a month curled up in a ball of misery and forget to live.

I take the long route up Mulholland Drive, in no rush to get there. Masters offered to accompany me, but I wouldn't let him.

This is something I have to do by myself.

Twenty minutes later, my tires crunch over gravel as I glide to a stop in front of the mansion. Oversized terra-cotta pots are evenly spaced along the driveway perimeter — at night, they're filled with dancing flames but now, in the mid-morning light, they stand like empty sentinels lining the walk.

My heart is slamming so hard against my ribs I'm worried they might crack under the pressure. I feel weak at the knees, like some swooning handmaiden in a fairy tale in need of smelling salts and a dashing prince to sweep her to safety. But this is no fairy tale, and I am certainly no princess.

I'm the villain.

I reach out and rap my knuckles against the door so faintly, I doubt the sound even passes through the thick mahogany. Hauling in a deep breath, I steel myself and try again. Three resounding bangs of my fist, booming in an indisputable announcement of my presence. If he's home, there's little doubt he heard me.

Two minutes pass. I count them down on my watch, berating myself a little more with each passing second that the doors remain closed. I waver, suddenly uncertain, and contemplate making a run for my car.

Sure, Cynthia will sue me for every cent in my bank account, and I'll wind up penniless, homeless, and jobless. Somehow that still sounds like a better alternative than waiting another moment on this stoop.

Perhaps it was a bad idea to show up without calling first. Perhaps he's standing just inside the door, staring through the peephole, waiting for me to give up and go away. Perhaps—

The door swings inward. "Katharine?"

I suck in a breath.

He's wearing a white bath towel wrapped low around his hips and nothing else. The stark contours of his pelvic bones form a deep v shape, framing a chiseled chest and defined abdominal muscles that are currently dotted with water droplets. His hair is unbound, hanging in a damp curtain to his shoulders. I watch a single bead of water roll from his neck all the way down to the line of hair that trails into his towel, my eyes tracing its journey with the purest form of envy. I'm overcome by the insane desire to lean forward and lick it from his skin with the tip of my tongue.

"This is a surprise." His voice is deeper than normal. "Sorry, I didn't hear your knock — I was in the shower."

I make an incoherent sound.

"Katharine, what are you doing here?"

Forcing my eyes to unglue from his abs, I glance up and find he's studying me with unguarded suspicion and something else — something I can't quite define. His gaze flickers down to the folder in my hands, and purpose returns in a swift instant.

"I'm sorry to bother you. I wouldn't be here unless I had absolutely no other choice, believe me."

He stiffens, insulted by my words.

Shit.

"No — I didn't mean—That came out wrong." I exhale sharply, trying to remember the speech I practiced over and over again on the drive here. It was the perfect balance of civil and composed. Friendly but factual. By the time I reached his street, I had it damn near memorized.

Yet standing here before him, every word has evaporated. My tongue is tied into knots.

"I— I have something I need to— to talk to you about." I pause. "Business! It's about business. Not about... other... things."

I bite the inside of my cheek to stop the babble.

Wyatt crosses his arms over his chest and levels me

with a stare. I could be imagining it — in fact, it's almost certainly a by-product of wishful thinking — but I'm reasonably sure there's a tiny bit of humor lurking at the back of his eyes as he regards me standing here melting down like a faulty nuclear reactor on his doorstep. Whatever the case, he decides to take pity on me.

Swinging the door wider, he steps back so I can enter.

"Just get in here. I'll go throw on some clothes and you…" His lips twitch. "Try to remember what you're doing at my front door at ten in the morning the day after Christmas." He starts ascending the extravagant staircase up to the second floor. "If you get stuck, I'd suggest looking inside that folder you're clutching like a security blanket."

"Right! *Right.*" I seriously contemplate slapping myself across the face. "I'll just… wait here then…" I call after him as he disappears upstairs. I think I hear the sound of a chuckle float back to me, but the fog clouding my psyche is so thick, I can barely function. None of my senses are remotely trustworthy.

I look around the foyer. My eyes involuntarily drift to the opposite wall, where Wyatt once hurled a full tray of pancakes, a shocking show of violence from such a pacifist. Lured despite my will, I find myself running a fingertip against the whitewashed wall, searching for any trace of that fateful morning. A smudge of residual syrup, an indent where the tray made contact.

There's nothing there, though. The space has been scrubbed clean.

As if that day never happened at all.

The thought bothers me immensely.

Memories crowd in from all sides, saturating the space, making me claustrophobic despite the twenty-foot ceilings soaring overhead. Unable to stay there another moment, I wander through a narrow archway into an adjacent room — Wyatt's home office.

If a room can feel like a person, this one feels like

him. Smells like him. Looks like him.

Rich leather and comfortable chairs, dim lighting and bookshelves on every wall. I suck in a deep breath and a pure dose of *Wyatt* invades my body, filling my every atom. It nearly knocks me to the floor.

It's not my intention to snoop; I just want a better look at his books. I've always thought the paperbacks a person chooses to keep on their limited shelf space says a lot about who they are, how they think, and what they want out of life. As I run my fingers along the spines of Wyatt's many books, I'm unsurprised to find a wide array of titles, ranging from whimsical — *Alice's Adventures in Wonderland, Grimm's Fairy Tales, The Little Prince* — to the classics — *The Sun Also Rises, A Tale of Two Cities, The Grapes of Wrath* — to the obscure — *A Clockwork Orange, Kafka on the Shore, Zen and the Art of Motorcycle Maintenance.* Unsurprisingly, I spot more than a few book-to-movie adaptations amidst his collection. A given, considering his deep love of film.

I can't say exactly how it catches my eye. I spot it unintentionally in my peripherals — its nondescript blue spine peeking out from the stack of papers on his desk. My fingers tremble as I pick it up, sending several sheaves fluttering into the air like vellum birds. I'm bending to retrieve them when the embossed letters on the front cover of the book make my heart skip a beat.

UNCHARTED

This is a first edition hardcover; vastly different from the worn paperback I've flipped through in the wee hours of the morning too many times to count. I wonder how Wyatt tracked it down... before remembering that he's Wyatt Hastings. His connections are endless, as are the zeros tacked on the end of his bank account. There are very few things in the world he cannot acquire, if he puts his mind — and money — to it.

I crack open the book like an old friend. Long before I was ever cast in the movie, I spent countless hours lost between these pages with Violet and Beck on their island.

There's always been something about their story that spoke to me like a drug, seeping its way into my system.

Is it possible to discover yourself in words penned by a stranger? Can you find your soulmate in the pages of a book?

If so, *Uncharted* is mine.

I reread a few familiar passages then flip it back closed, running a fingertip across the faded name on the front cover and wondering, not for the first time, about the author who penned it. *Tywin G. Hassatt.* A ghost, if the internet is to be believed, without so much as a biography for me to gather clues from during my gentle stalking session.

"What are you doing?"

His voice is softer than silk, but I jump as though he's shouted. The book tumbles from my hands to the floor as my eyes fly to Wyatt. He's hovering a cautious distance away, dressed in jeans and a fitted navy henley that brings out his eyes.

"Shit!" I curse, bending to pick up the book. My cheeks heat when I spot the other scattered papers on the rug — I've made an utter mess of his desk. "I'm sorry. I wasn't snooping, I promise. I just wandered in here and I saw the book.... I'd never seen a first edition before. Where did you get it? I'd die to have one of my own. Not that I need a first edition to enjoy the story, I'm perfectly happy with my old paperback, though the cover is starting to rip a little so I'll have to get another copy eventually..."

I'm babbling again as I shuffle the scattered pages into a short stack and set them back on his desk beside the book. The top sheet is a memo with his contact information stamped in bold, blocky letters at the top.

WYATT HASTINGS

I freeze. Almost in a daze, my eyes move back to the cover of the book sitting directly beside it, rearranging letters in my head like puzzle pieces snapping into place.

TYWIN G. HASSATT

W-Y-A-T-T H-A-S-T-I-N-G-S

An anagram.

A pseudonym.

My eyes fly to his. He's watching me warily.

"Holy shit."

He doesn't react.

"It's *you.*"

A muscle leaps in his jaw.

My mind is blown. "You're him."

His hands flex at his sides.

Wyatt — my Wyatt — wrote my favorite book in the world.

A gorgeous, incredible story of love and hope and heartbreak... written by a gorgeous, incredible man.

My hands grab for the book again, hauling the cover close to my face as though that might somehow illuminate things for me.

"You wrote this. Didn't you?" I look at him searchingly, and see the truth in his eyes. "You're the author of *Uncharted.*"

He still says nothing, neither confirming nor denying my accusation, but I know in my heart that I'm right. In fact, now that I've made the leap, I can't believe I didn't figure it out sooner. Details are sliding into place like a camera shifting into focus.

"This is why you had so much sway over casting decisions and filming locations. This is why you've been so involved with the adaptation, from beginning to end. It's *your* book being adapted." I can hear the awe in my own voice. I've officially slid into fangirl territory, but I'm too thrilled to be embarrassed.

Wyatt sighs heavily, as though I've just accused him of something terrible, and mutters just one word.

"...Yes."

"I KNEW IT!" I bounce on the balls of my feet, feeling adrenaline surge through me. "This is unbelievable!"

His lips twitch as he watches me jumping up and down like a child.

"But…" A million questions materialize in my head. "Why keep it a secret? Why not tell everyone? Why use a pen name? Why not scream about it from the rooftops every chance you get?" My hands tighten on the precious book in my hands. "Don't tell me you're ashamed of it or I will kick your ass from here to Sunday. You may be stronger than me, but I'm scrappy."

His lips twitch. "Scrappy?"

"Damn straight." I look back at the book in my hands and the whole world tilts again. "I can't believe you wrote it. This book… *everyone* should read this book, Wyatt. It's that good."

He runs a hand through his hair, still hanging loose around his shoulders. "I don't know about that. Frankly, I'm still surprised you'd read it before we cast you in the film. It's not exactly a commercial success."

"It will be after the movie comes out." There's not an ounce of doubt in my voice. "And, anyway why the hell would *commercial success* even matter?"

"It might surprise you to know it mattered a great deal to a great many people at my publishing house," he says wryly. "I barely earned enough to pay back my advance."

"No offense, Wyatt, but with a trust fund like yours, I sincerely doubt you needed the money."

"It wasn't about the money. It was about doing something outside the Hastings name. Proving…" He trails off, clearly uncomfortable with this conversation.

"Proving what?" I prod gently.

"Proving to myself that my worth isn't purely a side-effect of nepotism and family favors."

I stare at him for a beat. "Why did you write this story?"

"I don't know. It was a long time ago, Katharine."

"Bullshit. I don't care how long it's been. That's not the kind of thing that fades." I take a step toward him — forgetting, in my passion, that we're at odds, forgetting that I'm here for an entirely different purpose, forgetting

126

that I should stay away from him so he can move on with his life without me. "Tell me why you wrote it."

"Leave it alone."

"No."

"Katharine."

"*Wyatt.*"

"You're impossible," he growls, but his eyes have gone soft. He expels a sharp breath. "I grew up watching all these movies of epic love stories on the big screen. They were inescapable. Men and women who are destined to cross paths, fated to fall in love, predetermined to be together forever because it's supposedly written in the stars or steered by invisible winds or sparked by the prick of cupid's arrow. *Soulmates.* One, single person in the universe who is meant just for you." His eyes hold mine and I feel the temperature in the room kick up by several degrees. When he continues, his voice is fraught with tension. "But that's not real. It's fiction. It's the Hollywood spin. It's the fairy tale that never really comes true. Because while the idea that we all have a single soulmate is lovely... It's also bullshit."

"But you're a romantic! How can you—"

He cuts me off, mouth twisting. "You planning to let me finish?"

I clamp my lips shut.

"Trust me, I get the appeal of star-crossed lovers, fated to fall. Romeo and Juliet, Tristan and Isolde, Buffy and Angel."

"Did you just make a Buffy the Vampire Slayer reference?"

"Yes." His eyes narrow. "Why?"

I grin at him. "No reason."

Nerd-boy.

"Anyway..." He narrows his eyes at me. "Don't get me wrong. I love the idea of soulmates. It's thrilling to think about meeting someone, taking one look at them, and knowing in your heart that they're your other half. It's romantic as hell. But, to me... it's infinitely more romantic to think that, out of the seven billion people on this planet you could be with... you *choose* to be with just one." He steps a shade closer, almost without realizing it. "Love isn't some unavoidable destiny, some fate you can't sidestep. It's a choice you make — and keep making — every day of your life."

Shit. My eyes are stinging.

"That's why I wrote *Uncharted*. In these pages... Violet wouldn't die without Beck; Beck didn't take one look at Violet and simply know she was the one. There is no instant, inexplicable connection or unhealthy co-dependence." He shrugs. "There's just a story about two people who *choose* to be together — not because they have to, but because they want to. Even when it's hard. Even when the whole world is stacked against them."

My chest aches so intensely, it feels like I've been stabbed. Not for the first time — and probably not for the last — my mind is overtaken by a mournful lament.

Why does he have to be so damn wonderful?

He stares at me and I stare straight back, straight to his soul. I swear, in that moment, we have a full conversation without ever speaking a word. A million unspoken thoughts ping back and forth between us like a silent tennis match of things we're both too stubborn to say out loud.

It takes a minute to rein in my emotions. When I'm relatively sure they're back under control, I look up at him and speak in a voice that cracks despite my best efforts.

"It's not because of them."

He blinks, confused by the sudden shift in topic. "What?"

"Your success. It's not because of your family, Wyatt. Maybe they had a hand in helping you, maybe their connections gave you a leg up, when you were first starting out... but that only takes you so far. Some people with even better connections than yours don't do a damn thing with their lives. They piss away the chances they've been given because they're entitled and arrogant and lazy.

Why use your god-given talent when you can party all day instead?" I shake my head. "Those people, well-connected or not, lack the passion needed to create, to succeed. But *you* have passion — for your art, for your work, for every part of your life."

"Oh, really?" His voice is wry. "You've known me, what — two months?"

It hurts to hear him diminish our connection with a time constraint, even in a teasing way. I push on anyway.

"You forget, I've read your words. And the man who wrote these..." I trace the name on the front cover again, still stunned it's the same man standing three feet from me. "*This* man... he has a gift for words and characters and beauty. He has more passion than he knows what to do with. It's there in every sentence, buried in every line, enmeshed in every scene of Violet and Beck's story."

My fingertip presses down until the embossed letters dig into my skin. He doesn't speak, but suddenly the air is so full of tension, it's hard to haul breath into my lungs. I can't bear to look at him as I force out the rest of my words. My voice shakes.

"Don't dismiss your own hard work, just because your family happens to be in the same industry. Don't disregard your own talent, just because of your bloodline. My mother—" My voice breaks.

Wyatt shifts closer, as if to comfort me, but holds himself back at the last moment.

I clear my throat and try again. "My mother pushed me so hard to be someone I'm not that it nearly broke me. She forced a square peg into a round hole, determined to make me fit even if vital pieces of my soul were shaved away in the process. It's taken me a long time to realize how much that messed up my self-worth. Honestly, some days I still struggle with it. But I've finally figured out that the family you're born into doesn't define the person you become — no matter if you're the spawn of a crazed pageant mom or the offspring of Hollywood's wealthiest family. At the end of the day, the only person who determines who you become and what you do with your life is *you*." My eyes flicker up to his. "And.. you're one of the best people I know."

His Adam's apple bobs in his throat as he swallows several times. It doesn't help much — his voice is still gruff when he speaks. "When did you get so wise, Katharine Firestone?"

"Not wise. Just marginally less stupid." I let my eyes hold his for a breathless moment. "I've had a lot of time on my hands to think, this past month."

The comment hangs between us like a physical presence, saturating every particle of air. I want so badly to step into his strong, safe arms, to close that final distance between us and whisper all the things I'm scared of, all the awful doubts that I'll never deserve a man like this, so he can assure me otherwise. I want his hands on my skin, his mouth in my hair, his body pressed against mine like my own personal beacon of strength.

As if he can somehow read my thoughts, he takes a half step toward me, eyes never leaving mine. I grow roots; a hurricane could not move me, in this instant. My mouth opens. It's there, on the tip of my tongue — something crazy, something I shouldn't say, but can't seem to keep locked inside anymore.

Except I never get a chance to say it.

"Wy? Where are you?" a feminine voice calls from the hall. "Oh! There you are!"

The world freezes, mute and motionless, like the moment just before a lighting strike. My back snaps straight. My eyes, still on Wyatt's, go so wide it would be comical if my heart wasn't shredding inside my chest cavity.

Wyatt flinches as Caroline steps up to his side. His jaw is clenched so tight, the tendons in his neck stand out starkly. I finally force my eyes to leave his, to focus on *her*.

She's wearing a giant t-shirt, undoubtedly one of Wyatt's. She's barefoot, her long legs perfectly toned and tan. She's dressed as though she's just rolled out of bed, but her blonde hair is perfectly styled and her face is made up with more products than I own, so I'm guessing she's been awake a while.

"Oh! Wy, I didn't know we had company!"

The *we* kills me.

Her eyes are sharp. "It's Katie, isn't it?"

My tone is sharper. "Close enough."

She laughs without humor. "I've been seeing you on every newsstand and computer screen — it's a nice change of pace to see you in person! You're dating Grayson Dunn, aren't you? I saw your interview on *The Eileen Show*." She drops her voice to an excited murmur. "Do tell, is he as good in bed as they say?"

I see Wyatt stiffen.

My mouth goes dry.

"Oh, did I say something wrong?" She laughs again. "Wy is always telling me I go too far when I ask people personal questions. I can't help it! It's a hazard of my job. I work in film sales — you're way more likely to close a deal with a foreign distributor if you know what makes them tick."

I don't say a word; neither does Wyatt.

She shrugs, unfazed. "Anywho, what are you two up to in here?"

"Just going over a few things for the premiere." Wyatt's voice is empty.

"*Dull*." She leans against his side, wraps her hands around his arm, and pouts two perfectly pink lips at him. "I'm hungry. Can we go out for breakfast?" She looks at me fleetingly. "Whenever you're done with... *this*... I mean."

Another slice rips through the delicate flesh of my heart. I can barely breathe.

Wyatt removes her wrists from his arm and pushes her back gently. "Caroline, I need to finish talking to Katharine—"

"You know what?" I say brightly, blinking back tears as I glance at my watch. "I've overstayed my welcome anyway. Plus, I have another meeting to get to, so I better be going."

"Katharine—"

I'm already speed-walking toward the door. I've made it out of the study, into the foyer by the time he catches up to me. His fingers curl around my bicep in a steely cuff. I shake him off with a jerk, like he's burned me with his touch. His hand falls away.

Caroline wanders slowly toward the kitchen, expression bored but eyes alert. She lingers in the doorway just long enough to betray her desire to overhear our conversation.

"I mean it," I say flatly. "I have to go."

His eyes are on mine, guarded again. "Don't be ridiculous. You can't just leave."

I grit my teeth. "Watch me."

"You haven't even told me why you came, Katharine," he reminds me softly.

How silly am I, to think he stopped me from leaving for an entirely different reason...

"Right, of course." I snatch the folder off the small side table in the foyer where I left it when I first walked in, and hand it to him. "Here. My gift to you."

He flips open the folder and scans the first page, features darkening into a scowl.

"Yes. You're reading that correctly. Cynthia Firestone: *Mother of the Year,* twenty-two-time consecutive champion. I'm sure she'll be serving you a copy of your own in due course, but I thought I should warn you."

"Katharine." His eyes trap mine. It hurts to hold his gaze; he sees too much. All my jagged, bleeding edges. "Are you all right?"

No, I'm not all right.

You've got a gorgeous blonde staying over for sleepovers and I'm being sued by my own mother.

Oh, and did I mention the fake relationship, stalkerazzi, and accidental pregnancy?

132

I am most certainly not all right.

"I'm absolutely fine." My smile is frozen on my face. "But I really do have to go now."

"Katharine—"

"Wy!" Caroline calls from the kitchen. "Do you have almond milk?"

"That's your cue." I swallow hard and turn to yank open the door.

"Wait, Katharine—"

I step onto to porch before he can grab me again, but — glutton for punishment that I am — I can't resist a final glance back in his direction before the door swings shut between us. His mouth is a flattened line; his eyes are flooded with so many terrifying emotions, I could drown in them.

"See you around, Wyatt Hastings."

His mouth opens to say something else, but I'm already walking away. It takes all my resolve to keep the tears from leaking out as I climb into my car, strap up, and start the engine. But as his mansion disappears in my rearview, so does my self-control.

I weep the whole way home.

CHAPTER EIGHT

"I THINK I PUT IT IN THE WRONG HOLE!"
- Someone who is terrible at mini-golf.

It's that weird stretch of time between Christmas and New Year's, when nearly everyone in the country is off from work, spending time with family and celebrating the moments of their lives. Unless you're me, in which case you have no family worth celebrating and your world has fallen apart around your ears.

I mope around my house for three days after the encounter with Wyatt, binge-watching the first season of *Vampire High*, eating the entire contents of my refrigerator, and otherwise acting like a hermit until Friday afternoon, when Harper shows up at my door demanding a girl's night.

"I don't feel like going out," I protest, munching on a red pepper. Pregnancy cravings are *no* joke, hand to god.

"Don't care!" She plunks her makeup bag down on the vanity in my bathroom and grins wickedly. "I haven't been out in ages."

"Where's Masters?"

"At home. I forbade him from coming — this is an old-fashioned girl's night. We'll eat, we'll drink, we'll dance, we'll flirt shamelessly with college boys we'll never talk to again... It'll be great." Her eyes turn pleading. "Come *on*, Kat. Don't be such a stick in the mud. Neither of us has work tomorrow, I have a new eyeshadow palette I'm dying to try out, and you've got a closet full of brand new outfits just *begging* to be worn."

I sigh. She's got the same air of determination about her as the time she dragged me to a sample sale at a warehouse downtown at four in the morning, to get in line before every other fashionista in Los Angeles. There's no fighting her, when she gets like this. I take comfort in the fact that at least this time I won't have to sit on a sidewalk for three hours while my ass slowly goes numb waiting for the doors to open, all for the privilege of playing tug-of-war over clothing items I will never, ever wear but purchase anyway, just so I have something to show for my frozen butt-cheeks.

She strides into my walk-in closet, scans the many hangers, and selects a black dress she purchased for me three weeks ago, the day I handed over my wallet and gave her free range to style my wardrobe for the press tour. She came back with bag-laden arms and a shit-eating grin. I'm pretty sure my credit card was smoking, she'd swiped it so many times.

"No," I say, eyeing the dress.

"Yes," she counters, thrusting it at me. "You can't wear a bra, though."

Normally, I'd find this idea appalling. But for the past few days, my boobs have been so tender and swollen, I haven't bothered shoving them into the torture-chambers they call bra-cups at all. So, I must admit, there's some appeal in the idea of a dress that doesn't require me to struggle back into one.

I eye the garment.

It walks the razor-thin line between stylish and scandalous. The back is mostly nonexistent — a racerback panel of sheer lace tapers from the shoulders all the way down the spine in a narrow strip — but the front is rather simple and remarkably pretty, with its thin straps and fitted bodice. Years of previous experience have taught me that fighting with Harper about outfits is usually a losing battle. Plus, by objecting, I run the risk of her finding something even flashier in the depths of my closet.

Stripping down to my underwear, I slip the dress over my head and tug it over my curves, wincing slightly when the material flattens my boobs against my ribcage. I stand in front of the mirror and adjust them so they're slightly less confined — an unfortunate side effect of which is cleavage so deep, it makes the Mariana Trench look insignificant.

"Damn, I have a good eye! That dress is killer on you. Your boobs look humungous!" Harper wolf-whistles. "Seriously. Super hot. You're on *fire*, Firestone."

I roll my eyes. "Never heard that one before."

Smoothing my hands over my still-flat stomach, I can't help feeling bloated and paranoid. My body hasn't changed much, though my jeans are fitting a bit snugger. If I'm honest, though, that's more likely due to the entire bag of pita chips I consumed while powering through Season 2 of *Vampire High* at three in the morning.

Harper zips herself into a super-short, devilishly sexy magenta dress the exact shade of her hair. It's a stunning combination — she looks like some ethereal anime character who's wandered off the pages of a comic book. When our heels are on and our makeup is applied, we head downstairs, ready to hit the town...

...and find Masters leaning against my kitchen island, arms folded over his chest, regarding us sternly. I don't ask how he got in — the man designed my security system from the ground up.

"Please tell me you two weren't planning on going out dressed like that without me." His eyes narrow. "Because, if that's the plan, we're going to have issues."

Harper scoffs. "Kent, did we or did we not have a discussion about you being an overbearing caveman?"

"We did."

"And?" Harper plants her hands on her hips. "Do you recall the conclusion of said discussion?"

He shrugs. "You huffed and puffed about me taking care of you. I heard you out, because I think you're kinda cute when you're yelling your head off. Then, I decided to keep doing exactly what I'm paid to do, which is protect Miss Firestone and you, by proxy, whenever you're with her, which is most days because the two of you are a package deal. Though, since you and me are sleeping together every night and I'm practically living at your apartment, from now on I'll be protecting you wherever you go, regardless of your friends." He looks at me briefly. "No offense."

"None taken."

He swivels his head back to Harper. "Point is, you're my girl, and I protect what's mine."

She actually whimpers a little.

He leans forward. "Was that the conclusion you were talking about? Cause it's the only one I'll be reaching anytime soon."

Harper makes a big show of glowering at him, but we all know she's not actually mad. "You're annoying," she mutters unconvincingly.

He shrugs again, wholly unconcerned by her opinion, and grabs his keys off the counter top. "Where are we going?"

She's already beaming again. "Wherever the wind takes us."

Both Masters and I stare blankly at her until the grin falls off her face.

"Oh, *fine*, apparently being spontaneous is against the law." She sighs. "We have a table reserved at the *Limbo* supper club, then we'll hit their dance floor downstairs. A popular DJ is headlining — they all sound identical to me, if we're being honest, but supposedly he's a big deal because tickets have been sold out for weeks. Normally, we'd never get in, but now..." She trails off, staring at me.

"I'm Kat Firestone," I murmur regretfully.

"Exactly." Harper's grin returns. "I've been dying to get in there since I first moved to LA, and I finally know someone famous enough to get me through those red velvet ropes without waiting on the curb for six hours in hooker heels and a body-con dress, begging some brutish bouncer to notice me."

Masters' eyebrows lift, but he says nothing.

Harper pulls on her jacket. "My point is, we're obligated to at least test out the power of your new celeb status. It would be a waste, not to. So... I made a call."

"Shamelessly exploiting me?" I tap my hip against hers.

"Of course." She taps me back.

"Good. I'd hate to think this friendship was based on anything real, like mutual respect or love."

"Heaven forbid!"

We both dissolve into laughter.

Harper recovers first. "Did I tell you they actually bumped someone from one of their tables for us? How insane is that?"

"What?! Who?"

"Who *cares*?"

"Harper!"

"Oh, whatever, I'm nearly positive it was that snooty girl from *The Werewolf Chronicles* who broke Damian's heart last season."

"You do realize she's playing a character, reading lines she has no control over?"

"Tell that to Damian!" Harper folds her arms across her chest. "He spent six episodes moping."

"Again... he is a *fictional character*," I remind her, to no avail.

A snort echoes from Masters' direction.

"Oh!" Her eyes are swirling with possibilities. "Maybe I should try to name-drop our way into J-Lo's fitness class. I've wanted to know how she maintains that booty since I was six and she was still Jenny from the Block..."

"First of all, you should be a little embarrassed right now. Secondly, you're deluded if you think anyone in the industry would believe I'd willingly participate in a fitness class."

"Fine. No booty-camp." She pauses. "But what about Gwyneth Paltrow's ZenCycle class? It's full at the moment but I have a feeling if I leaned on them, there might be a *conscious uncoupling* between two current attendees and their reserved bikes..."

"Keep it up and I'll have to take away your name-dropping privileges. For your own good."

Harper glares. "You're dead to me."

"And you're drunk on power."

"So very true." She double-checks her small clutch purse, making sure she's got the essentials — ID, petty cash, cellphone, and, naturally, a full makeup kit in miniature. "All right, let's go make everyone hate us."

I sigh deeply but don't argue. When we turn for the door, we find Masters waiting there, staring at us with an indecipherable expression.

"What?" Harper asks.

He stares at us another beat, then turns and walks outside, muttering something that sounds like "batshit crazy" under his breath.

"What was that, honey?" Harper calls after him.

"I said I'll be in the car!"

"Uh huh." She catches my eye. "He loves that I'm crazy. He just doesn't know it yet."

We both break into giggles. Linking her arm with mine, she tugs me outside.

"Come on. You've been suffering all the shitty side effects of fame. I think it's time you enjoy a few of the perks."

* * *

I spent nearly a year slinging drinks and supplying bottle service to VIPs at an exclusive LA nightclub. It would be an understatement to say being on the opposite side of that equation is extremely strange.

When we get to *Limbo*, there's a line wrapping all the way around the block. Girls are shivering in their stilettos and short dresses, excitement palpable; their male companions are standing stoically, waiting to be admitted with all the eagerness of a death row inmate on his way to the chair. I'm not a huge fan of clubs, but even I can't deny there's a certain kind of thrill that rushes through me when Masters pulls up to the designated VIP drop-off area, throws his keys to a waiting valet, and pulls open the door for us.

The quiet of the SUV backseat explodes in an instant.

People at the front of the line scream and snap photos on their camera phones.

Look!

That's Kat Firestone! Did you see her?

Is Grayson with her?

Where is he?

I ignore them as best I can, keeping my eyes straight ahead as I stride for the doors, trying not to trip on the skyscraper heels Harper insisted I wear. The bouncers don't ask us any questions or check our IDs— they just clear a path and let us walk inside, where a hostess is quick to take our coats and lead us to our table.

The supper club at *Limbo* is famous, thanks in no small part to a popular rapper who included a line about their cheese puffs in his latest number one hit. The ritzy upstairs restaurant caters to the LA elite, with a wine list longer than my arm and an ever-rotating food menu that even the harshest critics are hard-pressed to find fault with. On the surface, the space is completely refined and romantic — low lighting, marble embellishments, geometric pendant lights suspended from the ceilings at asymmetrical angles.

But then you notice the opaque floor.

See-through and sound-proofed, the dining room offers unobstructed views of the raging club scene directly below us. It's a jarring juxtaposition — quiet elegance sitting twenty feet atop the writhing sub-level dance floor, where the flashing lights and madly-spinning DJ tracks keep the masses enthralled. I suddenly understand the name *Limbo* — this place is both Heaven and Hell, contained within a single space.

I imagine the people downstairs can make out our blurred shapes if they squint up at the ceiling.

I think I saw the bottom of Rihanna's heels! It was amazing!

"How fucking cool is this?" Harper hisses as we settle in at the table.

"Pretty fucking cool," I concede. "Though I feel bad for Masters."

"He didn't have to come." Harper shrugs. "He'll be fine at the bar."

I look for my security guard and find his hulking presence leaning against the sleek bar across the restaurant, his ever-watchful eyes scanning the room, his large hand gripping a glass of ice water. I sigh.

"I'm sure they could add a chair to the table..." My head tilts in thought. "But then he'd have to listen to us gossip about everyone in this restaurant."

"Did you see Chris Pratt in the corner?" she murmurs, eyes darting surreptitiously at the tables around us. "And I'm almost positive that's Ashton Kutcher, over there."

I nod, trying not to let it show that I'm freaking out a bit, just being in such company.

"Admit it," Harper whispers, leaning toward me. "Your life is pretty damn cool, Kat Firestone."

She is *not* wrong.

When the waiter returns, Harper orders a glass of wine. I stick to water, managing to play it off as another attempt at sobriety. We eat a delicious meal — fried zucchini flowers, shrimp risotto, and fresh fruit parfait. It costs a truly outrageous sum, but with a full stomach and a happy heart, I don't mind a bit as I sign the check. We decide to hit the bathroom before we descend the steps to Hell, knowing the club stalls downstairs will be far more crowded than the ones up here.

Harper turns sideways to examine her body in the mirror. "God, I'm stuffed. Suddenly regretting the skin-tight dress. You can see the outline of my food-baby through the fabric."

Better than my actual *baby*, I can't help thinking, staring at my own stomach.

"I should've worn my fat pants with the elastic waistband." She frowns at her reflection. "Next time."

"I thought you only broke those out on Thanksgiving?" I roll my eyes. "You look amazing. Relax."

I'm touching up my lipstick when I hear the sound of the bathroom door swing in. Stiletto heels click irregularly against the tile floor, as though the girl wearing them is having trouble walking a straight line. When she steps into sight, her lips painted the trademark blood-red shade I recognize from a message she once scrawled on my dressing room mirror, I realize two things immediately — she's highly intoxicated, and she hates me with a vehemence I've never before witnessed. I turn slowly to face her.

"Helena." My voice is soft. Behind Helena, Harper's eyes dart to mine, a question in their depths. I shake my head slightly, so she doesn't interfere.

"You," Helena slurs, stumbling closer. "You are a little *bitch*."

"And you're a little wasted."

Her perfect features, even prettier in person, contort into a mask of fury. "You stole everything from me. *Violet. Grayson.* You took it all."

"I didn't steal a damn thing from you, Helena. I never would've gotten your part, if you hadn't screwed it up in the first place," I remind her.

She's past the point of listening.

"You'll be sorry," she promises, leaning closer. I can smell the alcohol on her breath, see the abnormal size of her pupils, refracting the mellow light of the bathroom like dark glassy pools. Clearly, she's out of rehab — and off the wagon.

She leans even closer, pressing me back into the sink.

"Did you hear me bitch? *You'll be sorry.*"

"Oh, Helena. I am sorry," I tell her, my voice deadly soft. "I'm sorry you got your heart broken. I'm sorry you screwed yourself over. I'm sorry you're having a rough time. Truly, I am. But hear me when I tell you: if you threaten me again, my sympathies are going to expire faster than the low-carb leftovers in your refrigerator."

She doesn't seem to hear me. Not a single word. Standing there swaying uneasily on her heels, she looks almost... manic. It's frightening to witness. I study her for a moment, taking in the smeared lipstick, the vacant look in her eyes, and realize she has come completely unhinged — a door slammed too many times, no longer able to perform its most basic function. Equal amounts of disquiet and indecision churn through me.

Whoever this girl is, standing in front of me, it is not the Helena Putnam she used to be. It is someone unstable; someone in need of far more help than I know how to give her.

"You'll be sorry," she whispers again, like a crazed mantra, the smile on her face promising vengeance even as tears start leaking from her empty eyes. There's a hysterical edge to her words that sets my teeth on edge.

"You'll be sorry. You'll be sorry. You'll be sorry."

I look at Harper in alarm, wondering what to do.

She shrugs, at a loss.

Helena doesn't even seem to see me anymore. She's retreated inside her head, somewhere unreachable. I sidestep around her and walk to my best friend, ambivalence clawing at my insides.

"What do we do with her?"

"Who, Sylvia Plath over there?" Harper snorts, totally unsympathetic. "Um, how about... *nothing.*"

"She's having some kind of breakdown." I look back at Helena, who hasn't moved so much as an inch. "We can't just leave her here."

"Why not?"

"We're better than that."

"Are we, though?" Her nose wrinkles. "This girl has only ever called you names, spread rumors about you in the press, threatened you, and tried to make your life a nightmare. I say... to hell with her, let's go dancing. If she falls into a toilet and drowns while throwing up all the painkillers she washed down with her vodka soda, well, I for one will not miss her. Karma's a bitch and so am I."

"Harper!"

"What? It's true."

"It's *awful*."

"Since when are you such a bleeding heart?"

"Since I decided I'm going to try to be a better person."

Harper blinks at me, as though she can't wrap her mind around such a concept.

I sigh. "If we call a bouncer, they'll toss her out on the curb..."

"Sounds like a perfect solution."

I scowl. "Sounds like throwing her to the wolves. You saw all the paparazzi outside. It would almost be better to let her drown in a toilet."

"Doesn't she have a security detail? A driver? A babysitter? A sponsor, who's supposed to be preventing her from destroying her liver?"

"I don't know."

I'm trying desperately to think of a plan when the door starts to swing inward as a gaggle of girls enter the bathroom. Harper shoves it closed before they can get so much as a stiletto inside the frame. They squawk in protest as the panel slams in their faces.

"Out of order!" Harper yells, using her body weight to keep it shut.

I cross to help her hold them off. After a minute of indignant squeals, they give up and stalk away to find a different restroom.

I glance at my best friend. "I'll bar the door. You go get Masters — tell him what happened. He can stand guard, make sure no one comes in here."

Harper grimaces, but she doesn't argue as she steps out into the hallway. While she's gone, I run through every possibility I can think of... and grimace in frustration at the lack of good options.

If I call an ambulance, they'll roll up outside, sirens blaring, drawing the attention of everyone in a ten-block radius. Then, in all likelihood, they'll lock Helena up in a psych ward and throw away the key — which may not be an altogether terrible idea, given her current state, but it definitely isn't my call to make.

If I leave it to the *Limbo* staff to handle, it's only a matter of time before the story spreads to the servers, and then to the patrons, and then to the rest of the world.

If I walk her out the front door and put her in a town car, the paparazzi camped outside will notice... and take about a zillion photographs that will be plastered all over social media tomorrow.

The only viable alternative I can see is one I'd do almost anything to avoid.

Harper slips back inside a few moments later. "Kent is on door duty. Did you come up with a plan?"

"Not really." I sigh, deeply troubled, and run through the bleak list of options.

Harper's sigh echoes mine. "Crap."

"My thoughts exactly." I hesitate. "There is one person I could possibly call..."

Harper frowns. "If you're considering who I *think* you're considering, that's your worst idea so far."

"What choice do I have?"

"See this situation?" She points at Helena, who's still standing in a drunken daze by the sinks. "This is the definition of a human garbage fire. Adding Grayson to the mix and thinking it'll help matters is sort of like dousing flames with gasoline and expecting them not to explode."

"Give me another suggestion then. Tell me one reasonable, responsible alternative."

Her teeth sink into her lip in frustrated silence.

"That's what I thought," I murmur softly, pulling

my phone from my clutch purse. I scroll through my contact list until I reach his name. My lips twist; he's still programmed in as GIANT DOUCHEBAG.

I haven't called him on the phone since Hawaii; haven't spoken to him at all since the day of the camera-smashing incident. Yesterday, in a moment of weakness, I logged online to see if the story made the headlines — *DUNN ASSAULTS PAPARAZZO! CHARGES FORTHCOMING* — but there was nothing. Not one tiny blip about the smashed lens or show of rage. His lawyers must've bribed the shutterbug into silence.

Then again, the tabloids may just be sitting on the news until a slow day. From what I saw, they've got plenty of material concerning Grayson and me to keep the presses busy for months. This week alone, I've been accused of a teenage eating disorder, a decade of unreciprocated devotion, and an estrangement with my darling mother. I can only wonder what they'll come up with next week.

FROM BUSY BEES TO LOVE BIRDS... WE'VE GOT THE #GRAYKAT DETAILS YOU'RE DYING FOR!

INSIDER INTERVIEW: "SHE'S LOVED HIM FOR YEARS!"

KAT CRACKS DOWN: DUNN'S PARTY DAYS ARE DONE!

PHOTOS INSIDE: KAT AND GRAYSON, THROUGH THE YEARS

KAT'S SECRET STRUGGLE: FRIENDS OPEN UP ABOUT THE ACTRESS'S ANOREXIC PAST

UP IN FLAMES! FIRESTONE'S AGENT-MOTHER SEEKS LARGE SETTLEMENT FROM AXC

With clenched teeth and shaking hands, my eyes scanned all the horrendous things they'd written about me, not once bothering to check whether they might be remotely accurate before printing them as fact. Each bullshit story was capped with a cute little disclaimer:

"Firestone did not return our request for comment." As though that somehow validates them spreading lies.

If I had to bet on the identity of this "insider" who's provided a steady stream of stories and photographs, I'd put all my money on Cynthia. This practically reeks of my mother — stirring the embers of my stardom into a full-fledged inferno, not resting until my face is on every magazine rack, news feed, and Twitter stream. Even when we were still on speaking terms, she had no problem using my secrets as media fodder. Now that we aren't, there's no way she'd turn down an opportunity to make a quick buck by selling my childhood memories to the tabloids. The more I'm worth, the more she can ask for in the lawsuit.

Heart in my throat, I lift the phone to my ear and wait for it to connect. He answers on the second ring, his voice muffled. There's so much background noise I can barely make out his voice at first.

"Kat? Are you okay?"

"I'm fine," I assure him. "But Grayson... I need you to come to *Limbo*."

"Why?"

"It's Helena."

He doesn't ask any questions, but I hear him swear under his breath. "I'm on my way."

I click off.

Harper is staring at me, brows raised.

"He's coming."

"Oh *goodie*. I'm sure the playboy idiot will know exactly how to deal with Helena *Over the Cuckoo's Nest* Putnam."

I look back at the cuckoo-bird in question. She hasn't moved an inch. Swaying on her heels, the former model is transfixed by her own reflection, seemingly unable to look away from the sight of tears tracking down her beautiful face, leaving trails of watery mascara on each cheek before dripping into the sink. She isn't making a sound, but I see her lips mouthing the same words over and over again, like a prayer.

A chill of foreboding goes down my spine.

You'll be sorry. You'll be sorry. You'll be sorry.

* * *

Grayson shows up within fifteen minutes, so he must've been close by when he got the call. He's not alone when he steps inside the women's restroom — he's got an entourage of three heavily-muscled security guys who don't do much besides grunt. Their taciturnity is balanced out by the last member of the group to step into the room, who I know from experience never, ever shuts up.

Ryder Woods.

"Kit-Kat!" the musician yells as soon as he spots me, sweeping me into a hug. "You look fucking gorgeous!"

I pat him awkwardly on the back. "Hi Ryder. I didn't think you'd remember me."

"Remember you? I friggen *love* you! You bought me a cheeseburger at three in the morning. You saved me from a bar fight. Face the facts — we *bonded*, babe. No going back now." He shakes my shoulders so hard, Masters takes a warning step in our direction. Ryder pays him no attention. "How the hell have you been?"

"Can't complain." I laugh, staring into Ryder's unique eyes. One blue, one brown, both currently constricted to pinpricks, suggesting he's been partaking in more than just alcohol tonight. Unsurprising — the first time I met him, he was snorting lines of cocaine off a table at *Balthazar*, the club where I used to work. "How about you?"

"Been busy, babe. Did you know I'm recording a single for the *Uncharted* soundtrack? It's total shit, of course. I didn't write it, some studio-approved lyricist sent it over. I wouldn't be doing it at all, if not for my boy." He nods in Grayson's direction.

I follow his gaze to my co-star and find he's hovering a few feet away, his eyes on Helena, who we finally got to settle down on one of the plush chairs by the bank of mirrors a few moments before they arrived. Still lost in a stupor, her eyes are open but unseeing.

148

Grayson's gaze flickers to mine when he feels the weight of my stare.

"Hey," he says, lips tugging into a half smile.

"Hey." I take a breath. "Thanks for coming. I didn't know what else to do with her... I didn't know who else to call..."

"I'm glad you called me. We'll take care of her." He looks back at Helena, takes a deep breath, and crosses to kneel in front of her. She flinches when he puts his hands on her kneecaps, stroking her soothingly through the fabric of her leather pants like you might a skittish horse. "Hey. *Helena*. It's Grayson." He shakes her lightly. "Helena, can you hear me?"

She lifts her limp head at the sound of his voice. Her eyes seem to regain some of their focus.

"Grayson?" She sounds like a lost little girl, woken from a bad dream in the middle of the night.

"Yeah." Grayson expels a sharp breath. "It's me."

"You came." She smiles, still crying. "You're here."

"I'm here."

"I knew you'd come for me."

He runs a hand through his hair, looking distressed. Ryder nudges me. "She isn't looking great."

"No." I clear my throat. "She isn't."

"She should go to the hospital." Masters insists, not for the first time. "She's having some kind of psychological episode. She's too fragile to go home alone."

"I agree," Harper chimes in, folding her arms across her chest.

"Then I'll take her home with me," Grayson says flatly.

"Grayson—" I start.

"I'm not locking her up again." Grayson is on his feet, his hand wrapped around Helena's arm to keep her upright. She's swaying, but standing. Barely. "Last time, they just pumped her full of drugs and kept her sedated until she finally worked up enough strength to check herself out. It's no wonder that didn't help her. It's no wonder she's right back where she started."

"Grayson..." I trail off. "Look at her."

Helena has stopped crying. Her empty eyes are fixed on Grayson's face with a reverence that worries me.

"She needs help. More help than any of us know how to give her." I'm starting to regret my decision to call him. "You're too close to this situation — you aren't thinking clearly. If I'd known this was your solution, I would've called the paramedics straightaway. I only wanted you to help me get her out of here without too much fanfare, get her to someone who can actually help her..."

His eyes, so green it almost hurts to look into them, hold mine. His jaw clenches so tight, he can barely get the words out. "Don't you understand? I did this to her. *I did this*. It's my responsibility to fix it."

"Grayson," I gasp softly. "That's crazy."

"She's right, man," Ryder says, nodding in agreement. "You've got things twisted."

"She was fine, when I first met her. Normal. But then, when we got involved... I broke things off before they could get serious... and she couldn't handle it. She got violent on set. Throwing things, trashing her dressing room, fighting with Sloan every step of the way, showing up drunk for line-readings. She lost the part in the movie because she couldn't work with me anymore..." Grayson's face darkens. "It was my fault. It's my fault she's like this. It's my job to make it right."

I stare at him, and it's like I'm seeing him for the first time. For months, I've been caught up in thinking that I fell for this man because of his looks and his charm and his undeniable sex appeal. But in this moment, I realize I was entirely wrong. I fell for Grayson Dunn because he's *me*. The boy with the whole world at his feet, who can't see it because he's so consumed by the cloud of self-doubt swirling directly overhead. Thinking he's toxic to anyone who comes near.

My broken soul mirrors his. A kindred mess in the making. We are nothing more than two drowning fools who found each other in the depths — clutching desperately for survival and unintentionally winding up even deeper beneath the surface. Each dragging the other down until water filled both our lungs and we sank like stones into the abyss.

Not love.

Not fate.

Recognition.

Understanding jolts through me. Suddenly, I know how to handle this — how to handle him. It's like talking to myself in the mirror.

I step closer to him and wait until his eyes meet mine. Even from five feet away, I can see the shadow of guilt and self-loathing swallowing him up inside. I can't believe I never noticed it before.

"Grayson. Think about it. She *chose* to get involved with you. She *chose* to start a relationship with a co-star. She knew it might turn out poorly. She knew what she was getting into." I take another step. "You didn't take advantage of her. You didn't force her to quit the movie. Again — that was her choice. There's no way you could've known she'd..." I trail off vaguely, not wanting to say what we're all thinking.

No way you could've known she'd go crazy.

"There are normal responses when a messy romantic entanglement ends — drink a bottle of wine, eat a gallon of ice cream, have a one-night stand. Everyone has their own way of dealing with heartbreak. But this..." I glance at Helena. Her eyes stare straight through me. "*This* is not normal. Things like this don't just happen without a predisposition. You didn't do this to her, Grayson. Whatever Helena is going through right now... my guess is, it's been coming on for a long time. Brewing below the surface. Waiting for the right set of circumstances to bring it to the light." I take another step, close my hand over his, and slowly unwind his fingers from her arm. "You didn't do this. Do you hear me? It's not your fault."

He's a statue.

"Grayson — look at me."

He does and, in that moment, he's like a little boy who's broken his favorite toy. Sad and small and full of regret.

I squeeze his hand. *"It's not your fault."*

His jaw clenches even tighter. He doesn't say a word, doesn't even acknowledge I've spoken, but he does step aside to let me take his place supporting Helena.

I glance at the team of silent bodyguards.

"I'm going to need one of you to carry her out, one of you to make sure we've got a clear path out of here, and someone else to pull whatever car you're driving into the side alley. We'll walk her through the kitchen exits, get her into the backseat, and take her to a private doctor. Somewhere discreet, that's accustomed to treating high profile patients."

The three of them nod in tandem. I heave in a breath of relief as I pass Helena over to the nearest guard. She's a rag doll in his arms.

"Harper, I need you to talk to the manager. Make sure it's okay for us to use the kitchen exit."

"Will do," she says.

"Ryder..." My voice drops lower. "Stay with Grayson. Make sure he's all right."

The musician winks at me, which I take as a sign of agreement.

"Masters, can you handle the paparazzi?"

He nods.

"Great." I look around the bathroom and find every single person — with the exception of Helena — is staring at me. "What are you all looking at? We don't have all night. *Move.*"

Grayson's security team jolts into motion like I've fired a gun at the beginning of a race.

152

Harper smirks.

Masters flat-out grins at me.

It's Ryder, who breaks the silence though.

"Called it the first time I met you, Kit-Kat." His mismatched eyes gleam. "*Badass.*"

CHAPTER NINE

"THIS IS WHY I HAVE TRUST ISSUES."
*- A girl realizing her shampoo will never make her
look like the model in the advertisements.*

With the help of the *Limbo* night manager and
kitchen staff, we manage to get Helena out of the club and
into the car without any paparazzi taking notice. Grayson
and Ryder pile in after her.

"There's a wellness recovery center in Palm
Springs." Grayson's eyes meet mine. "I'll take her there,
stay a while to make sure she gets settled in."

I nod. "The press tour doesn't start up again for a
few more days, but if you need more time... just call. I'll
explain it to Sloan. Hell, I'll do the interviews alone if I
have to. I think I'm finally getting the hang of them —
there's a decent chance I might actually make it through
one without saying something inappropriate or idiotic."

"Kat..." Grayson's throat works. "I don't know what
to say..."

"You don't have to say anything." I shrug.

"You hate me most of the time," he murmurs. "And
yet, you're basically the best friend I have. Is that sad?"

"A little." A hint of a grin tugs at my lips. "I don't
know... We tried being enemies. It didn't really work out.
Maybe that means we have to be friends."

A strange look creeps into his eyes. "Maybe. Happy
New Year, Kat."

"You too, Grayson."

"What am I, chopped liver?" a peeved voice calls from inside the car.

I roll my eyes. "Happy New Year, Ryder."

"Back atcha, Kit-Kat."

I close the car door with a click and watch them drive off. A wave of exhaustion hits me, hard.

Turning to Harper, I grimace. "Listen, I know you wanted to go dancing, but..."

She waves my words away, linking her arm with mine. "Let's go back to your place. I'm thinking... we get into pjs, eat ice cream straight from the carton, and put on a rom-com we've seen a zillion times?"

"Sounds like perfection."

And it is.

Maybe twenty-two year olds are supposed to be out dancing till dawn, downing shots of tequila, and making questionable life choices... but I must say, I'm happy to be flouting convention, at least for tonight. After Masters drops us at my place, we make sundaes and serenade each other to old Whitney Houston songs in our pajamas, eventually collapsing onto my couch with our hairbrush-microphones abandoned at our feet.

"It's been way too long since we did this."

"Agreed." She sighs. "It's been way too long since you've been *able* to do this. For a while there, I was worried you'd never laugh with me again."

My mouth flattens. "I'm sorry."

"No! Honey, *no*, I don't want you to apologize. You were heartbroken. You were going through something. It was just really hard for me, as your best friend, to have to watch from the sidelines while you worked your way through it. I knew there was nothing I could do to help, but that doesn't mean it was easy for me to watch you struggle."

"You did help, though. You were here, every day. You helped me pick out every piece of furniture in this house. Hell, you helped me pick out the house, too. And the car in my driveway, and every article of clothing in my closet.

That was enough. That was *everything*."

Her eyes are watering. "Love you, you big slut."

"Love you too, you abominable whore."

"I have to say..." she murmurs after a while. "Grayson surprised me tonight."

"How so?"

She shrugs. "He really came through for Helena. Granted, his chivalry was a side-effect of being such an asshole and breaking the poor girl's heart in the first place, but still. Maybe he's changing."

"Maybe."

"Would it matter?"

My eyes narrow. "What do you mean?"

"If he could be different. If he could step up — commit to you. Actually be your boyfriend. Not as an act for the interviews... for real."

"That's never going to happen."

"But if it did," she pesters. "Humor me. Would you want him?"

I'm quiet for a long while. "I think... if you'd asked me a month ago, I would've said yes. But now..."

"Things have changed," she murmurs. "You've changed."

I nod. "It's more than just that, though."

"Okay, what else?"

"It's complicated."

"I have a very high IQ." Her eyes roll. "Explain it to me."

"Fine." I sigh. "On the surface, Grayson is light. He's fun. He's the good time guy — always down to party, always traveling, always working on a new movie. He's got women throwing themselves at him in every city in the world. He's got the swagger of a man who's insanely good looking and fully aware of it. And I admit, I'm not totally immune to that."

"You'd have to be a robot to be immune to that." Harper smirks. "Plus, there's the small fact that you were starring in an insanely romantic movie with him, falling

156

in love on camera, in possibly the most beautiful place on the planet." Her head tilts. "Probably didn't help the whole *resisting temptation* thing..."

"Definitely not." I grimace.

"There's nothing wrong with someone fun, you know. Maybe that's what you need, Kat. Someone endlessly fun."

"No, I don't think so. Being with someone like Grayson... It would be like living on a diet of only chocolate for the rest of your life. The premise sounds great, at first. But eventually you'd die of scurvy, wishing for a damn piece of broccoli. A diet of pure sugar is unsustainable. You'd slowly wither away into nothing, unable to survive without vital nutrients."

"So, no chocolate diet for me. Got it."

"You can tease, but my point is, we aren't meant to be happy all the time. I think we need sadness and pain and horror, otherwise all the joy we experience means nothing. If you never feel fear, you can't be courageous enough to overcome it. If you never have your heart broken, you have no barometer to measure the biggest love of your life. Without the dark, there's no light."

For some reason I can't look at her while I say these things without feeling like a total fraud. I stare at my hands instead and pretend not to notice the way my words shake when I continue.

"That's the biggest difference between someone like Grayson... And someone like Wyatt."

Harper sucks in a surprised breath. I've broken our unspoken rule. I've mentioned the unmentionable.

Wyatt.

I ignore her. "Grayson acts like there's nothing but sunshine in the world, ignoring the shadows altogether, like he thinks they might disappear if he pretends long enough. But Wyatt..." My voice gets so soft it's almost inaudible. "Wyatt knows the shadows are there. He recognizes just how much darkness consumes this world. And every single day he makes an active choice to see the flip side. The light. *He chooses sunshine.*"

Harper is quiet, saying nothing.

I try to gather my thoughts, but they seem more scattered than ever. "For a long time, I thought I was only worth a certain type of guy — a certain type of love. I've dated asshole after asshole, thinking they were my *type*, but maybe the truth is... I just didn't value myself enough to ever ask for something — *someone* — better. Maybe girls pick bad boys over good guys because there's something inside them that assumes being treated poorly is no more than they deserve."

Harper smiles sadly. "Honey, I've been telling you that for years. You deserve someone who treats you like you walk on water; instead you've been settling for guys who wouldn't buy you a freaking *bottle* of water if you were dying of thirst." She grabs my hand and squeezes. "And trust me, I'd have kicked your ass for it a long time ago, if I thought it would've made any difference at all."

"Nice." I laugh.

"True, though."

"I know. Self-esteem isn't something you can borrow like a pair of jeans and give back when you don't need it anymore. You have to stitch it together for yourself, thread by thread."

"At the risk of sounding like a pushy know-it-all—"

"Are you ever anything else?" I snort.

She glares at me. "*As I was saying...* at the risk of possibly overstepping... I think the reason you fell for Grayson is the same reason you haven't let yourself fall for Wyatt. Deep down, despite all the progress you've made, you don't think you're good enough for him. And, frankly, it's really starting to piss me off."

I flush. "You don't understand—"

"Katharine Firestone. I understand. I understand perfectly. You think you're toxic. You think you break people. But Wyatt Hastings is not a man easily broken. He's a Norse god with a casual billion-dollar net worth, for christ's sake. He's an extremely successful executive producer. He's thirty-five — a grown ass *man* who knows exactly what he wants. And, what he wants is you."

"But I hurt him—"

"So apologize."

"I've tried."

"Say it again. Say it until he hears you."

"Maybe he doesn't want to hear me."

"Of course he does! He loves you, you idiot!" Harper looks like she's about to smack me. "*He loves you.* And I think... I think, if you let yourself..." She doesn't finish the thought. She doesn't need to, when she sees the tears glossing over my eyes.

"I don't know how to fix it. He's with Caroline. And there's other stuff, complicated stuff..." My hand creeps to my stomach. "I have no idea if it's even possible to fix it. If there's even anything left to fix."

"You'll never know if you don't try, honey."

"You're right. I know you're right."

"Don't worry. I bet he'll be at Sloan's party tomorrow night. And, if he isn't... We'll figure it out. We always do." Her hand squeezes mine again. "I promise."

Even if she's only saying it to make me feel better, I don't care. It works.

My best friend is pretty damn amazing.

"So," she says casually. "Does this mean I can start wearing my #TeamWyatt t-shirt out in public, or...?"

I grab a pillow and smack her across the face with it.

My best friend is pretty damn annoying.

* * *

I'm full of nerves when I wake the next day. It's New Year's Eve, and there's a heady excitement in my veins that I can't seem to shake. Nothing's changed; not really. And yet, in my head, something vital has shifted. A puzzle piece, sliding into place.

It makes me want to get in my car, drive across town, pound on a door, and scream at the top of my lungs.

Instead, I pace in circles around my house, counting down the hours until Sloan's party.

The inaction is damn near killing me.

Harper is annoyingly calm, by comparison.

She's been working diligently on our costumes for the masquerade for the past week and is holed up in my walk-in closet making sure every last detail is perfect for tonight. After I nearly tread a hole through the floor, she banned me from the room, complaining that my pacing was driving her to distraction.

Whatever.

I pass the time by watching several more episodes of *Vampire High* while stalking the internet for news articles about Helena. To my relief, there's nothing new — which I take as a good sign that Grayson made it to Palm Springs without too much trouble.

I make a simple stir-fry dish for dinner — even my limited cooking skills are up to the task of chopping vegetables and tossing them into a wok — and carry a bowl upstairs to Harper. She's finally finished with the outfits, and accepts the food with a grateful smile.

I stare at the costumes laid out on my bed. Both are bird-inspired, but that's where the similarities stop. The one on the left is a gauzy affair of turquoise and emerald, adorned with a mask made of peacock feathers. It's pretty, but it doesn't capture my attention quite like the other.

On the right side of the bed, a stunning sheath of pure white silk is accompanied by a delicate, shimmery eye-covering that conjures up mental images of graceful waterbirds with gargantuan wingspans.

A heron?

No. A swan.

"Which one is mine?"

"Which one do you think?" she asks, curious.

"They're both beautiful... But I'm guessing the colorful one is for you, the classic one is for me."

"Ding ding ding!"

"Thanks for putting them together. I owe you one."

"Remember me in your memoirs, that'll be thanks enough."

"Seriously?" I ask.

"No, of course not." She scoffs. "You aren't getting off that easy. You totally owe me a cupcake from Magnolia. But not until after the *Uncharted* premiere. I already ordered our dresses, and I'd actually like to fit into mine."

I laugh, but a fissure of panic shoots through me. If Harper custom-ordered a dress using my old measurements, there's a chance it won't fit a month from now, when I have to put it on and glide down a red carpet as the whole world watches.

"What's my dress look like?" I ask, hoping she says something like *loose fitting* or *flowing* or *empire waist.* She doesn't say a thing. Her jaw does drop in disbelief, though.

"Since when do you have even the slightest interest in fashion choices?"

"I don't know, maybe since I have a giant movie premiere scheduled for a month from now."

"Ah." She grins. "Well, it's a surprise, so I can't tell you anyway. Sorry."

"You do realize I paid for the dress."

"Of course."

"Doesn't that mean I should get to see it beforehand?"

"Definitely not."

I sigh.

Harper is halfway through applying my makeup for the party when it starts. It's faint at first — a slightly queasy, stirring sensation in the pit of my stomach. I try to breathe deeply, to ignore the increasing nausea creeping through me in an unstoppable tide, but when a sudden rush of saliva fills my mouth, I know it's a lost cause. Bolting from the vanity stool, I practically leap the three steps across the tile floor to the toilet, where I promptly vomit up the entire contents of my stomach. The spicy stir-fry burns coming back up, making my eyes water and my nose sting.

Note to self: lay off the Sriracha. The tiny dictator is not a fan.

The room is utterly silent except for my occasional retching noises. When I'm finally done, I rise shakily to my feet and lift frightened eyes to my best friend. She's holding a cold cloth compress extended in my direction. My fingers tremble as I take it from her and press it against my forehead.

"How long?" she asks flatly.

My eyebrows lift.

"How long have you known?"

I blow out a breath. There's no use lying. The time for pretending is over.

"About three weeks."

Her jaw clenches. "You've known you were pregnant for *three fucking weeks* and you didn't tell me."

"Harper—"

"What, were you just planning to wait until the baby popped out and hope no one noticed? Maybe play it off as a new style — it's totally *in right now* to keep a basketball shoved up under your shirt at all times!"

I plunk down on the edge of my basin bathtub and press my fingertips against my temples. A headache is brewing.

"Harper, I'm sorry I didn't tell you. I haven't told *anyone*."

Her eyes narrow. "So... Wyatt... Grayson... No one else knows about this?"

"Well..." I hedge. "Masters kind of... figured it out on his own."

"Kent knows?!" she explodes. "He knows, before me?"

"It's not my fault you're dating a super-sleuth!"

"I'm your best friend! I should've been the first to know."

"I'm sorry! I didn't know how to tell you. Somehow, telling you would've made it more real. And I just... couldn't face it yet." I stare at the ceiling to keep from

162

crying. I am so unbelievably sick of my own useless tears. I'm not sure if it's the baby hormones swirling through me or simply the fact that everything in my life has fallen to utter shit, but it seems every time I turn around lately, the waterworks start up again.

"Well, it's certainly real now." She stares pointedly at my stomach. "If that eggo got preggo in Hawaii or just after we got home... you'd be about..."

"Eight or nine weeks," I say softly.

Harper's expression is solemn. "Do you want to keep it?"

I hesitate. "I don't know."

"Do you know who the father—"

"No," I cut her off. "I don't know."

"Are you going to tell them—"

"I don't know, okay?" A tear tracks down my face. "I don't know anything, so don't ask me."

"Okay." She leans back heavily against the countertop, like it's all that's keeping her standing. "Okay. It's all going to be okay."

I'm not sure if she's trying to convince me or herself.

"It's not okay, Harper. It's a mess. It's all a total mess. How can I possibly raise a baby?" My voice gets hysterical. After weeks of resolutely *not* talking about this, now that it's finally out in the open I can't seem to stop the torrent of words that rush forth from my lips. "I can barely take care of *myself*. There's no way I can handle this, Harper. I don't know anything about crying infants or little kids. I don't think I can do this at all, let alone by myself, as a single mom—"

"Honey! Honey, *stop*." Sitting down on the edge of the tub beside me, she circles her arms around my shivering frame and pulls me in close. "You're getting way ahead of yourself right now."

"But—but—" I blubber like an idiot. "I—"

"Shhh." She pushes my head down to lay against her shoulder and strokes my hair like I'm a little kid. "Just breathe for a minute. You don't have to decide anything right now. You've got months to figure things out. And you aren't alone, idiot. You've got me. No matter what you decide to do, I'll be with you every step of the way. I promise."

A shuddering breath escapes me — one I hadn't even realized I'd been holding. For the past three weeks, from the moment I open my eyes every morning until they finally slip closed at night, I've been so full of tension, so weighted down by the heft of this monumental secret, I didn't even realize the burden of carrying it alone until this second, when I've finally set it free. Something inside me unclenches. I feel lighter than I have since the moment the pregnancy test flashed the word *positive* as I sat right here on the edge of this tub and felt my world tilt on its axis.

I let Harper stroke my hair for what feels like forever, until my ragged breaths are calm and my eyes are dry. When I lift my head off her shoulder, she smiles faintly.

"I know you're scared. It's okay to be scared. But there are some things we need to do." Her eyes are gentle. "You should have an ultrasound, just to confirm you're actually pregnant and that everything is on track. You should also start taking pre-natal vitamins. And... it would probably be good to talk to someone who actually knows what the hell they're doing when it comes to babies, because frankly, this is out of my skill set."

I feel my panic returning and force it back. "I'll make an appointment for sometime this week."

"Good."

"Harper?"

"Yeah, honey?"

"Will you come with me?"

"Of course I will. You never even have to ask. Whatever you need, I'm there."

"Thank you."

"Don't thank me." She pauses. "But, for the record... if you have this kid, I get to be the godmother, right?"

164

I roll my eyes. "Glad your priorities are in check."

She snorts, but sobers quickly. "Hey, one more thing."

I lift my brows. "What?"

"That thing you said before, about how you can't handle this. That's crap. You realize that, right?"

"But—"

"No *buts*. You are not the same girl you used to be, crawling into a bottle whenever things get tough, refusing to acknowledge your own feelings, unable to ask for help when you need it. I watched you the other night. I saw you take command of a shitty situation. Ryder Woods may be a washed up coke head, but he was spot on. You're a badass, Katharine Firestone. You're honest and hard-working and, even if you don't like to admit it, you care deeply for the few people you allow to get close. You protect those who need help. You take charge in a crisis. You never take no for an answer. You stand up for yourself. You're a fighter." Her voice softens. "I hate to break it to you, but those are all the qualities that make for a good mother."

I suck in a terrified breath. "You think?"

"I *know*."

* * *

We get to Sloan's fashionably late, since Harper had to redo our makeup after the bathroom breakdown. The party is already in full swing.

"Ready?" Harper asks, adjusting the cleavage in her beaded turquoise dress. Her eyes peek out from between a flurry of peacock feathers.

"I think so." Reaching up, I give a slight tug to ensure my mask is tied securely then follow her out of the backseat, taking care not to trip on the loose limestone driveway in my razor-thin white stilettos.

I've never been to a masquerade before. There's something thrilling about a party where everyone is in disguise — the air is full of possibilities, saturated by the sensation that anything could happen.

Masters drops us by the entrance and drives off

to park the SUV somewhere along the dense row of cars lining Sloan's driveway. Despite Trey's fears that no one would show up on short notice, there must be at least a hundred people here. As we make our way down the walk to the front door, I can't help wondering if Wyatt is one of them.

No — he's probably ringing in the new year with his new girlfriend.

The thought makes my eyes sting, so I push it back and force a smile. Tonight, the last night of the year that changed my life, is for celebrating, not crying about things I have no control over.

A uniformed woman takes our coats at the door. The cool air hits my skin like a splash of water. The dress Harper picked out for me is stunning. Solid white, devastatingly simple in design, crafted of the purest, raw silk I've ever laid eyes on. It caresses me each time I move. A seductive kiss against my skin.

In this dress, I don't just feel like the swan I'm pretending to be — I *am* a swan.

Graceful. Romantic.

Flying.

The mask on my face is small but extremely well-crafted — all white feathers and intricate beading, a stark frame that seems to heighten the blue of my irises. I look around at the crowd and see I am a single drop of white in a sea of color. Flashy dresses, elaborate masks, and ornate costumes litter the room in a kaleidoscope. I recognize no one. I realize that's the point of a masked affair, but the anonymity still leaves me breathless.

With just over an hour left until midnight, Harper and I make the most of it. I avoid cater-waiters bearing trays full of brimming champagne flutes, partaking liberally in the stuffed mushrooms and mini quiches each time they come within reach. There's a photo-booth set up in the corner to commemorate the evening — we pose with outlandish props as a professional photographer snaps us in several different positions. Seconds later, his

166

assistant hands us a printout embellished with the words HAPPY NEW YEAR in elaborate script.

We stand in a corner, checking out the scene. Sloan is dressed as a horse and drunk off his ass. Every few minutes, he lets out a truly awful braying sound that makes everyone within a ten-foot radius either wince with annoyance or roar with laughter, depending entirely on the amount of champagne they've consumed. My heart stops at one point when I think I spot a familiar head of long hair in the crowd, tied back by a leather strap, but I must be imagining things because when I glance back mere seconds later, there's no sign of those broad shoulders stuffed into a tuxedo anywhere in the sea of masked strangers.

Harper and I are lurking on the side of the dance floor watching our equine, highly-inebriated director cut a rug with a woman dressed as a court jester, when Masters appears. He's not wearing a mask, because apparently macho tough guys don't partake in silly things like masquerade parties and costumes. He extends a hand in Harper's direction.

"Dance with me." He doesn't ask.

She doesn't object. "Okay."

They drift off onto the dance floor and I hover on the outskirts of the crowd, watching couples spin and rock and sway in time to the music. It's a slow song — the kind made for prom queens and inaugural balls. Your hands around his shoulders, your cheek pressed to his chest; his palms at your waist, his breath at your temple. I watch all the happy pairs and feel strangely alone.

It's five minutes to midnight and excitement is building to a crescendo. People are getting ready to countdown the seconds to a new year, to seal the start of a fresh calendar page with a kiss on the lips of the person you love most. Abruptly, it all feels rather wrong. Because the person I want most by my side, ringing in a new year, is somewhere else. *With* someone else. Starting his year with her instead of me.

And I have *tried.*

For weeks. Every day, every minute, every hour. An everlasting test of my emotional endurance.

I have attempted to let him go. To tell myself he's better off without me. To push him from my head and try to be okay without him. To be happy for him, because he's found someone who makes *him* happy.

But in this moment, watching everyone dance in a room filled to the brim with excitement and anticipation, I cannot try anymore. Cannot pretend I don't want him with me. Beneath this mask, expression hidden from the masses, I finally let my shield down and allow the utter devastation of the truth to sweep through me.

I am in love with my best friend.

And I have lost him.

Unable to witness the love around me, unable to stand here counting down the moments with the joyful crowd when I feel nothing but sorrow, I slip into the kitchen, dodging several cater-waiters, and make my way out onto Sloan's terrace. It's abandoned — everyone has gone inside for the midnight champagne toast. The silent air is a blessing after the crush of conversation.

I look out over the sprawl of Los Angeles far below and wonder which of those many, infinitesimal lights belongs to him. Which speck of brightness marks the spot where my heart beats, since it no longer resides in my chest and has flung itself foolishly into his unshakable hands.

Where are you?

Maybe it's selfish, maybe it's wrong, maybe it's weak... but in this moment, I need him like the ocean needs the moon to set her tides.

I hear them starting the countdown inside — a muffled chant. I don't think. I don't talk myself out of it. I don't even try to resist the urge that overcomes me.

59... 58... 57...

I pull my cellphone out of my clutch purse with shaky fingers.

54... 53... 52...
I scroll to the end of my contact list.
48... 47... 46...
I press his name.
43... 42... 41...
It rings. Rings. Rings.
37... 36... 35...
No answer.
Of course — what kind of person is checking their phone at midnight on New Year's Eve?
33... 32... 31...
His gruff voice implores me to leave a message. The voicemail picks up with a long beep.
28... 27... 26...
"Wyatt... It's Kat." I breathe deeply. "But you never call me that. You call me *Katharine*. Or *baby*. Or *crazy*. Or... you used to. Now, you don't call me much of anything. Now, I'm lucky if you even look at me." My voice breaks. I hear the chant inside, getting louder, picking up steam as more voices join in.
20... 19... 18...
"I don't know why I'm calling," I whisper into the phone. "Actually, that's a lie. I'm calling because it's New Year's Eve, and you aren't here. You're *never* here, anymore. And I get it — you're happy. You have her, and everything has changed between us. And I'm... I'm happy for you." My voice cracks again and I laugh brokenly. "Actually, that's not exactly true. I'm really, really *trying* to be happy for you. I swear I am. But it's really hard, because Wyatt... you're my best friend. And I miss you. I miss you so much I can't even *breathe*."
14... 13... 12...
"I hope, wherever you are, whatever you're doing tonight, whoever you're spending it with... you're happy. That's it. That's all." I take in a gulp of air that sounds a lot like a sob.
9... 8... 7...

"Happy New Year, Wyatt. I hope you know that I... that I..."

6... 5... 4...

I click off the phone and contemplate tossing it into the pool. I stare at my feet, breathing hard. Fighting down the last part of my message that I couldn't force myself to say. Three little words stuck in the back of my throat, suffocating me. I have to let them out.

"That I love you," I say to the night. Testing it out with only the shadows to hear.

3... 2... 1...

"I LOVE YOU!" I scream out loud, at the top of my lungs, anguish seeping into every syllable. The sound is swallowed up by the huge swell of voices inside.

HAPPY NEW YEAR!

They're cheering and clapping, kissing and hugging. And I am weeping.

Because I love, love, love Wyatt Hastings.

My Viking.

My novelist.

My sunshine.

My best friend.

He's not here. We aren't together. I don't deserve him.

But that doesn't change a damn thing. My choice is made. The thumping organ inside my chest has finally sworn its allegiance, and I fear there is no going back.

Love isn't some unavoidable destiny, some fate you can't sidestep. It's a choice you make — and keep making — every day of your life.

His arms, so safe, so strong. A home, made of flesh and bone. His eyes, so blue, so bottomless. A whole future in their depths.

No instant, inexplicable connection or unhealthy co-dependence. Just a story about two people who choose to be together — not because they have to, but because they want to. Even when it's hard. Even when the whole world is stacked against them.

I don't need him.

If I never feel his touch again, never kiss his lips or grip his hips as he thrusts into me in slow, delicious strokes, never run my hands through his hair or know the joy of making him laugh... I will survive. The world will not stop turning. My heart will not stop beating.

Years will pass, I will ache with each moment without him, but still, I will survive. Hollowed out, perhaps, but still breathing. Still living. Still existing.

I. Don't. Need. Him.

...But I want him.

I want him more than anything I've ever wanted in my life. Regardless of the mess I've made, regardless of the fool I've been, regardless of Grayson and Caroline and the tiny dictator and the press tour and all the other seemingly insurmountable factors in my life...

I choose him.

"There's no need to yell, baby."

The sound of his voice so close behind me, so full of hope and wonder and heartache, makes me go still. It is a bullet of calm fired through a night of chaos. It tears through me, a devastating death strike. My clutch purse tumbles to the terrace, my cellphone slips out of my grip. I don't bend to retrieve them. I whip around, barely breathing, barely allowing myself to believe it might be real. Telling myself I'm going crazy, because there's simply no way he's actually *here.*

But he is.

CHAPTER TEN

"I WAS TOLD THERE WOULD BE CAKE."
- An unwilling plus-one at a wedding.

He stands there, five feet away, ruining me without a single word.

It seems there are a million miles to traverse in that short distance as I stare into his eyes, locked on mine behind a simple black satin mask. He's dressed in a tuxedo tailored so sharply he looks like a magazine model, but I barely notice. My eyes are on his, and we're having another of our wordless conversations.

You're here, I drink in the sight of him. *I can't believe you're here.*

His mouth tugs up at one corner. *Of course I'm here.*

My voice shakes almost as badly as my knees. "I didn't see you inside."

"I know." His voice is carefully empty. He doesn't close the gap between us.

"Did you see me?"

His eyes answer. *I always see you, Katharine.*

My heart is pounding. "I needed some air."

He nods, saying nothing.

"I also... " I take a breath and string the words together. "I wanted to call you. I left a message."

His eyes ask a question he doesn't vocalize.

Why?

I take a tiny step, wishing my knees weren't trembling. Wishing I were stronger, that this was easier, as I listen to the crowd inside singing off-key, their voices slurring the familiar lyrics.

Should old acquaintance be forgot, and never brought to mind...

"Wyatt," I whisper. "I wanted to tell you... I had to tell you..."

A muscle jumps in his jaw, the only sign he's at all affected by my words. I see the tension brewing inside him, tightly reined, and I realize he's *waiting*. Not pushing. Never pressuring. Giving me time to find my voice. Because he knows me. He knows it's not easy for me to lay myself bare.

Allowing yourself to be weak is the hardest thing in the world. But maybe that's the whole point. Maybe, when it's damn near impossible, it means you have something to lose. Something that matters.

My eyes hold his.

He's still waiting. He'd wait a lifetime. He told me as much, a long time ago, back before I ever really knew him.

"I'm waiting for the right girl."

"What if she never comes along?"

"She will."

"You seem awfully certain of that."

"I am."

"You could be waiting a long time."

"It doesn't matter how long I have to wait. Because I'm waiting for my wife. And, however long it takes her to find me, I know she'll be worth every second."

The fear disappears. The self-doubt and nagging insecurities go up in smoke.

He will never push me.

He will never force me.

He will just love me, unfailingly, with limitless patience and quiet strength.

I can freely place my heart in those big, capable hands and know without a shred of uncertainty that he will never, ever drop it.

I steady my shoulders. I take that final step, until we're a hairsbreadth apart, the last remaining sliver of space between us so full of tension it's practically humming. And I say the words that finally bring an end to his wait.

"I might be bad at it. I might screw it up. I might make a mess of us. But here's the thing." My hands shake like mad as I reach up and slide them onto his shoulders. My palms barely skim the fabric of his tuxedo jacket, but I feel his whole frame shudder like I've electrocuted him. "I want an *us*. I want to try. I want to be with you." My voice breaks. "I know, last time, you thought I fell into your arms to get over someone else. I know you thought it meant nothing to me. But you were wrong."

My fingers brush the exposed skin of his neck as I press my body fully against his, my every curve plastered against the strong planes of his chest. He groans faintly, the only betrayal of his emotions, as though the merest graze of my fingertips might just be his undoing.

I press closer.

Closer, closer, closer.

And yet, not close enough.

"You were never a consolation prize, Wyatt. You were an unexpected gift, one I'd never allowed myself to hope for, except maybe in the darkest reaches of my heart, because I didn't think it was possible someone like you could ever love someone like me."

I stare into his eyes, two oceans on fire with heat. Somehow he's keeping it leashed so I can finish. And I find, when the time comes, I don't stutter. I don't flail. I don't babble. There's no hesitation — just a deep inner strength I wasn't even sure I had, until this moment, back in the arms of the man I was never meant to fall for, but somehow always meant to end up with.

"I love you, Wyatt. *I love you. I love you. I love—*"

His arms come around me so hard I worry they'll crush my ribs into dust. My words disappear on a gust of air as he lifts me clean off my feet, but I don't care because I no longer need words. Vowels and consonants and silly little syllables lose all meaning because his lips, curved in an undeniable grin, land on mine. He kisses me and I taste joy and heat and passion all blended into one on the tip of my tongue.

This is what love tastes like. Looks like. Feels like.

Love is the color of his bold blue eyes. Love is the sound of his heartbeat. Love is the taste of his mouth on mine. Love is a corporeal thing, something birthed into existence between two people whose passions combine. Love is tangible, implacable, irrepressible. It's him and me, light and dark, sunshine and shadow, choosing each other no matter the cost. Choosing to fight, regardless of the outcome.

His lips devour mine like a tornado, bowling me over. I surrender to the storm, clinging to his shoulders and allowing him to wreck me with each brush of his mouth. If not for his arms around me, I'd fall to the ground, unable to keep myself upright. We're both shaking with the intensity of our desire when he finally pulls back to let me breathe. The need is almost unstoppable. We've waited too long to taste each other again, let too many hours pass without the stroke of each other's hands.

We are fire and gasoline, ready to combust at the single strike of a match.

I know there are things we need to discuss. Important, vital, immeasurable things. And yet, I can't seem to think of a single one of them as he looks into my eyes with such longing, my heart nearly shatters at the sight of it.

I need you, I need you, I need you.

In my arms, in my bed.

Under my skin, under my sheets.

He sets me down on shaking feet and twines his hand with mine. And we run — through the sliding doors, past the clustered party guests still celebrating some holiday I cannot even recall the name of, straight by Harper and Masters, who stare at us with stunned smiles on their faces, and out the front door. We don't stop or speak as we race for his car, the night air sliding against my heated skin like a caress. The whole world has narrowed to a single feeling — his hand, wrapped around mine.

We zip out of the driveway. His house isn't far; a ten-minute drive through the winding bends of the Hills.

We make it in five.

The engine is barely off when he rounds the hood and yanks me bodily from my seat. I see the savage look in his eyes as he rips the satin mask from his face and tosses it to the ground. I recognize the raw carnality brewing inside him a second before his mouth lands on mine. My heart pounds at twice its normal speed as his hands fist in the silk of my dress and he hauls me up against his chest, then pins me against the side of the car without hesitation, his hips pressing into mine until I feel how hard he is beneath the fabric of his pants.

I gasp into his mouth; he swallows the sound with a kiss. As his lips ravage mine I realize, quite abruptly, that beneath all that steadfast patience and meticulous control he shows the world, there lies a beast of a man. The last time we were together, muted by alcohol and uncertainty, I only caught a glimpse of it.

No glimpse could prepare me for the full extent of his passion. For the wreckage he is about to inflict. A raider, a warrior, an invader. Burning me to the ground. Taking no prisoners.

His hands move down my thighs to find the hem of my dress, dragging it up to my waist in a fervent tug, and then his fingers are there, at the very core of me, his palm grinding slowly against my underwear, creating friction with the thin lace until I am no more than putty in his hands. I'm already teetering on the edge; a few careful strokes of his fingers and I know I'll slip over the side of the cliff, free-falling into a chasm of lust.

For a heart-stopping moment, I think he's going to make love to me right there, against his car. Throw me down on his driveway and fuck me in the dirt, in full view of anyone out for a midnight stroll, with a ceiling of stars and a bed made of gravel. And the craziest thing is, I'd let him. I'm so far gone, in this instant, he could do anything he wanted to me and I wouldn't utter a word of objection.

I'm on the brink, about to explode, when his hands shift away. A helpless sound of protest slips out as his palms slide under my thighs and hoist me up into the air. My legs wrap automatically around his waist as he carries me up the front steps, across the threshold, and straight up the massive staircase to the second floor. He kisses me the whole way to his bedroom, as if he cannot get enough, as if the thought of tearing his lips from mine even for a moment is not an option.

He throws me on the bed, almost violent in his need, and I've barely landed when my dress disappears up over my head, tossed across the room somewhere out of sight. My trembling hands aren't fast enough for him as they attempt to undo his buttons, so he takes over.

Patience has officially expired.

Waiting has unequivocally ended.

I see an apology in his eyes — he cannot be tender. There will be time for that later. For the slow, passionate exploration of each other, over lazy Sunday mornings and sunny weekday afternoons. But tonight is for lust. Need. Desire.

Total, complete, unfathomable wreckage.

Our eyes never look away as he pushes into me with a single, savage thrust. He moves like a man possessed, eyes burning with fire, and I bow beneath him like a reed caught up in a river's current, bent to his will. I am drowning in his eyes, reveling in the intimacy I see in their depths instead of running from it.

This is the undeniable consummation of a far-flung hope, the declaration of a long-suppressed wish never voiced. This is two people celebrating something that almost slipped away from them.

We find release in the same moment, clutching so tightly I'm sure we'll both be bruised. I don't care. He could break me in two and burrow inside my skin — it still wouldn't be enough. I've barely come down from my spiral into bliss, but the need is still there, clawing at me.

Insatiable.

The hunger in his eyes tells me I'm not alone.

We don't speak for hours. Not verbally. But our hands whisper a thousand secrets, our mouths trace a million stories as we toss beneath bedsheets, learning each other like a melody you already know by heart, but eventually buy sheet-music for so you can read the actual notes.

Dawn is creeping through his windows, staining the world pink on the first day of this new year, by the time we are finally spent. I lie there, tangled around him as he runs his fingers through my hair with the last bit of energy that hasn't been sapped from his system, and think it's rather perfect that so far, he is the only person I've spent time with this year. It is a clean slate, upon which nothing is written except our burning, unblemished love story. And if day one is any indication of the remaining three hundred sixty-four, I walk into this future with hope and happiness in my heart.

"Happy New Year," I whisper against his skin, the first words I've spoken in hours, as my eyes drift closed and I slip into slumber.

His lips land on my temple.

"Happy New Year, baby."

* * *

This time, when I wake up in Wyatt's bed, I'm not alone.

A smile touches my lips before I'm fully conscious. My eyes crack open and I find he's already awake, watching me with soft eyes. He lets out a low *oof* sound as I roll suddenly on top of him, so I'm half-sprawled across his chest, and press a kiss against his lips.

"Good morning," he says, chuckling.

I look at the long shadows creeping across his bedroom floor. "Afternoon, I'd guess."

He shrugs. "I don't care what time it is. I have nothing else on my agenda today besides a very long appointment with this bed and you."

"Oh? Trying to keep me captive here, Mr. Hastings?"

"*Trying?* No. Just keeping."

"That's kidnapping."

He shakes his head as an amused light fills his eyes. "It's not kidnapping if you're a willing captive."

I kiss him again, soft and sweet. There's no rush. No need to hurry. I savor this moment with him, recognizing how precious it is even as it's unfolding around me. There's something beautiful about being here with him, wholly exhausted from a full night of love making, but buzzing with excitement down to a molecular level. I feel supercharged from the inside out. Fatigue may've deadened my limbs, but it cannot damper the thrill of being in his arms.

I shift against him and my muscles cramp painfully. "God, I'm sore. Every bone in my body aches."

He laughs. "And you call *me* an old man. You're a sprightly twenty-two-year-old. Keep up, will you?"

I attempt to punch him on the arm, and am rewarded with a cramping bicep muscle.

"Ow," I moan.

He rolls his eyes and sits up, bringing my body vertical with his. "Come on. I'll make you breakfast."

"Really?"

"Really. What do you want?"

"Everything." My stomach rumbles.

His hand laces with mine as we climb out of bed. He pulls on a pair of sweatpants, then tosses a giant t-shirt in my direction. He even helps me pull it over my head when my aching arms protest, only making fun of me a little.

"You did this to me," I remind him, tugging the hem of the shirt down to my thighs.

His eyebrow quirks. "Are you complaining?"

Every raw, hot, mind-numbing moment of last night flashes through my head. I feel my cheeks get warm.

"No." I swallow, feeling desire sluice through me. "Not complaining."

"Thought so." His jaw clenches. "Stop looking at me like that, baby."

"Why?"

"Because I'll throw you right back in that bed and this time, I won't stop until you're so sore you can't stand."

I gulp. I try to tell myself I *don't* want him to do exactly that.

It's not working.

"Katharine." His voice is warning.

"Fine!" I scowl. "But they better be some damn orgasmic pancakes, that's all I'm saying."

He smirks like I'm an adorable inconvenience, crosses to me, and before I realize what's happening, he's hoisted me over his shoulder so my ass is in the air and my limbs are dangling.

"Wyatt!" I squeal, staring at the small of his back as he starts to move. "What the hell are you doing?"

"Bringing you downstairs."

"I could've walked!"

"Probably. But I'm thinking you're going to need to save your energy for later." His hand squeezes my ass playfully.

"You're insane."

He doesn't deny it, but I can feel laughter rumbling through him as he carries me like a firefighter rescuing a victim from the flames. He sets me down on his kitchen counter, presses a quick kiss to my forehead, and proceeds to make us breakfast.

Fleetingly, I wonder why it doesn't feel strange or uncomfortable to be here with him, why I don't have that slightly panicked energy coursing through me like I would after any other sleepover with a man. It doesn't take me long to realize why.

This isn't any man.

It's Wyatt.

I watch him moving around the kitchen with ease, cracking eggs and sifting flour and squeezing orange juice. I feel totally at home. Like we've done this a million times. Like we're a genuine couple, who've fallen into a comfortable pattern. It makes me happy and sad at the same time. I feel the weight of our wasted weeks, pressing down on me.

He sees the twisted expression on my face and drops the spatula with a thud, sending batter flying in all directions. He crosses to me and stands between my knees, so we're eye to eye.

"What is it, baby?"

My voice is clogged with unshed tears. "This is how it should've been. That morning, after the cast party. If I'd just waited another five minutes... but I thought you regretted it, I thought you'd left me there..."

"Hey." His hands cup my cheeks, tilt my head up so my eyes are locked on his. "Things happen for a reason. Maybe, a month ago, you weren't ready for this. I don't know. I don't care. You're here now, and that's all I care about." His lips brush mine. "We're together. No more secrets. No more lies. No more miscommunications."

A pang of guilt shoots straight through my midsection, where my one last secret has taken root.

I need to tell him.

I know I need to tell him.

I just need to find the right moment.

"I love you," I whisper, crying a little.

"I know, baby." His arms wrap around my back, pull me in close so I can hear the thudding of his heartbeat beneath my ear as it presses against his warm, bare chest. Its tempo stutters as he whispers something else, something I've never heard him say out loud before, but already know in my heart.

"I love you too, Katharine."

Exhausted or not, I summon the energy to tug his lips to mine, to peel the shirt up over my head and kick his sweatpants to his ankles. Breakfast burns to a crisp on the stove as we make love on his countertop. I don't care in the slightest. Things like food and water and sleep lose all meaning as we gasp and sigh and cry out. Any needs outside the singular need to consume each other have dissolved away into nothingness.

Later, when we've managed to eat and shower and stop tearing each other's clothes off, we're sitting in Wyatt's favorite spot — a tiny gazebo nestled in the middle of a pond at the edge of his property — watching the sun slowly sink toward the edge of the horizon. I'm leaning back against his chest on the padded bench, his arms are wrapped around my midsection, and everything feels remarkably simple.

Still, as the sky turns cotton-candy pink signaling the end of the day, I know the bubble we've been living in is about to pop. Real life is returning with an alacrity I'm not ready to face. Wyatt seems to realize it too — his hold tightens around me, as if I'm already slipping away from him.

"You have an interview tomorrow?" he asks after a while.

I nod. "Just one, in the afternoon."

Neither of us mentions what that means, though I know we're both thinking about it. Me, in Grayson's arms. Keeping up appearances for the cameras.

"You'll be great." Wyatt's lips find my temple.

"Thanks. What are you up to?"

He sighs. "Unfortunately, I have a full schedule of meetings that will probably run late. And..."

"What?"

"I also have to talk to Caroline at some point."

I blink, surprised. "Oh...*Oh.*"

"It's not what you think. We were never serious. She always knew I had feelings for someone else." His voice is full of stark honesty. "But I still feel like I owe her an explanation. I don't want her waiting around for a call that isn't ever going to come. Things have changed; it's only fair I let her know."

182

I look at him and see the worry in his eyes. I hate that he's fearful of my reaction — hate that he thinks hearing this might make me bolt. I slide a hand over his heart and lean in close, so he can't miss the truth in my words.

"You're a good man, Wyatt Hastings."

The worried look vanishes. A smile tugs at his mouth. "Can I take you to dinner afterward?"

"Of course. Dinner sounds good." My lips twist mischievously. "But, instead of going out, maybe we could stay in... and cook.... and also *not* cook...."

His eyes glitter. "I like the way you think, baby."

I nuzzle against his chest. He's so warm, I wouldn't be at all surprised to learn he's got a thermal conductor under his skin.

His hand slides beneath my sweater, coming to rest directly against my stomach, right over the spot where my tiny dictator has taken up residence. I feel myself stiffen.

"Hey, you okay?"

"I'm fine," I lie, heart hammering. Trying not to think about the small nuclear bomb rooted inside me, ticking down on an invisible timer. About to explode my newfound happiness into bits of irreparable debris.

Only a matter of time.

I know I need to tell him. But in this perfect moment, I cannot find the words. I cannot bring myself to wreck the beauty of this fragile start between us. Not when it took us so long to find our way back to each other.

I swallow down the words.

I'll tell him tomorrow, I think, relaxing against his chest again. *One more day won't change anything,*

* * *

Wyatt drops me off at my place on his way to work the next morning. I watch him drive off from the end of my driveway, already counting down the minutes until I'm back in his arms. When I spot the SUV parked under the tree in front of my garage, I brace myself for what's to come but it's ultimately useless. Prepping for Harper is like sheltering in place during a tornado. All you can do is close your eyes and hope like hell the roof doesn't cave in.

"Hello?" I call, stepping inside my own house like a guest. "Harper? Masters? You here?"

I hear a sound to my left and jump about a foot when I see my best friend standing there, silently beaming at me from the archway of the kitchen.

"Jesus, Harper, you scared the crap out of me!"

"Sorry!" she sings, not looking at all apologetic. In fact, she looks downright giddy as she closes the gap between us, grabs my hand, and starts jumping up and down. "It happened! You and Wyatt!" Her expression twists and she stops jumping. "Wait... That *was* Wyatt you took off with the other night, wasn't it? You haven't been holed up somewhere with a long-haired lookalike in a mask?"

"Of course it was Wyatt," I confirm, laughing.

The jumping starts up again. "I need to hear everything!"

"Okay, okay, but please stop bouncing. You're giving me vertigo."

I walk into the kitchen and spot Masters leaning against the far counter. He nods in greeting.

"Miss Firestone."

"Seriously, Masters?" I snort. "Call me *Miss Firestone* one more time and you're fired."

His lips twitch. "I'll take my chances."

"Don't bother with him," Harper says, hopping up on a barstool. "He's utterly impossible."

"True," Masters agrees, stony-faced.

Harper pins him with a look. "That's not a *good* thing, you idiot."

He shrugs, unconcerned.

I laugh.

"Impossible man," Harper growls. "Anyway. Back to Wyatt. I want to hear everything."

"It's already nine — I should go shower, start getting ready for the day..."

184

"Katharine Firestone, sit your ass down on that stool and spill."

Glowering, I do as I'm told. Before she can scold me again, I tell her about the past two days — the PG:13 version, because Masters is listening. When I finish, Harper's eyes are glossy with happy tears.

"I'm proud of you, honey. And happy that you guys finally worked it out."

"Thanks."

"What did he say, though?" Her eyes dart to my midsection. "About... you know. The grape."

"The *what*?"

"The grape," she repeats tiredly, as if I should know exactly what she's talking about. "You know..." She gestures again at my stomach.

I blink slowly. "Are you referring to the tiny dictator growing inside me as a *fruit*?"

"As if calling it a *tiny dictator* is somehow better than a *grape*." She rolls her eyes. "I Google-searched pregnancies, okay? Apparently, if you're around ten weeks, your baby is approximately the size of a grape right now."

"Oh." My hand touches my stomach absently. "Huh."

Harper stares at me, a strange look in her eyes.

"What?" I ask, hand dropping away.

"Nothing." She shrugs and tries very hard to hide a smile. "Nothing at all."

"Whatever."

"You didn't answer my question."

I stare blankly at her.

"About Wyatt," she prompts, none too gently. "What did he say about the grape, when you told him? I'm sure he was shocked, but this is Wyatt we're talking about..."

"What do you mean by that?"

"Just that I can't picture him flipping out over this. He's far too even-keeled."

"I'm not so sure about that," I murmur, the memory of the morning after the wrap party flashing through my head. I'll never forget the look of rage on his face when he threw that tray against the wall. My Viking is a frozen river — solid at the surface, but wild underneath. "He's got a temper."

Harper stares at me, a knowing light creeping into her eyes. "Kat... what did he say?"

I avert my gaze, feeling guilty. "I, uh... haven't exactly told him yet."

"WHAT?!" she explodes.

"There wasn't a good moment!"

"There will *never* be a good moment to drop this bomb on him. That doesn't mean you don't have to drop it — sooner, rather than later."

"Maybe I don't have to tell him this instant, Harper. I don't even know what I'm doing about the *grape* situation yet. I don't know if I'm ready for the grape to turn into a kumquat or a mango or a potato or worse, an actual *baby*, okay?"

"Potatoes aren't fruit," Masters chimes in.

"*Helpful*, Masters, thanks so much for the contribution," I snap.

He smirks.

"My point is, I shouldn't tell him until I've decided how I feel about this situation." I sigh. "I haven't made up my mind about what I'm doing."

"Honey..." Harper shakes her head. "Yes, you have."

"How can you say that," I cry incredulously. "How can you know what I'm going to do, when I don't even know myself?"

"Because I know *you*," she says softly. "Do you realize, every time we talk about this pregnancy, your hands creep to your stomach, like you're cradling that little life inside you?"

"That's nothing. That's just—"

"And do you realize," she barrels on. "That you gave up alcohol and caffeine — two of your favorite pastimes — without blinking, the minute you found out you were pregnant?"

"But, I didn't—"

"And furthermore, do you realize that you are already so hugely protective of the *tiny dictator*, as you are so fond of calling it, that knowing you were pregnant was what finally enabled you to turn your back on your own awful mother?" Her voice gentles. "Honey, you told me you were never more sure it was the right decision to walk away from Cynthia than when you realized she might someday influence your child if you let her stay in your life. That's called a protective maternal instinct."

"But..." My whisper is weak. "But..."

"I think you want this baby." Harper's voice is quiet. "And I think that scares the shit out of you. Because as scary and terrifying as it would be to *not* want this baby, to actually exercise your legal right to choose — which, by the way, I am in no way against, should you ever change your mind — I think you're more afraid of giving up a chance at something that could be really great." She pauses. "Scary as hell, definitely... but also really great."

"Every minute of every day, I am terrified." I bury my head in my hands. My words shake. "I'm terrified to want this. I'm terrified I'll be bad at it. I'm terrified I'll turn out like my mother. I'm terrified of telling Wyatt and watching him walk away. I'm terrified to do this alone. I'm terrified *not* to do this. I'm terrified of how it will change my life. *I am terrified.*"

"Welcome to motherhood," Harper says wryly. "My mom used to say if you aren't afraid you're screwing it up, you're not doing it right."

I'm quiet for a moment. "This... this.... *thing*... has already changed my life so much, and it's the size of a freaking fruit. What's it going to be like when it's an actual baby?"

"I don't know. But I know you. And I know you're never one to run from a fight, Kat Firestone." She smiles. "You can do this. If you want to do it, you can. I have no doubts."

My smile wavers.

"You still have to tell Wyatt, though," she insists. "And, you also have to tell..."

She doesn't finish the thought, but we both know exactly what she was about to say.

Grayson.

God, I don't want to think about that possibility. Not yet. Because, while there's a slim chance Wyatt won't freak out when I tell him, there is literally *zero chance* that Grayson won't melt down when he hears this news.

The man-child, having a child.

I shake myself out of those terror-inducing thoughts.

"I'll tell Wyatt. Soon," I murmur. "Tonight, maybe."

"Maybe?"

"Harper. Please stop."

"*You* stop." She lifts her hands defensively. "I'm not the one in denial, here."

"What if I tell him and..." My voice cracks with fear. "And he walks away? What if he doesn't want me anymore, when he realizes I'm pregnant with a baby that might not be his?"

"Then he's not the man you thought he was." Masters' voice cuts through my fear like a knife strike. "He walks away, he doesn't deserve to stand by your side anyway."

I look up at my bodyguard — I wasn't even aware he'd been listening, but it's clear from his expression that he's paid attention to our every word.

His eyes are intent. "For the record, though, I don't think he's gonna walk away. Men who look at their women the way Hastings looks at you when you're not paying attention... they don't bolt. Not for anything."

"UGH!" Harper glares at her boyfriend. "Why can't you ever say anything mushy and sweet to me, huh?"

"Babe." He grins at her. It's a good grin — the kind that lights up his whole face, made altogether more effective because he reveals it so rarely. "You don't like mushy and sweet. If you did, you wouldn't be with me."

She huffs, but doesn't argue, because it's the truth. Turning back to me, her face twists back into a mask of worry. "I'm not your mother — thank *god*, that woman is a tyrant — so I'm not going to tell you what to do. But I will gently remind you that you have a doctor's appointment scheduled for noon today at a private practice downtown. If you're still up for it, I was planning to go with you before your interview this afternoon."

I stare at her for a few seconds, then cross the room and pull her into my arms. She goes still, clearly surprised by my show of affection. Typically, she's always the one to initiate contact.

"Thanks," I whisper. "For knowing me better than I know myself, sometimes. And for loving me even when I drive you crazy. Even when you hate me."

She sniffles and her voice is thick when she responds. "I always hate you. Just using you for free fame perks, remember?"

"Oh, right. I forgot." I pull back, grinning. "I'm going to take a shower. You'll help make me look semi-attractive for my interview, right? We both know if I try to do my makeup alone, I'll wind up looking like a troll."

She nods.

"You're a gem, Harper Kline. Don't know where I'd be without you."

I wink and walk out, whistling *Auld Lang Syne* as I go. I'm nearly to the stairs when I hear Harper's hushed tones, full of concern as she consults her boyfriend.

"Do you think she's okay? She *hugged* me. And *complimented me without sarcasm*. And she's *whistling*."

"She's not okay, babe." Masters chuckles. "She's *happy*."

CHAPTER ELEVEN

"PATIENCE IS A VIRTUE."
- *Someone defending their lack of other virtues.*

Two hours later, my happiness is gone.

All I feel is nervous.

I stare up at the fluorescent ceiling light. The paper sheet crinkles beneath me each time I fidget. Suddenly, I'm wishing I hadn't forced Harper to stay out in the waiting room of the discreet clinic downtown where I've come to get my first glimpse at the tiny dictator. It might be nice to have someone in here with me, holding my hand.

If I'm being honest, though, it's not Harper I want holding my hand. It's Wyatt.

This might be his baby, and he's missing it.

I should've told him, should've trusted him. No matter what happens, I'm telling him tonight. No more excuses. No more fear.

No more secrets.

"Are you ready, Katharine?"

The doctor with the ultrasound machine smiles down at me in a perfunctory sort of way. She's not exactly warm, but she's not cold, either. She's exceedingly professional in a way that suggests she likes her job, but has been doing it for long enough that the shine is starting to wear off.

I nod. "As I'll ever be."

"Are we waiting for someone? Husband, boyfriend..."

"No." I swallow hard. "No, I'm alone. It's… just me."

Her eyes soften a bit. "All right. This is going to be a bit cold."

There's a squirt sound, like squeezing the last bit of ketchup from the bottom of the bottle. A dollop of chilly gel lands on my stomach. Goosebumps appear on my arms, though they could just as easily be from nerves as the cold.

"Okay, this will just take a minute… If it's still early, it can take a while to find a rhythm…" She's looking at a monitor as she moves the ultrasound wand over my stomach, seeking something. My eyes press closed and as the seconds tick by, a thousand thoughts flit through my head.

Maybe it was a false positive.

Maybe I'm not actually pregnant.

Maybe all this worry and stress and heartache has been for nothing.

I'm not sure whether that possibility instills more relief or regret inside me. Before I can figure it out, a foreign sound makes my eyes fly open. Twice the speed I was expecting. Muffled, like it's coming from underwater… but, undeniably, present.

Thump-thump.

Thump-thump.

Thump-thump.

"There." The doctor is smiling. "That's your baby's heartbeat."

I turn my head to the screen, wide-eyed and breathless as I take in the sight of the blurry, black and white image.

"Right here." She points to a tiny shape that looks a bit like a kidney bean. "That's your baby. Do you see it?"

"I…" I suck in a sharp breath, trying to keep my emotions under control. Tears fill my eyes anyway. "Yes. I see it."

I see it.

I see you.

Hello there, tiny dictator. I can't wait to meet you.

* * *

Harper and I are sitting so close in the backseat our hips are practically fused together. We're on our way to my only press tour event of the day — a talkshow interview about *Uncharted* for an episode of *Late Night with Reggie* that will air sometime next week. She's staring down at the picture in my hands, a look of awe on her face.

"That is one good looking grape," she murmurs.

I roll my eyes. "It's a blurry smudge of black and white. We have no idea what it looks like. For all we know, it could pop out looking like Al Pacino."

"Hey!" she protests. "Leave Al Pacino alone. He was a legend in his prime, and he's arguably quite the fox now."

I roll my eyes.

"Anyway," she adds thoughtfully. "There's no way this kid will be anything but hot. Whether it's Wyatt's or Grayson's, the potential gene pool is frankly almost unfairly attractive to the rest of us."

"Please, stop talking."

"It's true," she insists. "You'll end up with the cutest spawn on planet earth. Your eyes, Wyatt's hair... your spunk, his smile... Can you imagine?"

Yes. I can, actually. That's what makes this so hard.

"Don't worry, babe." Masters catches her eyes in the rearview mirror. "Our kids will be cuter."

She blanches. "We've been together a month. You have to stop saying things like that."

"Nah," he says, merging left onto the highway. "Don't think I will."

I giggle.

She tosses her hands up. "He's impossible."

I start to say something else, but my words are drowned out by the sound of an engine revving close behind us. We turn around to look through the back windshield and spot a man on a motorcycle racing toward

192

our bumper, a large camera strapped to his saddlebag. His features are concealed by a visored black helmet.

"What the hell?" I mutter, totally at a loss as the man comes up alongside us, trying to peer into the backseat.

"Is he *chasing us?*" Harper exclaims.

Masters doesn't say anything, but I notice his hands are gripping the steering wheel a bit tighter. He presses down on the gas pedal to increase our speed, attempting to lose the paparazzo as we race down a stretch of four-lane highway. We turn to watch as the motorcycle falls behind, but a moment later the rider's gloves curl around the handlebars and he rockets forward again. He swerves and shifts lanes without signaling, trying to come up on our opposite flank. Two cars beep angrily, braking hard to avoid a collision as he cuts across the highway like a madman.

"Oh my god, he is!" Harper hisses, sounding excited. "He's chasing us!"

"I don't know what he expects to see." I shrug as if my heart isn't pounding twice its normal speed within my chest. "The windows are tinted."

"He probably wants to be the first one on the scene when we pull up at the studio. Really gives a new meaning to the phase *chasing down a lead*, doesn't it?" She snorts.

I, for one, see very little humor in the situation as we careen too fast around a bend, the SUV leaning at a precarious angle, the motorcycle keeping pace with us despite Masters' evasive maneuvers.

"This is my mother's fault. She's been stirring the press into a frenzy with all these stories about me and Grayson and our *decade-long love affair*." I shake my head. "There's a new tabloid story out every day."

"I thought you didn't bother reading those?" Harper asks.

"I don't, usually. But I was checking to see if there was anything new about Helena."

"Have you heard from Grayson?"

"Not a word." I wince at the thought. "Today will be the first time seeing him since that night at *Limbo*. Hopefully he got Helena some help. When we saw her she was..."

"Emulating Angelina Jolie in *Girl, Interrupted*?" Harper supplies.

"Basically, yes."

Masters hits the gas pedal again and I feel my stomach lurch as we take a sudden exit off the highway. The motorcycle, not anticipating our departure, misses the turn and flies past our left side.

"Lost him," Masters mutters.

"Yeah, well, I almost just lost my lunch all over your seats," Harper grumbles. "Can we please focus on getting there in one piece? We've got a baby on board for god's sake."

I roll my eyes. "The tiny dictator is just fine."

"That's my god-baby grape, in there." She gestures at my stomach.

"I don't technically think godmother duties start until after the in-utero part of the program."

"What kind of crap is that?" she asks. "I plan to watch out for it every step of the way. Even when it looks like an alien."

I decide it's best not to argue with her.

Thankfully, no more paparazzi attempt to tail us as we make our way to the studio. We pull into an underground garage without fanfare and take an elevator upstairs to the recording stage. A production assistant greets us with bottles of water before leading us to a small lounge to wait. Settling in on one of the plush chairs, I ask if Grayson has arrived yet; she's not sure. I ask when she thinks we'll start filming the interview; she has no idea. I ask if we can expect a debrief with Reggie, the show host, before we start recording; she can't say definitively.

Essentially, she is utterly useless as a PA.

"I'll come get you a few minutes before we start. It shouldn't be too long," she informs us blithely, drifting out the door with a dreamy look.

"Who did *she* bang to get this job?" My best friend snorts.

"Harper!"

"What? I'm genuinely curious. There's no way she landed this gig on merit."

"Go find your seat," I implore her. "Please."

"Fine." She sighs. "But if there's a makeup person backstage, don't let them cover you with setting powder. It makes you look like you sneezed in the warehouse of a cocaine cartel."

Masters winks at me as they disappear out the door to find their seats.

Alone at last, with no one around to mock me for my sentimentality, I pull out the ultrasound picture and stare at the black and white image. A strange sensation creeps over me as I trace the tiny shape with the tip of my finger. There's no single word to describe what I'm feeling.

Fearjoyguilthappinessanxietyterrorhoperegretlove.

I slide it back into my purse and grab my phone, scrolling to Wyatt's name and sending a quick text message.

KAT: *I MISS YOU.*

He responds almost instantly.

WYATT: *I MISS YOU MORE, GUARANTEED. THESE MEETINGS ARE A SLOW DEATH.*

KAT: *SORRY. I'LL REVIVE YOU TONIGHT. HOW DOES THAI TAKEOUT SOUND?*

WYATT: *PERFECT.*

KAT: *AND THEN MAYBE WE CAN TAKE A LONG HOT SOAK IN MY GIANT BATHTUB...*

WYATT: *YOU'RE KILLING ME.*

KAT: *DON'T DIE YET. I NEED YOU TO FUCK ME FIRST. PREFERABLY IN THE TUB.*

WYATT: *BABY...*

KAT: *I LIKE WHEN YOU CALL ME BABY. I LIKE WHEN YOU DO ALL SORTS OF THINGS TO ME.*

WYATT: FUCK, KATHARINE.

KAT: ...THAT CAN BE ARRANGED.

WYATT: THAT'S IT. I'M CANCELLING MY LAST MEETING.

KAT: GOOD. WE CAN HAVE A MEETING OF OUR OWN. MY MOUTH. YOUR COCK.

WYATT: I'M HARD AS A ROCK.

KAT: THAT WAS MY INTENTION.

WYATT: DID I MENTION I'M IN A MEETING WITH THREE AXC EXECUTIVES? INCLUDING MY FATHER.

KAT: LOL!

WYATT: NOT LAUGHING OVER HERE.

KAT: I'M SORRY!

WYATT: YOU CAN MAKE IT UP TO ME LATER. I HAVE A FEW IDEAS...

KAT: KEEP BRAINSTORMING, LOVE. I'M ALL YOURS.

WYATT: GOOD LUCK AT YOUR INTERVIEW, BEAUTIFUL.

KAT: SEE YOU TONIGHT. XX

I'm still grinning like an idiot when the door swings inward. Grayson's familiar frame fills the entryway. His gaze finds mine instantly.

"Hey."

"Hi." I tilt my head at him as I shove my phone back inside my purse. "How are you?"

I only ask because he looks like a total wreck. There are deep shadows beneath his eyes, making his emerald irises stand out starkly in their sockets. If I had to guess, I'd say he hasn't slept since I saw him last.

He shrugs. "You know me. Always good."

I'm not buying it. "Grayson..."

"Kat. I'm fine."

"You don't look it," I say bluntly, climbing to my feet. "How's Helena? Did you get her settled in?"

His mouth opens to respond, but he doesn't have a chance to answer because the spacey PA appears in the doorway.

"Reggie is ready for you," she informs us. "If you'll just follow me..."

We walk in silence down the hall and find ourselves backstage. I can hear the crush of voices from the live audience upstairs as they file into their seats. Nervous jitters take hold of me.

Grayson reaches out and squeezes my shoulder. I startle at the sudden contact and his hand drops away.

"Sorry." He swallows hard. His eyes are on mine, and there's a lost look in their depths. "You nervous?"

"Always," I murmur.

"You'll be fine. Reggie is a ratings shark, but he's not a bad guy. His jokes are pretty terrible, though."

"Hey! I heard that!" A nasally voice interjects. "Blame my writers, not me, hombre."

We turn to face the man himself — Reggie Vasquez. His late-night show dominates the ratings year after year, in part due to his ever-rotating roster of celebrity guests.

He looks so much smaller in person than he does on a television screen. Not a particularly handsome man, nonetheless he has a certain kind of charisma that commands your attention. His dark brown eyes are locked on me, appraising.

"Katharine Firestone," he murmurs, extending a hand. "It's great to meet you."

I slide my palm into his, trying not to flinch at the sweaty warmth of his skin. "Thanks for having us on the show. I'm excited to be here."

His grip tightens, not releasing mine. "Excited to have you."

A fissure of unease spirals through my chest. Grayson shifts closer to me, sliding an arm around my back. I notice he doesn't shake hands with the host — they trade taciturn nods of greeting instead. As the seconds tick on in silence with me trapped between the two of them, I begin to feel like a doomed chew toy caught in a game of tug-of-war between two rival dogs.

"Reggie." Grayson forces out, shattering the stagnant moment.

"Dunn," Reggie returns, smirking like he's won something as he finally releases my hand. "Happy to have you back. It's going to be a great show."

Grayson smiles, but it seems forced. "Always is."

There's no quiet moment to ask about the sudden tension in the air — not with the PAs and cameramen and tech crew hovering all around us, making sure the show goes off without a hitch. Grayson keeps up the appearance of a supportive boyfriend, his arm slung casually around my shoulders, and I try not to feel guilty about it. In my head, I know I'm not cheating on Wyatt, but it feels remarkably like a betrayal in my heart.

Reggie heads onstage, gives his opening monologue to the cheering crowd, and launches straight into our introductions. I hear a relentless buzzing sound coming from my purse on the small vanity behind us, as though someone is calling over and over, desperate to get ahold of me, but there's no time to check my phone because the interview is about to start.

I'm sure it can wait.

A crew member signals for us to step from the wings. I take a breath, paste on a smile, and follow Grayson out, my hand wrapped tightly inside his.

The audience goes wild when they spot us. Their thunderous applause slams into me like a punch to the stomach.

We grin and wave at them as we walk across the stage. Reggie is already seated behind his desk, clapping along as we approach, easily embodying the overjoyed host. There's no sign at all of the backstage tension; his expression indicates nothing except his thrill to have us with him as we settle in on the twin wingback chairs beside his desk. The uneasiness inside my stomach fades a bit.

"Grayson Dunn and Kat Firestone, everyone!" Reggie revs up the crowd again, until their applause practically rattles the roof off the building. "Or, as you have all been manically tweeting at me for the past few days since I announced this show... #GRAYKAT!"

We laugh good-naturedly, as if it isn't totally strange to be one half of a trending hashtag.

The interview proceeds much like our others. Reggie makes jokes at our expense — *Hey, what do you call an actress starring in a Grayson Dunn movie? Topless!* — and we pretend they're the funniest things we've ever heard. We play a game where Grayson and I have to guess obscure facts about each other, like at what age he had his first kiss and whether or not I'm allergic to anything, his childhood pet's name and the color of my first car. We get most of the answers wrong, of course, but that's the point of the game; even if we were actually dating, I'm not sure I'd have been able to properly answer a single one. The audience thinks it's hilarious, though. They're eating up everything we serve them, falling for our act hook, line, and sinker. Desperate to believe in our star-crossed love story.

Kat and Grayson. Couple of the decade. Aren't they just dreamy?

After we talk about *Uncharted*, Reggie plays a promo clip from the movie — the scene where Violet and Beck realize they're alone on the island. I watch the girl on screen, see the passion in her eyes as she looks at Grayson, and feel strangely separate from my own body. So much has changed since we filmed those scenes. So much has altered, in the months since I stood on a white sand beach and begged him to stay.

Watching the scene play out before my eyes is like picking up an old diary and flipping through the pages, recognizing the girl who scrawled such heartbroken words but no longer identifying with her. I see the pain and passion in my own expression onscreen, seeping through the character I was playing, bleeding between the lines of a script that seemed to so perfectly mimic my life, and feel nothing except a detached sort of sympathy for her.

That sad, broken girl with no self-confidence is a stranger to me.

Grayson's thumb traces slow circles on my hand as the clip plays on. Once, that small touch would've sent me into cardiac arrest. Now, all I feel is a remote sort of acceptance. The passion I used to have for him, fueled by delusional dreams and a self-destructive streak, have burned through me like a wildfire, the flames leaving nothing behind in their wake. Lust has run its course. All that's left is a memory, trapped within the reels of a movie. A time-capsule of heartbreak, immortalized forever on film.

"Wow!" Reggie claps, turning to face us. His beady brown eyes are unreadable. "I, for one, cannot wait to see this movie! It looks like quite the whirlwind romance."

"Oh, it definitely is," I agree, glancing at Grayson with a practiced smile. "We had an amazing time in Hawaii filming it. Our cast and crew got so close — we're all like family, now."

"Close is an understatement, I'd say," Reggie counters. "You two have had quite the whirlwind romance yourselves, these past few months!"

The crowd goes wild again.

"We're just happy we found each other." Grayson's voice is warm. "Every day, I thank my stars that I have this girl by my side."

My fake smile stretches wider. "Same goes for me. I'm incredibly blessed."

"That's just so sweet — isn't it sweet, folks?" Reggie asks the crowd. They cheer and clap. "But things will be different now, won't they?"

Grayson tenses, as though anticipating some kind of blow.

"What do you mean, Reggie?" I ask, suddenly nervous.

"Well..." He leans in like he's sharing a secret between friends, but his voice is booming when he speaks, ensuring that every person in the room hears his words. "Now that you've got the baby coming, I mean."

I freeze. I feel Grayson go still beside me. The

audience gasps, then falls into silence. It's so quiet on the stage, I can hear the cameraman breathing as he zooms in on my face.

Grayson's grip grows so tight it's cutting off circulation to my fingers.

I don't look at him. I keep my eyes on Reggie — that sniveling snake of a man — and smile benignly.

"*Funny*, Reggie!" I say, striving for a light tone. "You're full of jokes today."

No one is laughing, though.

Grayson hasn't said a word. I don't even think he's breathing.

Reggie leans closer, eyes glittering, and adopts a tone of phony contrition. "Oh, Kat, I didn't mean to catch you off guard!"

The audience members are whispering and checking their phones. Their murmurs have crescendoed to a dull roar.

I feel panic sweep through me.

They know. Somehow, they all know.

"Anyway!" Reggie claps abruptly, the sound making me flinch. "My apologies! We'll move on to another topic."

Rising to my feet, I stare down at him like he's a piece of toilet paper stuck to my shoe.

"No, we won't. This interview is over." I tug on Grayson's hand, still wrapped around mine like a vise. He looks pale with shock as he staggers to his feet. "Come on, Grayson. We're going."

Without another word, I yank him behind me and storm off stage. I hear Reggie speaking to the crowd and do my best to ignore him.

"*Well, folks, it seems we're cutting our interview a bit short today...*"

My teeth clench.

Harper is there, waiting in the wings, an expression of rage twisting her features.

"I'll kill him! He is *dead*! You hear me, Reggie?" she yells at the stage. "You're *dead*!"

"Harper. Not now." I look at Masters. "Let's get out of here before the paparazzi descend on us."

He nods and starts walking.

I follow, trailing Grayson like a dog on a leash. Harper is right behind us as we file into the elevator.

"He's coming with us?" she asks, looking at Grayson.

"Yes. His security team can deal with his car. Right now, we need to get out of here, though, because I have a feeling we're about to be at the center of a media storm."

Grayson emits a low grunt.

Harper winces at the sound. "Is he okay?"

"Sure he is."

"He looks like he's going to throw up."

"He's fine," I assure her unconvincingly.

Grayson is *not* fine. He's gone pale. His hand is limp inside mine. He's staring straight ahead, jaw clenched, eyes active with scary thoughts.

I sigh as we descend down to the parking garage. "How did they know?"

"That pap, on the motorcycle — he must've followed us from the clinic. There are pictures everywhere, plastered all over the internet." Harper types a few keystrokes, then holds up her phone. Peering at the screen, I see a series of images of me sneaking out the side door of the doctor's office. I thought we'd been so careful...

Apparently not.

"Fuck," I curse quietly.

"I called you, tried to warn you before you went onstage, but it was too late." Harper's voice is mournful. "I saw the pictures right before the interview started. I was worried Reggie would pull something like this."

"I heard my phone buzzing, but there was no time..." I expel a sharp breath. "He saw an opportunity and didn't hesitate to use it to his advantage. Can you imagine the ratings boost we just gave him?"

"Cutthroat, but effective." Harper scowls.

We walk to the SUV and pile inside — Grayson and

me in the back, Harper and Masters up front. No one says a word as we pull out of the underground garage onto the street. I've never been more grateful for tinted windows; there are at least thirty paparazzi gathered on the curb, hoping for a shot of me and Grayson as we emerge.

I duck my head down as the world explodes in a mob-scene of camera flashes and screams. They're pounding on the glass windows, rocking the car back and forth in their ferocity. Masters pumps the brakes to avoid running several of them over as they lean onto the hood of the car, snapping their shutters crazily.

KAT, IS IT TRUE?

ARE YOU PREGNANT?

DO YOU PLAN TO KEEP THE BABY?

GRAYSON, HOW DO YOU FEEL ABOUT THE NEWS?

I grit my teeth and try to tune them out, ducking low to hide my face. Masters slams his palm against the horn, blasting an ear-splitting warning into the air. The paparazzi have only seconds to leap out of the way as he guns the engine and we leave the horde behind.

We careen through the streets at twice the legal speed. The world feels muted in the absence of raining fists and bellowed accusations. Only when the SUV has slowed to a normal pace am I certain we're in the clear. I sit up in my seat and look around. We're in an unfamiliar part of the city — somewhere off the grid of Hollywood's glamour and glitz, packed with rows of dingy warehouses and nondescript cars. A relieved gasp slips out from between my lips.

We've lost them.

Belatedly, I realize my hand is still wrapped around Grayson's. I start to extract it, but his fingers suddenly twist and tighten on mine, trapping them.

My eyes meet his — dazzling green, swimming with ghosts.

He finally finds words. Or, *word.*

"*Kat.*"

My brows lift.

"Is it true?" He grits out the question through clenched teeth. "Tell me it's not true."

I gulp for air. "I... I..."

He releases my hand with a rough jerk.

"God, this is a fucking nightmare." His eyes are wild with fear and anger. "I can't believe this. I cannot *fucking* believe this is happening to me again."

I anticipated that he'd react poorly, but I wasn't expecting this level of rage. Granted, it might've gone better if I'd had the chance to drop the baby-bomb myself, rather than him hearing it from a sleazy talkshow host, but he still doesn't have to be such an asshole about it.

He scoffs bitterly. "I just went through this with Helena and now... Again! Twice! It's un-*fucking*-believable."

Anger sweeps through me. "Convenient how you seem to assign the blame exclusively to me and Helena... because apparently the choice not to use protection isn't at all *your* fault?"

"So, it's true then." He looks at me, mouth flattening. "Great. Fucking great."

"First of all, even if I am pregnant, I never said it was yours."

"Of course it's mine." He scoffs bitterly, as if the idea of me being with someone else is totally ludicrous to him. "Who else would it belong to?"

How typical of Grayson Dunn — expecting my loyalty while offering none of his own.

My teeth clench so tight, I'm giving myself a headache. "Grayson—"

He cuts me off. "You're not planning to keep it, though. You have to get rid of it. At least tell me you recognize that."

I go completely still. "I can't believe you just said that."

"Kat, come on. You cannot possibly think either of us is equipped to handle a child. You cannot possibly think that this is what I want." His voice is flat. "I won't be

204

trapped into a relationship just because you're having a baby. I won't, so if that's what you're thinking—"

I bristle at the accusation. "How dare you say that to me? How dare you even suggest that I would ever try to... to... *trick you* into a relationship?"

He shakes himself. When he speaks again, he sounds a bit more like himself. "I'm sorry. That came out wrong. I know you'd never do this intentionally. I'm just... *fuck*, Kat, I'm panicking over here."

My body trembles with rage. I turn away, to keep from smacking him.

His voice is quiet. "Helena thought, if she invented a pregnancy, it would make me stay."

"I'm not Helena," I snap, not looking at him. "And I've never asked you for a damn thing, since the day we met."

He's silent for a moment. I can hear his labored breathing.

"That doesn't change the fact that I don't want this," he says slowly. "I'm sorry if that's not what you want to hear. I'm sorry for my part in this. But... I think you should get rid of it. For my sake, for yours, and especially for the sake of the..." He clears his throat, as if he cannot bear to say the words. "The *baby*."

I suck in a breath. Tears are pricking at my eyes.

"It's for the best, you see that, don't you?" he asks. "You can't take care of a kid. You're still a kid yourself, Kat. People who have kids need to have their shit together. They have to be responsible, all the time." He pauses. "That's not you. It sure as shit isn't me."

I think about the picture of the tiny dictator sitting inside my purse.

What if he's right? What if I mess up that tiny little life?

The terror I battled back earlier rises up inside me again. I turn to face him. I'm not even sure what I'm about to say, but before I can get out a single word, Harper's voice cuts me off.

"Kat, as much as I appreciate you doing this, I can't let him continue berating you for my problem."

My head swirls in her direction. "Huh?"

She shakes her head at me, eyes intent. "You can stop covering for me. You can tell him the truth."

I blink at her, totally confused.

Grayson is equally baffled.

She turns to him and lies through her teeth. "Kat isn't the one who's pregnant. *I am.* She was just being a good friend, coming to the clinic with me for my first checkup because I was nervous. So you can stop yelling at her like a psychopath, because you're off the hook. She's not pregnant with your demon spawn — and thank goodness for that because it would probably come out with your personality. Frankly, one Grayson in this world is *more* than enough." Her smile turns sweet. "Get over yourself, Douche — I mean, *Dunn.* And apologize to Kat, while you're at it."

With that, she turns promptly back around in her seat.

I see Masters glance at her, an amused smirk on his lips. "I get to pick the name."

She shoots him a dark look.

"Well... shit." Grayson sounds undeniably relieved. "I'm sorry, Kat. Truly, I'm sorry if I was an asshole just now. But... *shit*, I nearly pissed myself, thinking you might actually be pregnant. Can you imagine what a total goddamned *nightmare* that would be?" He laughs.

"Yeah," I murmur absently, looking out the window. "Total nightmare."

* * *

We drop Grayson off at his place in Malibu. He's back to his happy-go-lucky self, buoyant with the knowledge that I'm not carrying his child, grinning at me as he climbs from the car and waves goodbye. The drive back to my house passes in utter silence. When we pull into my driveway and climb out, I meet Harper's eyes and ask just one question.

206

"Why?"

She shrugs. "I didn't like the way he was talking to you. I don't care how upset he was — that doesn't give him the right to make you feel small or inferior or scared. Just because he'd be the shittiest parent on the planet doesn't justify him telling you you'd be one too. He was trying to intimidate you into a choice you don't want to make, and I wasn't going to stand by and let him do it."

I fight back tears. "But what happened to all your *you have to tell him, honesty is the best policy* crap?"

"Maybe I was wrong." She sighs. "The way he was acting, he doesn't deserve the truth. If he pulls his head out of his ass in the future and decides to come around, I'll be the first to reconsider. But as far as I'm concerned, if he can't act like a mature adult, he shouldn't be included in adult decisions."

A tear slips down my cheek. "You're a real cow, Harper Kline."

"Yeah, well, you're a big priss."

Masters steps up to her side. "Hate to break up this love-fest, but Kat... I want to talk to you about security."

My brows lift. "What about it?"

"I'm thinking we might need more." He glances around the perimeter of my house. The security gate, a wrought-iron fence, and a few hedges are all that's keeping us separated from the outside world. "They were already pretty rabid — you saw the man on the motorcycle today, the paps outside the studio. When news of this baby spreads... they're only going to get more frenzied for pictures. We need to be cautious. Make sure the gate is locked at all times, maybe think about setting up some extra cameras. Never go out by yourself. They'll be waiting to ambush you — at the grocery store, on the walk to your car, everywhere you go. Constant vigilance is the only way to combat them."

A wave of exhaustion crashes through me at just the thought.

"Enough doom and gloom for one day," Harper says, linking her arm with mine and tugging me inside. "What are we doing for dinner?"

My feet freeze halfway up the walk as a thought occurs to me.

"What?" she asks, alarmed. "Kat, what is it?"

Dinner.

Thai takeout.

Wyatt.

There's no way he hasn't seen the news by now — it's all over the tabloids. As soon as the story broke — *KAT'S OUT OF THE BAG! #GRAYKAT SECRET LOVE CHILD!* — it started circulating on every social media platform.

Fuck, fuck, fuck.

"Kat?" Harper prompts, concern etching her features.

"Wyatt," I whisper hollowly. "What the hell am I going to tell Wyatt?"

CHAPTER TWELVE

"TREAT OTHERS AS YOU WANT TO BE TREATED."
- A girl who's just given a really great blow job.

The Thai food grows cold in its containers as it sits on the counter. I ordered it more for show than anything — a prop, carefully arranged, setting the stage for the scene about to play out. I have no appetite. Unmoving, I stare at the clock in the darkening kitchen and wait for him to come. There's no question in my mind that he'll show up. It's just a matter of when.

He knows the security code for the outer gate, and I've left my door unlocked. I'm not sure how long I sit there before I hear the crunch of tires on my gravel driveway. The steady march of his feet across my porch. The swing of the front door as he steps inside. The soft click of it closing at his back.

It doesn't take him long to find me, sitting in the dark, staring at the congealed noodles through the plastic cover like they might offer up some answers. A part of me wishes Harper and Masters were still here, but I know that's a selfish desire. This is something I have to face on my own.

He stops in the archway. I can feel his gaze on me, but I'm scared to meet it.

"Is it true?"

There is no anger in his voice. None of Grayson's fury or fear. Just a stoic sort of sadness, blanketing his words.

I look up at him, standing there in the doorway, his broad shoulders silhouetted in the fading beams of sunset shining through the windows behind him. My breath catches as I study the gorgeous planes of his face. I have traced its every feature, from the elegant slope of his nose to the tiny dimple in his left cheek. I have kissed him until my lungs were aching for air, more willing to asphyxiate than pull away.

"Yes," I say, voice hollow. "It's true."

I'm confirming something he already knows, but my words still jolt through him. His head bows a bit, as if he's no longer able to look at me directly. As if the very sight of me is too painful to take in.

My eyes fill with useless tears.

"Is it mine?" he asks, voice like gravel. "Or is it... *his?*"

I try to breathe around the thick lump in my throat. My voice is a warbling mess when I force out the words.

"I don't know."

My admission rolls through him like a tsunami. His hands clench into fists. I know he's doing his best to steel himself, to keep calm in spite of the fact that everything between us is crumbling into chaos. But I see the veins standing starkly in his neck, the corded muscles bulging in his arms, and know how much that composed facade is costing him to maintain.

"Wyatt—"

"Just—" He cuts me off with a sharp gesture. "Just give me a minute."

"Okay," I whisper.

He takes a few steps into the room, until we're only a handful of feet apart. I watch him carefully, waiting for him to speak. It would almost be better if he'd rage and yell and curse my name. If he'd flip a stool or smash a plate. Anything at all, except this frozen silence, slowly turning me to ice.

I get to my feet, shaky and numb. His eyes flicker up to mine and he goes rigid when I take a step in his direction. I turn to stone.

"I'm sorry I didn't tell you," I whisper. "I didn't know how... I didn't want to ruin it... I was waiting for the right time." I swallow harshly. "And then it all blew up, before I had a chance."

He nods.

"Wyatt... *I'm sorry*. I never meant for this to happen. I definitely never meant to hurt you again..."

But that's all I ever do.

Hurt him.

Some unintentional sadist, an accidental sociopath, inflicting pain without intent.

"I'm sorry," I say again, two ridiculously inadequate words to convey the regret tearing me up inside. "I'm sorry. I'm sorry. I'm sorry. I'll say it until my lungs give out. I'll say it until you hear me, until you believe me."

"I do believe you. And I understand why you didn't tell me. I do." He watches me blankly and speaks in an equally empty tone. "I'm not angry."

I blink, stunned. "You aren't?"

"No." His eyes are steady on mine, but I can see the pain in their depths. I hate the sight of it there. Hate knowing I caused it.

"Wyatt..."

His Adam's apple bobs. "I'm going to need some time."

"Time?"

He nods. "To think about what this means — for me, for you, for us. For the future."

"Please, Wyatt..." I stare up at him, wanting to throw myself into his arms but holding back because the thought that he might push me away is too hard to contemplate. "Say that this doesn't change anything. Say that we'll figure it out. Say that everything is going to be okay."

His face seems to crumple, at that. "I can't say that nothing's changed, baby. That would be a lie. And I'm not going to lie to you, ever."

"I love you," I whisper defeatedly.

"I know you do." His eyes look a little glassy. His voice is almost unrecognizable, as if the strain of keeping all his emotions under wraps is physically killing him. "And I love you, Katharine. But that doesn't change the fact that I need time."

"How much time?"

"I don't know." His eyes are remote. Bleak. "Enough to figure out how I fit into all of this."

"What do you mean?" I whisper. "*With me.* You fit with me. By my side. At my back. In every corner of my heart, just as I fit in yours."

"*Katharine.*" His eyes flash with such anguish it levels me. He can barely speak. "If this... if the baby—" His voice cracks. "—If it isn't mine... if it's Grayson's... I'm not going to tear apart a family. I'm not going to stand between you and Dunn. I'm not that guy."

"There is no *me and Dunn.* There's only you and me."

"I want to believe you. I really do," Wyatt says softly, in a voice that breaks my heart. "But... How can I, when every time I turn around, you're with him?"

"I didn't want anything to do with the fake relationship!" I protest, tears filling my eyes. "It wasn't my choice."

"I know, baby. That's not what I'm talking about at all."

I sniffle. "It's not?"

"No. I know you didn't want any part in that. I know Dunn manipulated the situation. But it doesn't change the fact that every time I see you with him, every time his hands are on you, or his lips, or even his damn eyes, I want to break him in half. And, if this baby is his, it will never end. He'll be in your life forever, one way or another. Inexplicably enmeshed in every part of your existence." His shoulders heave like he's carrying the weight of the world on them. "I need to think about whether or not I can handle that."

"Wyatt..." Tears stream down my face unchecked.

"Wyatt, please…"

I don't even know what I'm begging for, anymore. I just know I don't want him to go. I know, if he walks out my door, there's a very good chance he'll never walk back through it.

I'm losing him.

I'm losing the love of my life, after I've finally found him.

He crosses to me and presses a kiss to my forehead. I feel a tear hit my skin, and I know I'm not the only one with wet eyes.

"I love you," he says fiercely, voice muffled as he buries his head in my hair.

"Then why does it sound like you're saying goodbye?" I whisper.

His arms wind around my back and he pulls me close, just for a moment. I squeeze my eyes shut and breathe him in. *Old books and aftershave.* I memorize the way he feels wrapped around me. *Safe. Strong. Like home.*

Far too soon, he lets me go.

He steps back, putting careful distance between us. His eyes are red when they find mine.

"It's not goodbye. Not forever. I just… I need some time. I need some space, away from you, to think about this. Because, when I'm near you, my head is so caught up in loving you, I can't even see straight. I can't think. I can't breathe. I can't do anything except love you."

I nod, not trusting myself to speak again. Knowing, if I open my mouth, I'll beg him to stay.

He stares at me for one, two, three long seconds — the longest seconds of my life — and then he turns and walks out.

This morning, I woke up in his arms.

Twelve hours later, I have already lost him.

* * *

I sit in the dark, crying until I run out of tears. The sun set long ago and I haven't turned on any of the lights. Even with every switch in the house fully illuminated, nothing would be different.

I carry the darkness inside me. No 60-watt bulb can change that.

When I hear the click of my front door opening, my heart leaps.

He came back.

I'm so relieved, I don't think about the fact that I didn't hear a car pull into the driveway. I don't consider the very real possibility that it might not be Wyatt at all, as my feet race across the hardwood floor. I round a bend, barely breathing, already planning to rush into his arms and kiss him until he realizes that we're meant to be together...

And stop short when I catch sight of the figure standing in my living room. The only light comes from a small lamp in the corner — just bright enough to see that it's not Wyatt. The shoulders are too narrow, the build too slender.

It's a woman, I think stupidly. My brain feels sluggish, moving at half speed as I process what I'm seeing.

Her hair is messy, almost matted, as if she hasn't been bathing regularly. Her typically stylish attire is gone, replaced by a hodgepodge of clothes that don't match — pajama bottoms with a leather jacket and flip flops on her feet. Her eyes have that same vacant look I remember from the other night, though there's something else in their depths now, as they shift to stare into mine. Something infinitely scarier.

"Helena," I say slowly, holding out my hands in front of me like a shield. "What are you doing here?"

Her head tilts. She doesn't answer.

My pulse starts to pound.

"Helena, why are you here?" I repeat, backing away. My mind is racing, trying to remember where I left my cellphone.

Is it still sitting at the bottom of my purse? Or charging on the kitchen counter?

She takes a step toward me, hands shoved deep inside the pockets of her coat. Her absolute silence is eerie.

"How did you know where I live?" I try to stay calm as I back away and she follows me deeper into the house. "How did you get through the gate?"

"I waited for him to drive away," she says, sounding empty. A broken doll with a voice-box. "The door was open."

"Helena, you shouldn't be here. You should be in Palm Springs. Didn't Grayson take you there?"

Her head shakes. "He told me it was secret. That he was going to make me better. No more doctors. No more medicine. No more, no more, no more," she sing-songs crazily, laughing at nothing.

Fuck.

Grayson didn't take her to the medical center; he took her to Malibu. Tried to fix her himself, the idiot.

When I get my hands on him, I will break his freaking neck.

I shuffle a few steps backward, wary of turning my back to her. She's may well be harmless... but the unhinged aura surrounding her is making every hair on my body stand on end.

"Okay, Helena," I aim for a soothing tone. "I'm going to call Grayson, he'll come get you."

She perks up at the sound of Grayson's name, like a dog who hears the word "walk" in casual conversation and knows, without context, that the rest of the gibberish somehow applies to it.

"Grayson," she echoes dully.

"Yes." I lick my parched lips. "It's going to be okay."

"Okay?" Her head tilts and she laughs again — that maniacal, mad laugh that sends a chill down my spine. "It's not okay."

"I promise, it'll be all right."

"You took it all." She starts to close the gap between us, eyes on my face. "My Grayson. My movie."

Tears are leaking from her eyes as she advances. Her voice grows anguished. "My *baby.*"

My hands fly to my midsection. "Helena..."

Run, run, run.

All my instincts are kicking into survival mode. Fight or flight. If it was just me, maybe I'd fight. But it's not just me, anymore. And I'm not about to risk the tiny dictator's life in a scuffle with a crazy bitch a foot taller than me who, more than likely has snorted opiates up her nose at some point in the recent past, rendering her essentially immune to pain. I'd have better odds wrestling a professional MMA fighter to the ground.

"Wait here, Helena," I say with a calmness I don't feel, picking up speed as I backpedal away. I'm nearly to the kitchen. "I'll be right back."

"No." Her voice is totally hollowed of all emotions. She sounds inhuman. I suck in a breath when her hand moves out of her coat pocket and I see the dull gleam of a knife clutched in her fingers. It's big — the kind you keep in a wood block on your kitchen counter. Even from here, I can tell it's sharp.

"Helena," I whisper, feeling fear flood through me. "Put that down."

Her eyes meet mine, focusing for a nanosecond, and I see the pure madness there. Even before she speaks, I know there's no reasoning with her.

"You took my baby," she says again in that terrifyingly empty voice. "*You took my baby.*"

I don't attempt to dissuade her.

I don't wait another second.

I *run.*

Feet flying on wings of terror, I bolt for the kitchen in search of my phone. I hear her chasing me, that high-pitched, horrifying giggle resounding from her throat. My desperate eyes fly around the kitchen island, seeking salvation in the shape of a smartphone, but it's nowhere to be found. I whirl around and see her right behind me, only the island separating us. She lunges right; I counter by leaping left. She changes course; I do the same. We are a seesaw, lurching back and forth, her knife slicing the air between us.

"Think about this Helena," I gasp out, wondering if I can make it to the front door. "You don't want to do this."

She's past the point of listening. There's no reaching her. No reasoning with her. She's had a full psychotic break. I can imagine it easily — her fragile state, after the hysterical pregnancy, exacerbated by drugs and drinking, coupled with the tabloid stories that I'm having Grayson's baby... It was too much. She snapped like a twig under the strain of it. Her grip on reality is gone.

She will kill me and my child in some insane attempt to get hers back.

She lurches again, and I make a run for it.

Around the island, through the archway, toward the front door. It's still ajar. I can see the porch light, a beacon of hope just beyond the threshold. If I can get outside, I can scream for help. If I can get to the street, I'll be safe.

I'm almost there, almost free, when something hits me from behind, square in the back — a lamp from a nearby table, hurled with brute force. It knocks the breath from my lungs as I topple forward onto my hands and knees. I hear it shatter into fragments against the hardwood and try to scramble to my feet, but she's already there, looming over me like a reaper from hell. Her foot comes down on my wrist, pinning it to the floor. I think I hear something snap as her weight slams fully onto the fragile bones, grinding them beneath her heel.

I scream as red-hot pain flares through me. An unrecognizable, banshee-like wail, so loud it echoes back at me through the dark.

I blink away tears as she flips me over onto my back. She towers above me in the darkness, straddling my hips, pinning my wrists. I don't see the knife, but I do see the look in her eyes.

Pure, unequivocal madness.

217

"Helena," I plead, thrashing. Trying futilely to buck her off. "Helena, please."

She presses my hands harder against the floor, squeezing my snapped wrist until my eyes are smarting with tears. The pulverized bones are so painful, I can hardly see straight.

"Helena, let's call Grayson, okay?" I gasp out between sobs. "Let's call him and he'll come for you and everything will be okay."

She stills. Her head tilts.

Maybe I can get through to her.

"He doesn't love me, he loves you, Helena." My heart is pounding so hard I can barely breathe, my wrist feels like a hot brand is stabbing through it, my eyes are watering with agony. "Please, just let me go. Let me go, and we'll call Grayson, and everything will be okay."

"He loves me."

I nod, weeping from pain and fear. "Yes, he loves you."

"We're a family," she tells me vacantly.

"Yes, you are."

"Once we have our baby back, we'll be together."

She releases my maimed wrist, and I know she's reaching for the knife. It's my only chance.

With all my might I heave upward, knocking her off balance, at the same time swinging out with my fist to catch her across the temple. Pain explodes through me — I've done more damage to myself, with my strike — but I ignore it. For a single second, she freezes, stunned into stillness. My unexpected attack caught her off guard. Her weight shifts, just enough to unseat her.

I don't hesitate.

Shoving Helena aside, I roll out from under her, eyes streaming. My hands shred on the broken glass from the lamp when I push up off the floor, smearing blood against the hardwood as I scramble to my feet. I barely feel the pain. I hear her moving behind me, but I don't turn to look. My eyes are on the door. On escape. On *survival.*

218

I'm almost there, when it swings open.

Masters is standing there like my avenging angel, gun drawn. His ice-blue eyes assess the situation in under a second.

"Duck!" He yells to me.

I don't question him; I hit the deck.

He fires off a round and I hear Helena scream in pain, followed by the thud of her body as she collapses to the floor. Typically, I'd be concerned, but the fact that she was about to carve me open like a Thanksgiving turkey has essentially eradicated any semblance of sympathy. I watch Masters approach her, a set of handcuffs materializing from his back pocket. She's restrained in under a second. With grim proficiency, he tears a strip of fabric from the bottom hem of his t-shirt and tourniquets her leg so she doesn't bleed to death.

The shock of the bullet in her thigh is enough to quell her struggles. She lies on the floor, whimpering in pain, as Masters picks up the knife and moves it far out of her reach. When he's sure she's not going anywhere, he crosses back to me. I'm still crouched on the floor, barely daring to breathe.

"Are you okay?" His voice is gentler than I've ever heard it as he stoops down to my level so we're eye-to-eye.

I nod. "Oh, I'm just grand. Thanks for asking."

His eyes crinkle a tiny bit, but his mouth is pressed into a solemn line. "The police are on their way. They should be here any minute."

I stare at him. "You saved my life."

Shrugging like it was nothing, he pushes to his feet. He flips on the nearest light switch, illuminating the room. The sudden brightness makes me blink. When my eyes refocus, I look around my living room. Between the shattered glass littering the floor and the bloody handprints trailing from Helena's whimpering form to the front door, it's like something straight off a scary movie set.

I look back at Masters and find he's staring at me worriedly. I don't say a word as I cross to him and throw my arms around his muscular frame. He goes still at first, but eventually his arms come up around me to return the stiff hug.

I don't care if it's awkward. I don't care if he thinks it's weird that his boss is hugging him. I don't care about a thing except making sure he knows how grateful I am.

"Thank you, Kent," I whisper, using his name for the first time since we met. "Thank you for saving my life."

It could be my imagination, but I think his voice is a little thicker than normal when he speaks.

"Nice try, Firestone — getting yourself nearly murdered just so I'll call you by your first name. Not gonna work, but I applaud the effort."

I laugh through my tears — a hiccupping, horrible sound that catches in my throat and quickly turns to a sob.

He drops his arms and steps back, patting me on the arm like he doesn't quite know how to handle my emotional display. We both hear the sirens at the same time, growing louder as they race down my street. Masters crosses to the security panel and punches in the code to open the gate. Flashing red and blue lights flood my driveway as two cruisers pull up in front of my house, followed closely by an ambulance. Uniformed officers leap from the vehicles like ants at a picnic, talking into radios and barking orders as they survey the scene.

Standing on my porch, I watch the paramedics load Helena onto a stretcher and wheel her toward the waiting ambulance — a lifeless, empty-eyed girl with no fight left in her. She stares straight up at the sky without a care in the world.

I try to summon sympathy.

None comes.

Masters is in the driveway talking to the police, gesturing from me to the house to Helena. I know I should join their conversation, should allow someone to look at my bleeding hands and ravaged wrist, but I am floating outside my body, experiencing everything as it unfolds like a passive bystander. It's as if I'm watching a horror movie instead of living inside one.

There's a crowd gathering at the end of my driveway — neighbors, news crews, paparazzi. All eager for details of Katharine Firestone's horrific ordeal. Camera flashes mingle with flashes from the police cars, until the world turns to one giant strobe of color.

I'm not sure who arrives first. I just know that they all roll up, one after another — Harper in her used sedan, Wyatt in his shiny Audi, Grayson in the sleek Bugatti. The police attempt to stop them, but Masters waves them through. I try to conjure the strength to walk, to meet them halfway down the steps, but my feet aren't cooperating. I have grown roots in this spot, beneath the dim porch light.

Wyatt moves faster than I've ever seen him. One second he's behind the wheel and the next he's there in front of me, face a mask of horror. He's breathing rapidly, chest rising and falling like he's just run a marathon. I see how his hand trembles as he reaches out and pushes a strand of hair behind my ear, so gently you'd think I was made of glass, liable to shatter under the merest pressure. His fingers hover by my ear as his eyes hold mine, communicating wordlessly. Asking permission without making a sound, because he doesn't trust himself to speak without breaking down.

That's all right. We've never needed words, anyway.

In total silence, I turn my head to lay my cheek in his big hand. A shudder of relief moves through him as his fingertips press into my skin.

I'm fine, my eyes say. *I'm breathing.*

The stubborn set of his jaw expresses the words he cannot say.

I could've lost you.

I know he's aching to pull me into his arms — that he needs the crush of physical contact to remind himself that I'm real, that I'm alive, that I'm still breathing. I also know that, because he's Wyatt, he's holding himself tightly in check, putting his own needs behind mine until he's one hundred percent sure I want his arms around me.

I'd roll my eyes at him, if I could find the strength. Instead, I look at him and force out a single word. A broken plea.

"*Wyatt.*"

A growl of need rattles inside his throat as he pulls me into his arms. He hugs me for a long stretch, standing there breathing me in like a man starved for air, until a wry voice interrupts the moment.

"Hastings, you're not the only one who wants to hug her, you know." Harper sounds impatient.

Wyatt drops his arms, but doesn't release me fully. He keeps a hand on my waist as he steps aside so Harper can throw her arms around me. Her hug is full of warmth and strength.

"You good?" she asks simply.

I nod.

"Good." She dashes tears from her eyes and looks around for her boyfriend. He's still speaking to the police. Grayson's joined them, which means they're probably talking about Helena. He tries to catch my eyes, but I avoid his seeking gaze.

"I should probably talk to the police."

A grumble of protest sounds from Wyatt. "No. You need to get checked out by the paramedics first. Another ambulance is on the way."

I wrinkle my nose and turn to face him, a comment about his overbearing protective streak poised on my tongue, but he's not paying attention. He's too busy running his hands over me, checking for damage. I yelp when he reaches my wrist. He pulls it up to inspect it and I hear him suck in a breath.

"*Baby.*"

"I'm fine."

"You're hurt." His hands delicately feel the bones in my wrist. "I don't think it's broken, but you still need to see a doctor."

"It's probably just a sprain. Doesn't even hurt that much," I lie. "I'm okay."

"You're *not* okay."

He turns over my hands, sees the deep gashes scored into the skin, and swears under his breath. Before I can say anything else, he's scooped me up into his arms and carried me inside.

"Wyatt!" I protest. "I can walk!"

He ignores me, stepping over the threshold. The sight that greets us makes him stop short. I feel the tension inside him building like a storm as his eyes sweep from the wreckage of my lamp to the puddle of Helena's blood, seeping across the hardwood.

"Wyatt, *breathe*. And put me down, please. I'm fine."

He doesn't listen. He strides through the house until we reach the sitting room, untouched by signs of struggle, and sets me down on the couch carefully. His hands stroke over my hair.

"I'll be right back," he murmurs. His eyes cut to Harper. "Stay with her."

Harper doesn't object. She settles on the cushion beside mine and sighs.

"Quite the drama queen, aren't we? You know, if you felt you weren't getting enough attention between the crazed paparazzi and accidental pregnancy and movie premiere and messy romantic entanglements with multiple men, you could've just gotten a bad haircut or rashly decided to get a tattoo you'd later regret. You didn't have to go and get yourself practically shish-kebabed by a crazy girl with excellent bone structure and questionable sanity."

I snort. "Noted. Next time, I'll just get a really ugly pixie cut and call it a day."

Wyatt reappears, the small first aid kit from my bathroom cabinet in his grip. He crouches between my knees, grabs my hand, and starts to pull tiny pieces of glass from the cuts with a pair of tweezers.

"Ow!" I wince and try to tug my hand away. "That hurts!"

He holds my hand still, concentrating.

"Wyatt, you really don't have to—"

"Katharine." His eyes flash up to mine and I see the fresh horror still swimming in them. "Let me do this. Let me do *something* so I don't feel so goddamned useless. Please."

I nod and my voice goes soft. "Okay, love."

A few minutes later, my hands are glass-free and we're joined by Masters and Grayson. Two police officers follow them in, along with a fresh crew of paramedics. They nod to Wyatt as they take his place by my feet, inspecting my wrist and hands. The wrist isn't broken, but it's severely sprained and there's so much swelling under the bruised flesh, they err on the side of caution by wrapping it in a tight splint.

"Are you hurt anywhere else?"

"My back," I murmur, rising to my feet. Now that the adrenaline has worn off, I'm starting to feel aches and pains over every part of my body. I turn and lift my shirt so they can examine my spine. Wyatt steps in front of me, creating a human privacy shield to block the view of the others.

I smile at him, appreciation in my eyes.

He frowns back at me, deep concern etched on his gorgeous face.

"Just bruising," the paramedic says, lowering my shirt. "But if you experience any dizziness, excessive fatigue, or blood in your urine, make sure you get to a hospital ASAP. Otherwise, drink lots of fluids and take Advil as you need it. You should be back to normal in a few days."

"Thank you," I murmur, examining my new splint as they gather their med-kits and head for the door.

The police are next. They ask me to describe the

ordeal from the moment Helena arrived to the second Masters showed up on my doorstep. I try to keep my voice steady, dispassionate, as I relive the horror, but I don't think I succeed because Harper starts to cry and Wyatt's hands are fisted so tightly by the time I finish, I worry he's lost circulation. Grayson has gone pale. Even Masters looks effectively shaken.

With efficient nods, the officers snap their notepads shut and turn to go. Masters walks them out. The rest of us sit in silence. My eyes are starting to droop; it's been a long day.

"You know, this is getting kind of old," Harper says, shattering the quiet. "My boyfriend having to rush out of bed at odd hours, to save you. I'm thinking I should move in, like I did when you first bought this place. For wholly selfish reasons, of course."

I smirk. Typical Harper — she recognizes I don't want to be alone in my house, after this ordeal, but also knows me well enough to realize I'd never ask for her to stay.

"I'm hoping this was the last time," I murmur, laying my head on her shoulder. My tired eyes find Wyatt's and I see he's watching me intently. His too-blue stare never leaves my face, as if he fears I'll disappear should he shift his attention away even for a moment.

"What I want to know is how the hell she got in here in the first place," he mutters darkly.

Walking back into the room, Masters answers before I can. "Saw her come in on the security feed. She slipped through the gate while you were leaving. Must've been camped out in the hedges, waiting for an opportunity."

Wyatt flinches.

"It's not your fault," I whisper, knowing it's useless even as the words leave my mouth. He'll blame himself for this, despite the fact that he couldn't have possibly known what would happen when he drove away. I see his jaw clench even tighter. The thoughts in his eyes are clear as day.

If I'd stayed, you'd be fine right now.

"I thought she was in rehab," Harper says. "How the hell did she escape a loony bin in Palm Springs and make it here in the first place?"

"She wasn't in Palm Springs." I sigh tiredly. "She was in Malibu."

The air goes still. I don't realize I've just dropped a bomb until I see Wyatt turn to Grayson.

Up till this moment, my co-star has been hovering on the fringes of the room, looking vaguely guilty. Now, seeming to realize I've just thrown him into the spotlight, he shuffles a bit father inside.

"I didn't take her to Palm Springs," he admits, voice suffused by remorse. "I thought I could handle it. I thought I could help her on my own, if I watched her round the clock and brought in a private doctor for home visits. I was trying to do something good. I had no idea she'd go after you, Kat." He steps closer to me, those infinite green eyes contrite. "I *swear*, if I'd known she was this bad, I—"

I never get to hear the rest of his words, because Wyatt's fist flies out and punches him in the mouth. Grayson goes reeling from the force of the blow. He catches himself just in time to prevent tripping over an end table.

"Fuck!" Grayson curses, clutching his bleeding lip. "Hastings, what the hell is your problem?"

Wyatt is red-faced and seething. His words vibrate with fury as they leave his mouth. "You put Katharine in danger with your shitty choices. I don't want to hear your excuses. I don't even want to look at you. You're leaving, right now."

"Kat—" Grayson's eyes fly to me. "Kat, I'm sorry—"

Wyatt takes a threatening step toward Grayson and he backpedals a bit.

"Just go, Grayson. It's fine." I rise to my feet, exhaustion saturating my every atom. "Really. I'm not mad. But I am tired. You two having a fist fight in my

226

living room really isn't helping matters." I glance at Wyatt. "You need to calm down, love. You're freaking me out."

He grunts, his glare never leaving my co-star.

Grayson looks from me to Wyatt and back. I see comprehension fill his eyes. For the first time, he seems to realize that I'm not *his* anymore. That I haven't been *his* for quite some time, now.

His throat muscles contract. His mouth opens to say something, then closes again without vocalizing a single thought. I think he knows there's nothing else he *can* say, in this moment, to repair things between us. Too much has happened.

Hawaii. The baby. Helena.

Running a hand through his hair, he looks down at his feet. "I'm sorry. I truly am."

"I know," I whisper.

His sad eyes meet mine. "For all of it."

"I know," I repeat, even more softly.

Nodding, he turns and walks out my door. And it's strange, because I know I'll see him again soon with the movie premiere rapidly approaching, but as I watch him walk out I get the sense that it's the last time I'll see him. An indisputable goodbye.

I shake off the ridiculous sensation and look around from Masters to Harper to Wyatt. They're all watching me warily.

"So... this was a pretty stellar day, huh?"

Masters smirks.

Wyatt looks to the heavens, as if seeking patience.

"You aren't funny." Harper elbows my side. "And you look like crap."

"Thanks."

"I mean it," she insists. "You should go upstairs. Get in bed."

"I won't be able to sleep."

"I'll stay over so you aren't alone," she offers.

"No." Wyatt's firm tone interjects. "She's coming home with me."

My eyes widen. "Excuse me?"

"You. Are. Coming. Home. With. Me." He over-annunciates each word, eyes narrowing. "Which part of that statement did you not understand?"

"You aren't the boss of me."

"Technically, I sort of am," he reminds me. "But even if I wasn't your boss, you'd still be coming home with me, because I love you and I'm worried about you and you could've died today. And until that image is out of my head, I'm not letting you out of my sight. Got it?"

"You're being very domineering, old man."

"I don't give a shit."

My voice gets quiet. "I thought..."

His brows lift. "What, baby?"

"I thought you needed *space* and *time*."

"Fuck space. Fuck time." He takes two steps, closing the gap between us, and bends so our eyes are level. "I was an idiot earlier. I was scared and stubborn. I let my own selfish needs distract me from what's important — *you*. I choose *you*, Katharine Firestone. Even when it's hard. Even when it's complicated. I choose *us*."

My eyes are stinging, but he's not done.

Carefully, so carefully it breaks my heart, he reaches out a hand and places it flat against my stomach. When his eyes meet mine, they're filled with something like wonder.

"When I look at my future, I see you. At my side, in my arms, in my bed. I want to build a life with you. I want to start a family with you. This baby..." His voice cracks. "*Our* baby... will be so loved. Unbelievably loved. It doesn't have to be a burden. I was wrong to even think that. This... it's an incredible gift."

"But..." I bite my lip to keep from blubbering. "What if it's—"

"Shhh." His eyes flash. His fingers flex against my stomach. "I don't care about biology. I don't give a shit what a piece of paper from some lab says. From this moment on, I'm in. I'm one hundred percent in."

Tears are streaming down my face. Forgetting about my bruised limbs and ruined hands, I hurl myself into his arms. He drags me up against his chest, so my feet dangle in the air, and tucks his head in the crook of my neck.

"Wyatt?"

"What is it, baby?"

"Take me home?"

He brushes his lips against mine. "Let's go."

CHAPTER THIRTEEN

"ONE INCH LOWER, AND SLIGHTLY TO THE RIGHT."
- A girl giving her boyfriend very explicit directions...
about where to hang her new painting.

I glare at the television so vehemently, I'm surprised it doesn't combust into flames. The woman on the screen smiles serenely, her bleached teeth so white they're nearly blinding. The bright blonde of her hair catches the light as she shifts on the interview chair and answers Eileen Dillan's question.

"Yes, I'd say we're very close," Cynthia murmurs sweetly. "Like all mothers and daughters, we have our ups and downs... but at the end of the day, we're connected by an unbreakable bond."

"Unbreakable? *Unbreakable?* HA!" I throw a piece of popcorn at the TV, hitting her right between the eyes. My voice drops to an angry mutter. "I know something I'd like to break, all right..."

A kiss lands on my temple as a big hand reaches down and plucks the remote from my grip. Turning off the talk show, Wyatt leans over the back of the couch and wraps his arms around me from behind. His hands settle against my stomach, an unconscious gesture he seems to be making more and more frequently as weeks pass and the tiny baby bump begins to swell. It's small, but undeniably there.

Harper calls it the *lime*, now.

I turn around on the couch and sling my arms over Wyatt's shoulders.

"I didn't know you were home."

"Just got back." He kisses me softly. "How was your day?"

I glower. "Any more mandatory *taking it easy* and I'm going to have to kill you."

"Where's your splint?" he asks, eyeing my naked wrist with disapproval. "It's only been two weeks. You're supposed to keep it on for three."

"Wyatt, my wrist is fine. Look." I demonstrate the full range of motion. Only a tinge of pain shoots through the healed appendage. "I'm *fine*. And I am eventually going to leave this house, regardless of your attempts to keep me hostage."

"I was hoping you'd develop Stockholm Syndrome."

"I don't need Stockholm Syndrome. I already love you, you idiot." I roll my eyes. "And I've been here every night. I should go home."

"Or you could stay."

"For how long?"

He shrugs. "Forever."

"You aren't funny."

"I'm not joking."

Heart hammering, I pull out of his arms and change the topic to something less insane than the possibility of me moving in with my boyfriend after a few short weeks of dating.

"Can you believe the audacity of my mother?"

"It's your mother. So yes, I can." He sighs. "Another interview?"

"Yes." My tone is sour as I grab the popcorn bowl off the coffee table and start walking toward the kitchen. The week after Helena attacked me, the AXC legal team made quick work of tearing Cynthia's lawsuit to shreds. Her claims of unfair compensation and breach of contract couldn't hold up, considering she had no paperwork to substantiate a single one of her claims.

At first, she put up a fight, but when Wyatt personally threatened her with a countersuit for years of manipulating my career and pocketing earnings without consent, she backed off faster than a vegan at a steakhouse.

"She can't seem to turn down any opportunity to exploit me. This must be the third talk-show she's booked in the past two weeks. Plus, all the tabloid stories…"

"They'll lose interest in her eventually," Wyatt assures me. "Once the hype dies down."

"You see that happening anytime soon?" I snort. "My life is a circus. I think us cancelling the rest of the press tour made them even *more* rabid for stories about me, not less."

"Eventually, things will calm down. Don't let it get to you, baby," Wyatt advises, grabbing a handful of popcorn before I dump it into the sink.

"I'm not." I sigh. "I just thought, if I stayed out of the public eye for a few weeks…"

His brows lift. "That your life would go back to how it was before all this? I'm sorry, baby, but that's never going to happen. There's no going back. This is the new normal."

My lips twist in a scowl, but I don't argue. I know he's right. Setting the bowl on the counter, I spin around and catch sight of a tell-tale brown paper bag on the countertop.

"No!" I hiss, turning my glare on him "Not takeout again."

"Baby, be reasonable."

"I've *been* reasonable for weeks. Now, I'm done being reasonable. I want to go out. I want to breathe fresh air and see people again." I look up at him, pleading. "I love you. And I know you're worried about me. But I'm *fine*. Helena is locked up in a psych ward. My cuts are healed. The baby is okay. We're okay. You have to relax."

His expression darkens as he pulls me into his arms. "I worry."

"I know you do."

"I think about what almost happened…"

"Don't." I squeeze him tighter. "Don't think about the past. Think about all the exciting things in our future."

Turning in his arms, I catch sight of the refrigerator. The sleek stainless steel is interrupted by a small black and white photograph, taped in the center. My latest sonogram.

"Come on." Wyatt laces his hand through mine and leads me upstairs.

"Where are we going?"

"I'm taking you out to dinner."

"Really?" I squeak. "You mean it?"

He nods. "I want to protect you. I want to keep you safe. But that doesn't mean I want you to feel trapped. I'll never smother you, Katharine. If you say you're fine, I believe you. If you want to go out, I'm not going to keep you prisoner against your will."

Guilt washes over me.

I'm a bitch.

We're halfway up the stairs when I tug him to a stop. He glances over his shoulder at me, brows raised.

"What?"

"Have I thanked you lately?" I ask, stepping up so we're on the same level. "For everything you've done for me?"

"Baby..." He swallows, eyes dilating as they sweep over my face. He reads the desire in my eyes. "You don't have to thank me."

I slide my hands around his waist. "I do, though." I press a kiss to his neck and he groans. "I do have to thank you. And you haven't been letting me."

"Katharine..."

"You've been hovering and worrying and treating me like I'm made of glass." My mouth trails up to the hollow beneath his ear. "For weeks you've been kissing me sweetly on the forehead and tucking me into bed. And as much as I appreciated that while my wrist was damn near broken and my back was covered in bruises and my nightmares woke me up screaming the middle of the night... I'm all better now." I let my teeth graze his earlobe before sucking it lightly between my lips.

He shudders.

"I'm not made of glass, Wyatt," I whisper. "I'm not going to break if you put your hands on me."

A groan of desire rumbles through his chest as my hands slide lower, down to his belt loops. I press against him, experiencing first-hand the throbbing need he feels for me. My patient Viking, my selfless warrior — he would put his own desires last until he broke beneath the strain, rather than push me before I was ready for him.

"Put your hands on me," I murmur, my mouth brushing over his again, my eyes staring into his stormy ones. "If you don't, I'm going to explode."

He doesn't need any more encouragement.

Before I can move, my dress is gone — up over my head, tossed over the railing. I undo his belt buckle as he rids me of my bra. He shrugs out of his shirt as I step out of my underwear. We are shaky with impatience — gripping hands and desperate kisses.

It's been an insufferably long two weeks.

We don't even make it to the bedroom. He makes love to me right there on the grand staircase, with raw desire and an unyielding passion that turns my bones to water. I see stars as I stare up at the glittering chandelier, my head thrown back in ecstasy. And, as an orgasm crashes through me, I think I might reconsider my ideas about going out tonight, after all.

* * *

Two days later, I've finally negotiated my release from captivity.

Dressed in an elegant evening gown of pale coral with my lips painted red and my dark waves swept into an elegant twist, I watch the limo pull up outside Wyatt's house. A dark SUV follows at a meticulous distance.

"Ready?" Wyatt asks.

I nod, grinning with excitement. We're on our way to an advanced screening of *Uncharted* at one of the most exclusive film festivals on the West Coast. The nerves I should be feeling at the prospect of a room full of critics watching the full cut of our movie have been tamped down by my thrill at the prospect of finally escaping house-arrest.

"Did you take your prenatal vitamin today?" Wyatt asks sternly, as I grab my clutch purse and walk to the door.

I roll my eyes. "Yes."

"Did you drink enough water?"

"Yes."

"Did you kiss me goodbye?"

"Ye—" I stop short, spinning around to smile at him. "No. I did not do that."

His lips are curved in a grin as he leans down to press them against mine. "I'll see you there," he murmurs, nose bumping mine playfully. "Try not to look at me too longingly across the crowd, you'll blow our cover."

My smile fades. "I wish we were going together."

"I know."

"I'm tired of pretending not to love you for the sake of the cameras."

Wyatt's eyes are carefully blank. "The premiere will be here in a few weeks. After that, it won't really matter whether the public thinks you're with Grayson or not. But you heard what Sloan said, when he called yesterday. He wants to keep up the act, especially now that we've cancelled most of your remaining interviews."

"I know. I understand the logic behind it. But that doesn't mean I have to like it."

Wyatt sighs and grabs my hand. "Come on. They're waiting."

We part ways in the driveway — he climbs into the SUV with Grayson's security team while I clamor into the back of the limo. Grayson is inside, sprawled across a leather seat on the far side, looking gorgeous in a tuxedo.

There's a flute of champagne in his grip; not the first he's consumed, if the half-lidded look in his eyes is any indication.

"Hi," I say, settling in. The driver closes the door behind me with a soft click. It's quieter than a tomb in the backseat. "Long time no see."

Grayson is watching me intently. I fidget under the weight of that bottomless green stare.

"Okay, then. Guess we aren't making small talk," I murmur, reaching for a water bottle. I slug down a few sips. The dress Harper chose for tonight is blessedly loose around the midsection — a dreamy, empire-waisted affair that looks like pale flames when I walk — so I can drink and eat as much as I'd like, with the added bonus of hiding my tiny bump from the red-carpet cameras.

"You look beautiful, Kat."

Grayson's sudden comment makes me jump. I look back at him and see he's moved to the seat directly across from mine, so only a few feet separate us. His eyes never leave my face.

"Thank you. You look very handsome too, Grayson."

He takes another gulp of champagne. "Don't be nice to me, Kat. I don't deserve it."

My brows lift. I've never heard such defeat in his voice. "What? Why do you say that?"

"I fucked up." He runs his free hand through his hair. "With Helena, with you." A sharp breath bursts from his lips. "I destroy everything that comes close."

It's strange, hearing the same thoughts that used to haunt me come from someone else's lips. I stare at him — this imperfect man, who hurt me so thoroughly, and revel at how much has shifted in a few short weeks. I don't feel any anger, looking at him now. In fact, I feel only sympathy.

"You aren't a bad guy, Grayson," I whisper. "I've been where you are. I've felt that relentless sense of self-loathing that burns you up inside. Don't let it destroy you."

236

His eyes find mine, fragile hope in their depths.

"It gets better. I promise," I whisper, smiling.

"Kat…" He shakes his head, sets down the champagne flute, and leans forward so his hands are braced on his knees. "You always see the best in me. Even when I don't deserve it. Especially when I don't deserve it."

"That's the thing, Grayson. One day, you'll realize you *do* deserve it," I say softly. "You deserve to be happy — to be with someone who makes you happy."

"You make me happy." He exhales a ragged breath and leans closer. "I want to be with *you*, Kat."

I suck in a startled gulp of air.

"I know." His voice grows pained, but his eyes are deeply serious. "I know I missed my shot. I know you're with Hastings now, and it's all twisted between us. I know I don't have a chance at changing your mind. But if I let you go without ever saying it, I'd regret it for the rest of my life."

I go still, sensing what's coming before he says it.

"I— Kat, I— *I love you*," he blurts, looking more stunned than I am that those words have come out of his mouth. As if he cannot fathom that he's actually voiced them.

Time slows to a crawl.

I stare across the limo at this beautiful man, hiding a soul full of demons, and make my voice as gentle as possible as I lean forward and lay my hand over his.

"You don't love me, Grayson." I smile sadly. "You just think you do."

His head shakes, a denial. "But—"

"What you feel for me, right now? That gut-churning nausea? It's not love. It's the first blade of grass, creeping up through the pavement after a nuclear apocalypse. I don't say that to be mean — I say it because I've been there." My lips twist. "You think you love me because the feelings between us were real, and intense, and gave you a glimpse of a different kind of life for yourself — one with real commitment and honesty and emotion. You took a step. But that doesn't mean you're ready to run, yet."

"Maybe I am ready, though," he mutters unconvincingly. I don't even think he believes his own words.

"One day, you'll be ready. One day, you'll meet the right girl and realize that this, what you're feeling for me, is nothing compared to the contentment you experience when you find someone you're truly compatible with. When that day comes, when you have the option of choosing a life with that girl or one without her by your side, there won't be a doubt in your mind. You'll just know."

He sits back with a sigh, watching me curiously. "That's how it is for you. With *him*."

I nod.

His eyes regain a little of their sparkle as he winks at me. His voice is wry. "First blade of grass after an apocalypse, huh?"

I laugh. "Yep."

He runs a hand through his hair and murmurs, "Can't wait to see what the whole forest looks like."

"You will. One day, you will. I promise."

We don't speak much for the rest of the ride, both lost in our own thoughts. It's a relief, in a way, to finally close the chapter on Grayson Dunn once and for all. Maybe now, we can actually be friends.

I watch him from the corner of my eye as he sips another gulp of champagne, wondering about the woman who will tame him. His far-flung *someday* girl, out there somewhere in the world, still a stranger to him.

I used to think settling down wasn't a matter of *who* so much as *when* — that meeting the right person and deciding to spend the rest of your life with them had very little to do with them being that elusive *one* for you and instead was simply an indication that you'd reached the point in your life where things like marriage and babies seem remotely less terrifying, while dying alone looms scarily on the horizon. I used to think it was just a matter of chance — whichever girl a man happens to be dating at the time that switch from playboy to potential husband flips, winds up being his wife.

And, hey, maybe that's partly true. But mostly, I don't think it's a matter of finding someone else; I think it's a matter of finding yourself.

People are always waiting around for that magical person who'll walk into their life and fix them, who'll offer up some vital piece they've been missing and make them complete. They spend years trying to fit their broken edges against another person's and call themselves *whole* and *healed*. The only problem with this, of course, is that expecting anyone else to fix you is an unequivocal disaster.

You can't wait for a man to come around and put you back together. You have to put yourself back together first, and become the kind of woman who deserves a good man.

You can't settle for someone; you have to strive for them — strive to be better, to do better, to love better.

Wyatt Hastings makes me a better person.

He always has, since the first moment our paths crossed. I look at him and I see a whole future, laid out before us. Once, that would've terrified me. Now, it thrills me.

The limo pulls up to the theatre and I see the red-carpet rolled out before us, so much bigger in person than it looks on a TV screen, already jam-packed with actors and industry members whose films are part of the festival. We creep forward, waiting for our turn to disembark, and I feel my eyes widen at the splendor of the gowns and the beauty of the celebrities wearing them, as they float gracefully across the sea of red.

Starstruck is an understatement.

It's nothing like what you see when watching from the comfort of your couch. It's infinitely more chaotic, the very air buzzing with a frenzied sort of rush — and we're not even out of the limo yet. I swallow down my nerves as we finally reach the drop-off point.

Grayson gets out first, his hand holding mine steady as he leads me from the car. I try to stay calm as we pose for the cameras, remembering all the tips Harper impressed on me yesterday.

Don't grimace. Don't squirm. Don't over-smile. Don't cross your legs. Don't touch your dress. Don't play with your hair. Don't adjust your shoes. Don't trip. Don't curse. Don't make eye contact with anyone for too long.

Basically, I'm not allowed to do anything except stand completely still and smile in a poised, pleasant manner.

I hover by Grayson's side, eyes sweeping the crowd. A-list celebrities litter the carpet like diamonds, intimidatingly beautiful as they pose and stride and smile for the press. Awards season is officially in full swing — the crush of press behind the velvet ropes on either side proves that beyond a shadow of a doubt.

I'm thankful for Grayson's well-practiced presence at my side as we make our way through the gauntlet. It takes me a few minutes to focus on much of anything as he steers our course, keeping me steady as camera flashes blind us. We stop to chat with three different reporters, answering questions on autopilot.

Who are you wearing?

What films are you most excited to see during the festival?

Have you heard the Oscar buzz over your performances?

They're tactful enough not to ask about the Helena situation — or, more likely, they've been threatened with legal action by AXC, should they attempt it.

The thought makes me smirk.

It takes an extraordinarily long time to traverse the carpet. We're barely halfway down the stretch when I finally spot two familiar sets of shoulders in the distance.

Sloan and Wyatt, posing together for a photograph. My gaze cut across the sea of people between us. As if he feels my stare, he glances up abruptly. Those blue eyes lock on mine, asking a question.

What are you doing, baby?

My feet move unconsciously. I hear an interviewer firing a question about my dress at me, but pay her no mind. I keep my eyes locked on Wyatt as I walk away. Smiling, he detaches from Sloan's side and meets me in the middle of the carpet. There's a swarm of people all around us, but the only one I see is him.

"Hi," I say, when we're a foot apart.

"What are you doing? Where's Dunn?" he asks, confused. "I thought we were supposed to be keeping a low profile."

"Yeah. I thought so too." I step into his space, sliding my hands over his chest, and crane my neck to look up into his face. "Then I decided that was pretty much the stupidest idea ever."

"Oh, really?" He chuckles and the sound warms me down to my toes.

"Yes, really." I stretch up and brush my lips against his, not caring about the zillion camera shutters clicking down all around us, barely hearing the collecting gasp from the crowd as they take in the sight of me kissing the man I love for all the world to see. "I love you, Wyatt. I'm not going to pretend I don't just to sell movie tickets or promote my career. I'm not going to do that for anything in the world."

He doesn't say anything. He just presses a kiss to my forehead, then laces his hand with mine and squeezes tightly.

"Plus," I tease softly. "You look super hot in that tux. I can't promise I'll be able to keep my hands off you all night..."

"Katharine."

"What?" I say innocently.

"*Behave.*"

"If only I knew how…"

He shakes his head in amusement and starts walking. Hands clasped, we make our way to the towering theatre doors. There's nothing forced about my smile anymore, as we pose for the press for picture after picture, pretending not to hear the questions they hurl at us.

What does this mean for the baby?

How long have you two been together?

With the man I love at my side, and the whole world finally aware of it, all is right in my universe.

Katharine Firestone and Wyatt Hastings are indisputably, undeniably, irrevocably together.

Nothing anyone says or does tonight can burst the happy glow shining inside me like a beacon, lighting me up from the inside out.

* * *

The night is about as perfect as I could've hoped for. The first ever full screening of *Uncharted* is met with resounding applause. I sit wedged between Sloan and Wyatt, tears in my eyes as Violet and Beck's story plays out on the screen before us. It's an indescribable feeling, to be part of something so beautiful.

When the credits roll, I look at the man who owns my heart, filled with so much pride I want to burst.

"You created that," I whisper, low enough that only he can hear. "You. Your characters. Your story. Your book."

He glances at me. "And you brought it to life."

A perfect balance.

"Don't you think it's time you gave up your secrets, *Tywin*?" My eyes are teasing, but I couldn't be more serious. "Don't you want the credit you're owed? The recognition you deserve?"

"I don't need the credit. I don't need the recognition." He leans over and kisses me. "I already have everything I've ever wanted."

There are still several more movies to be screened, plus a slew of afterparties scheduled that will rage late into the night. I know I should put in an appearance, but after we make the rounds through the theatre and I'm introduced to what must be every living soul in the Screen Actors Guild, I'm starting to fade. Wyatt, ever perceptive, takes notice.

"You don't have to stay. We can go any time you want."

"No! No. I don't want to drag you away."

"I'm happy to leave with you, baby." He shrugs. "This stuff... it's all the same, after a while."

"This is your movie, Wyatt Hastings," I insist. "Enjoy your moment. Stay. I'll have Masters take me home."

His brows lift. "My home or your home?"

I go still, realizing my slip-up, and feel my cheeks get red. "*My* home. Obviously."

"Uh huh." He grins, heart-stoppingly handsome. "Admit it. You want to move in with me."

"Why would I admit something so egregiously wrong?"

"I'll wear you down."

"You can try." I tilt my head. "You know, you might persuade me quicker if you incorporated some sexual favors into your bargaining strategy..."

"Good tip. I'll consider that."

I laugh and kiss him. "Okay. I'm leaving now. A bubble bath is calling my name. If you can figure out which *home* I'm heading to, you should come join me when you're done here."

"I won't be too late." His eyes hold mine. "If you wait another twenty minutes, I'll come with you. I shouldn't leave until Sloan introduces me to one of the foreign distributors. He's just gone to track him down..."

"No rush. The bubbles will wait." I wink goodbye at him, then turn to find Masters. He and Harper aren't far — I spot them hovering by the wall on the other side of the theatre. He looks thoroughly bored; she looks utterly captivated.

"Hey," I call, approaching.

Harper's excited eyes meet mine. She looks stunning

— her hair is back to blue-black, a stunning contrast to her ivory gown. "This is *incredible*. The makeup! The jewelry! The dresses!" She sighs dreamily. "Seriously. I'm never leaving."

"That's inconvenient..." My lips twist. "I was about to ask Masters to drive me home."

"We haven't even hit an after party yet!"

"I know. I'm just exhausted. This much activity after two weeks of house arrest... It's a little overwhelming." I stare pointedly at the champagne flowing freely around us, as waiters carry trays through the crowd. "Plus, I can't drink. Perks of the pregnancy. And as fun as it is to stand around, completely sober, while everyone else gets toasted... I think I'd prefer a long soak in a bubble bath with a good book."

Harper sighs. "You're a wet blanket, you know that?"

"Fully aware."

"Good. So long as you recognize it." She looks around wistfully. "This is pretty amazing, though. Even you have to admit that much."

I nod. "You know, you don't have to come with me. You can stay — in fact, you *should* stay. Grab a ride home with Wyatt. He's not leaving yet."

She squeals, eyes wide. "Really?"

"Really."

She turns to Masters. "You don't mind if I stay a bit longer, do you honey?"

"Let's see..." His eyes glitter as he tugs at the collar of his tuxedo. "I get to escape early and take off this penguin suit you forced me to wear, while you stay here and wear yourself out talking about dresses and fashion, so later you're happy and complacent when you crawl into bed with me?" He practically grins. "Yeah, babe. Safe to say I don't mind."

She glares at him. "You're a jerk."

"You love me."

"Stop saying things like that!" she hisses. "It's way too soon!"

244

He shrugs. "Nah."

"Impossible man." She throws up her hands.

"Love you too, babe."

She screams again as he presses a kiss to her temple. "Again — *way too soon,* you lunatic!"

Masters ignores her.

"I'll get the car," he tells me, just before he turns and stalks away.

As soon as he's out of sight, my best friend glances at me desperately. "If I didn't love him so much, I'd hate him."

I grin. "Good thing you love him, then."

"He's going to be the death of me, I swear to god."

"But you'll die happy," I point out.

"Try to talk some sense into him on the ride home, will you? Tell him to stop moving at light speed. There's no rush." She shakes her head. "We have all the time in the world."

I don't think about her words, as I kiss her goodbye and make my way to the exits.

That's the thing about real life, as opposed to the movies.

The bad omens are never obvious until it's far, far too late.

CHAPTER FOURTEEN

"ONCE MORE, WITH FEELING."
- A lover hoping for better results the second time around.

We're halfway to Wyatt's, the SUV winding its way through the curving hills that look out over Los Angeles. It's dark and damp outside — a rare rainstorm has settled over the valley in the past few hours. The roads are clear; the late hour and miserable weather are keeping most people indoors. I stretch out my legs across the vacant backseat, exhausted down to my bones. Masters meets my eyes in the rearview.

"Tired, Miss Firestone?"

"Exhausted."

"It's been a long day."

I snort. "It's been a long day, long week, long month. I'm about ready for this movie premiere stuff to be over. Frankly, I'd be happy to step away from all this fame for a bit, after *Uncharted* comes out."

"Don't think that's an option." His voice is wry. "You can't just turn off the attention like a switch. Comes with the territory, unfortunately."

"You know, it's funny — when I was younger, I'd have given almost anything to have people know my name. To be recognized for something. To be notable. Famous. Popular." I laugh. "Now, I'm starting to realize there are downsides to having everyone on the planet know your name."

"Grass is always greener," he murmurs.

246

"Exactly." I sigh. "I think I'd rather have a boring life with a handful of people who matter than all the acclaim in the world from nameless strangers."

"Hate to break it to you, but I think you've got both." He winks at me.

I grin and glance back out my window.

Far below us, the city lights shine brighter than stars, sprawled out like a glittering constellation. I've got a smile on my face as I stare out, watching water droplets track slowly down the glass, thinking of the look on Wyatt's face when he walks into his bathroom and finds me naked in his bathtub.

The perfect end to a perfect evening.

It starts as a dull roar in the distance, but soon grows louder. I see Masters look up sharply, his eyes on the rearview. I turn around in my seat and see the single headlight of a motorcycle appear around the bend behind us, racing closer with each passing second. His helmet and backpack come into view, and I know this is no average rider.

"Not again," I mutter, annoyed. "Why won't they leave me the hell alone?"

Masters puts pressure on the gas pedal, increasing our speed, but the paparazzo keeps pace with us. The roaring sound increases in pitch. I turn around to look again and blink hard, barely believing my eyes when two more spotlights appear in the darkness. They zip down the straightaway to join the biker already on our tail.

I scoff, disgusted at the show of utter stupidity — three mounted paparazzi, racing each other for the money shot, all equally determined to get the exclusive photo of Kat Firestone after a night on the town. They change lanes at will in a deadly game of chicken, swerving wildly, speeding faster. Each trying to intimidate the others into a forfeit.

"Idiots," Masters growls, his eyes flipping between the dueling motorcycles in his rearview and the winding road ahead. The steering wheel jerks roughly in his hands as he brings us around a particularly sharp bend in the road. I feel my stomach lurch into my throat. My seatbelt strap cuts into my chest, holding me in place.

The bikers follow us around the curve, their speed increasing all the while. My heart begins to pound as I watch them getting closer and closer to our back bumper.

Masters blows the car horn in warning — a long, angry note that pierces the rainy night.

Heedless, they keep coming, so close the entire SUV is filled with light from their zig-zagging high-beams. Relentless in their pursuit. Pushing us — *faster, faster, faster* — until we're careening around the bends at breakneck speed.

With wide eyes, I watch the fat water droplets on my window slither away like translucent snakes. I hardly hear Masters yell over the pounding of my own pulse between my ears.

I can't pinpoint the exact moment we switch over from driving to hydroplaning, our momentum too great to rein in. I can't determine the specific sliver of time the SUV slips out of Masters' control and sails toward the guard rail, instead of turning round the next bend. I can't calculate the precise instant our tires leave the slippery road and spin uselessly against air instead of earth.

I just know that it happens.

There's a horrible wrenching sound, metal against metal, as we tear through the highway divider like it's made of foil. And then there's nothing — no sound, no light. Nothing but the sheer, paralyzing terror of free-fall as we plummet down an embankment, into utter darkness.

* * *

When I come to, the first thing I feel is the rain, which I think must be a mistake.

How can I feel the rain if I'm still inside the car?

My eyes flicker open and I see the whole world has gone sideways. It takes me a minute to realize that's because the SUV is lying on its left flank, wheels spinning uselessly in the air, sides crunched in like a beer can in the hands of a fraternity brother.

I blink at the back of the passenger seat headrest in front of me, feeling dazed. I'm suspended in the air, limbs dangling, my body held in place by the seatbelt against my chest. I feel another raindrop hit my cheek and turn my head to the right, up to the sky. I see the window above me shattered on impact. Rain falls freely through the open panel.

Something trickles down my temple. I reach up to wipe it, expecting water, but my fingers come away covered in bright red blood.

It matches my dress, I think ludicrously.

A distant part of my brain suggests I might be in shock, but it's hard to focus on much of anything with the dense cloud of panic obscuring my thoughts.

A moan of pain snaps me back into reality.

Masters.

I lift my head to look for him, but there's no one in the front seat. All I see are the deployed airbags, already half-deflated, and a gaping hole in the windshield, the remaining glass splintered and stained with red.

The moan pierces the air again. I realize it's not coming from inside the car. My head empties of all thoughts except one.

I have to get to him.

My hands shake as they move to my seatbelt buckle. If my head wasn't so dazed, perhaps I would've thought through the logistics of my extraction a bit better; as it is, I simply press the release button and drop like a stone, without even throwing out my arms to catch myself. I hit the ground with a painful thud, landing in a pile of shattered glass and twisted metal.

I push aside the agony that wrenches through my jarred wrist and ankle bones. There is no time to dwell on useless things like pain right now. I start to crawl, dragging my body over the center console, lowering myself into the ripped remains of the driver's seat.

249

I am graceless, gasping; I gulp for air and grasp
for purchase against the leather dashboard as I haul my
frame over the steering wheel, through the jagged hole in
the windshield. I spare no time trying to avoid the sharp
glass shards as I worm my way out. They tear at my bare
arms, catch on the long train of my dress, gouge deeply
into my skin as I crawl from the wreckage on my knees
and elbows.

My dress snags on a twisted bit of metal. I tug and
kick and tug still harder, until it gives with a sudden rip
that sends me sprawling out onto the earth in a final
aching jolt. My hands hit the damp earth, steady rivulets
of my blood mixing with mud as I pull a breath into my
screaming lungs.

The moan comes again, fainter despite the fact that
I'm closer to him.

I lift my head, searching the night, and spot him
ten feet away, lying on the ground, illuminated by the
headlights. I don't think I can stand, so I drag myself to
him. My own pain pales into a distant ache as I look down
at my friend, lying broken in the dirt.

The first thing I ever noticed about Masters was his
size. He's a big man. A strong man. All muscle and brawn
and brute strength. And yet, he seems so incredibly small
as I look into his face, wiping blood and dirt and rain
from his skin as best I can. His eyes are pale blue slivers,
watching me.

"Kent, *Kent*, oh my god," I whisper in a voice I don't
even recognize as my own. "Don't worry, I'm here. I'm
here. You're going to be okay. Tell me where — tell me
what to do. Tell me how to help."

I look for the source of the bleeding, but he's
bleeding *everywhere* — from his nose, from his ears, from
his mouth. His head, his abdomen, his legs. He tries to
speak and I see his white teeth are stained red.

"No use," he gasps out, chest shuddering with
the effort. Like there's a boulder pressing down on him,
growing heavier with each breath.

"What? *No.* No, don't you dare say that," I snap, crying as my hands move over his stomach, trying to staunch the flow of blood with my fingertips — a river of blood, an ocean of blood, an unstoppable tide my ineffectual hands can do nothing to yield. "You're fine. You're going to be just fine."

My desperate lies don't convince him.

"Kat," he says — the first time he's ever used my name, and it sounds like a prayer on his lips. "Kat—"

I bite through my lip so I won't scream.

Keeping one hand on the worst of his wounds, the big one in his abdomen where glass and metal ripped through him like a knife through a block of cheese, I reach into his pocket and pull out his cellphone. My fingers are so wet with blood, it takes a few tries before the screen recognizes my keystrokes. I push the emergency button and wait for the call to connect, cursing each passing second.

"911, what is your emergency?"

"There's been an accident," I yell into the receiver. "Please, you have to come, straightaway!"

"What is your location, ma'am?" The disembodied voice is so composed I want to reach through the line and strangle the woman it belongs to.

Doesn't she realize how bad this is?

Doesn't she know my friend is dying?

I do my best to give a description of our location, slightly relieved when she informs me another motorist already called it in.

"Emergency personnel should reach you within five minutes."

Five minutes.

An eternity.

Too long, too long, too long.

My heart is splintering inside my chest.

"We're down the embankment. My friend — he's hurt. You have to come. Please come... he's... I think... I think he might be..." I shake myself.

"Please, just get here!"

Masters wheezes in pain.

I drop the phone into the dirt and move both my hands back to the gaping wound, applying pressure as best I can. I pull my soaked dress train up and try to use it as a compress; his blood saturates the fabric so fast there's little point.

"Don't worry," I lie to him, trying to sound positive despite the tears coursing from my eyes, falling onto his face, mixing with the steady flow of raindrops from the sky. "They're coming, Kent. They're coming."

His eyes meet mine again, hazy with pain.

"Tell her..." He coughs, blood flying from his lips, spraying against my face as I lean close to catch his words. "Tell her..."

I grab his hand and squeeze it as tight as I can. "Tell her yourself, when you see her later."

A sound rattles in his throat.

A sound like death.

A second later, I watch his eyes lose focus, the life draining out of them as the blood drains from his body into the earth. His face goes slack. His chest stops moving up and down in labored breaths.

"No!" My voice breaks on a scream. "Don't you dare leave, Kent Masters. You hang on. Do you hear me? You just hang on for a few more minutes. Just hang on, and everything will be okay."

But it's not okay.

He can't hang on.

He's already gone.

* * *

The rain falls, but I don't feel it.

The flashing lights arrive, but I don't see them.

The paramedics scramble down to us, shouting questions, but I don't hear them.

I am numb.

I stare unseeing at the body of my friend. There are twin streaks of red on his eyelids from where my bloody fingers closed his vacant eyes, unable to bear looking at them anymore. Unable to see them staring lifelessly at the sky.

The first responders pull me to my feet and shine a light into my pupils. Their words make no sense. They are unrecognizable. Another language, another place.

Their nonsensical syllables belong to a world that still makes sense. A world where good men don't die for no reason and your best friend gets to live happily ever after with the man she loves.

A world I no longer exist in.

A paramedic is examining the wound on my head, mouthing words at me. I watch his lips, their funny shapes forming vowels and consonants, articulating and annunciating. Like a game you play in the pool on a hot summer day, shouting at your friends beneath the surface, trying to get them to guess your meaning. If you're lucky, you might catch one word out of a dozen.

"He's DOA... in shock... possible head trauma... contusions... glass... stretcher..."

They move Masters' body onto a stiff board and carry him up the embankment, to the waiting vehicle. I start to trail after them, my strappy heels sinking into the mud with each step, now that I'm on my feet. I quickly find my progress halted by a steely grip.

"Ma'am, can you hear me?"

Sluggishly, I glance at him — the brave paramedic. He's young. My age, maybe. Twenty-two and invincible. A whole life ahead of us.

There's no rush, Harper's voice says inside my head. *We have all the time in the world.*

A sound slips from my lips. A hysterical, horrible sound I cannot contain. Not a laugh, not a sob, not a scream. Some terrible mix of all three.

"Ma'am, I need you to sit, okay? They're bringing down a stretcher for you. Can you sit? I promise, it's all going to be okay."

My throat closes abruptly, cutting off the noise in an instant. I blink at him.

"He's dead."

My voice is empty.

My heart is shattered.

"Masters. He's dead."

The paramedic nods. "I'm very sorry for your loss, ma'am, but right now we need to take care of you. You might have a concussion and you're bleeding pretty profusely."

"I am?" I ask, looking down at myself. In the light of the SUV high-beams, I see the pretty coral shade of my dress is drenched darker red down the front and along the hem.

"That's not my blood," I murmur, feeling light headed. Suddenly, sitting down doesn't seem like such a bad idea. "It's not my blood," I repeat softly, as he lowers me to the ground.

"Where the hell is that stretcher?" the paramedic yells up the embankment. "She's fading!"

I hear a ripping sound and look down to see the young medic has sliced my dress wide open with a pair of razor-sharp shears. He's feeling my legs, running his hands up and down my flesh, muttering to himself.

"Where is all this damn blood coming from?"

And then... *I know.*

"I—" I start, but can't get the words out. "I think—"

He looks up at me, concern etched on his features. His face alternates red then blue then yellow as the world flips between the steady SUV headlights and flashing ambulance strobes.

"I think..." I look up at the sky and say the words to the stars, so I don't have to see the look in his eyes. My voice is a broken whisper. "I think I'm having a miscarriage."

The stars swim for a moment, fuzzy and unfocused, and then everything goes totally black.

* * *

I float in the darkness. It's not entirely unpleasant.
No more pain. No more sorrow.
Maybe I should stay here.

"Female crash victim, approximately twenty years old, lost consciousness in the field!"

I was always meant for the shadows, anyway. Some people say I gravitate toward them, but I think they have it backwards: the shadows have always gravitated toward me.

"Multiple contusions to her arms, legs, and temple. Pupils are equal and reactive to light."

There's something soothing about the dark. People let their secrets out, in the small hours of the night. Their masks come off. Their guards come down.

"We've got a pulse, but it's irregular."

You can be totally yourself in the witching hours; maybe because there's no one else awake to judge you.

"She's losing pressure."

I am a creature of shadows. Some people like *the dark; I'm* made *of the dark. The dark is in my blood, in each beat of my heart. So it's not totally disturbing to find myself adrift here, detached from the flashing lights and screaming sirens and creeping absence of a friend I was not prepared to say goodbye to yet.*

"She's lost at least a liter of blood. Possible miscarriage. Get someone from OB down here."

Yes. Maybe I will stay here. Maybe it's where I belong.

"She's in v-tach! Get the crash cart!"

The light is too hard. Too harsh. Too bright.

"Code blue!"

Bringing all your flaws sharply into focus.

"We're losing her!"

You cannot hide, in the light. Not from pain or sorrow or loss or despair.

"Push one of epi and atropine!"

Why would you choose to feel any of that? Why would you pick blinding pain when you could float in the dark forever?

"Charge to two hundred!"

The dark is comforting. Swaying. Lulling.

"CLEAR!"

A flash. A flicker. A strike of lighting, in the darkness.

"Push another epi!"

There's something I'm forgetting. A fragment of a memory at the corner of my mind, on the tip of my tongue, just out of reach.

"Charge to three hundred!"

Choose sunshine, baby. Always choose sunshine. You look so much prettier with the light in your eyes.

"CLEAR!"

Wyatt. Wyatt. Wyatt.

"Again!"

I grasp onto the thought. A faint touch of dawn in the night sky. A flickering candle, guiding me back.

"We've got sinus rhythm. Pressure is returning."

The sun is rising.

"We got her back, barely. Let's get her to the OR, stat. She's still got a long fight ahead of her tonight."

* * *

When I was ten years old, I borrowed a tattered copy of *Gone with the Wind* from the library after school one day. I didn't want to — the librarian thrust it into my unwilling hands when I discovered the latest volume of *The Babysitters Club* had already been checked out by brown-nosing Susie Lowell and wouldn't be returned for fourteen insufferable days.

I fully expected to hate every word of the dog-eared volume, which felt thicker than the dictionary in my hands. I remember walking home, backpack near to bursting, zipper straining under the effort, vowing not even to crack it open. Surely nothing so long-winded and old-fashioned could be of interest to my barely-formed brain.

And yet...

I opened it.

I flew through the pages until my eyes were shot with red, until my lids were drooping closed, until the flashlight clutched in my fingertips ran out of batteries and I was forced to close the cover and fall asleep, otherwise risk waking Cynthia and whichever husband she was married to at that point.

For the next week, I lived between those pages. Every spare minute. I couldn't put it down. I was captivated. I'd never read a story like that in my life. Up till then, it had all been perfect heroines and infallible princes. The villains never won. Good always prevailed over evil, no matter what.

Not in that book, though.

War and deceit and betrayal and agony saturated those pages. There were no clear-cut lines, no perfect characters. Just a flawed heroine who does what she can to survive, whatever the cost. A woman who spends half her life in love with the wrong man, too stubborn and self-destructive to recognize her own folly until it's far, far too late to rectify things.

I cried, when I finished — big, miserable, crocodile tears. And the next day, I marched that stupid, horrible, awful book straight back to the library, shoved it into the amused librarian's hands, and demanded answers.

Where's the next one?

She said there was no *next one*. I'd reached the end.

I tried reasoning with her.

Surely, the story cannot end like that. Surely, Scarlett finds her way back to Rhett. Surely, the author did not mean for me to live the rest of my life hanging by my fingertips on the edge of a cliff, wondering what happened to characters I've come to love so deeply.

I glared at the librarian when she shook her head no.

I didn't understand. I thought, frankly my dear, the author *must* give a damn. She must write a better ending. A happy ending, where all the characters get the things they deserve. Otherwise, what was the point of reading the dumb book in the first place?

The librarian laughed and said it was good practice.

For what? I hissed, full of piss and vinegar.

For life, she said, handing me the Babysitter's Club book that I no longer had a lick of interest in.

I never read Gone with the Wind again.

But I never forgot the lesson it taught me.

Not all stories have happy endings.

Sometimes, the villains win.

Sometimes, the heroes die.

Sometimes, life breaks your fucking heart into so many pieces, you think you'll never be whole again.

But you carry on.

You push through.

You keep trying.

Because life is all one big, endless cliffhanger — riddled with uncertainties and inconsistencies, each page suffused with complex characters and heart-aching plot twists that take your breath away. There's nothing you can do to change that.

All you can do is choose the sunshine instead of the shadows. All you can do is hang onto the knowledge that no matter how dark the night, the sun always rises in the morning and chases away the doom.

Because... no matter what.... tomorrow is another goddamned day.

CHAPTER FIFTEEN

"**You can trust me.**"
- *A super-villain.*

"Baby, what the hell do you think you're doing?"

"Carrying in the kitchen stuff." I roll my eyes. "What the hell does it look like I'm doing?"

"I hired movers for a reason." Wyatt scowls at me, crosses the room, and yanks the box from my grip. "To *move* things."

I cross my arms and glare at him. "Bossy."

He grins. "Beautiful."

"Stubborn man."

"Stunning girl."

"It was one tiny box. Did you not hear me say *kitchen stuff*?" I snort. "We both know I don't cook. All that's in there is an ancient garlic press and stale box of Girl Scout cookies from my pantry."

"Not the point," he grumbles, pulling me into his arms. "We aren't taking any more chances."

I tilt my head up to look at him, scrunching my nose but deciding not to argue.

He kisses me fleetingly, then crouches down, puts both his hands on my stomach, and plants another kiss there. My fingers slip into his long hair, stroking absently.

"Hear that, watermelon?" he whispers. "*No more chances.*"

A smile touches my lips. I've grown so massive in the past few months, my stomach now protrudes out over my jeans, bigger than a basketball.

"I'm huge," I complain, frequently.

"You're beautiful," Wyatt counters, always.

The doctors told us it was a miracle I didn't lose the baby, the night Masters died. The stress of the crash coupled with my other injuries and a partially-ruptured placenta meant there was something like a ninety-five percent chance of termination when I finally arrived at the hospital and was rushed into surgery.

I was the five percent.

The miracle case.

Recovery from my physical injuries — a concussion, two sprained wrists, severe bruising, and lacerations over twenty percent of my body, many of which needed stitches — took a long time.

Recovery from my emotional injuries — well, we'll call it a work in progress.

Every morning, I wake in Wyatt's arms. I watch the sun rise from the gazebo in his yard as I drink a cup of decaf coffee and re-read his book for the hundredth time. The new version, republished with his honest-to-god name on the front, not my tattered old paperback.

Every morning, I ask myself the same question.

Can I survive this pain?

And, every morning, the answer is the same.

I can survive.

I will survive.

Because I am not the sad, broken girl who swooned despite her better judgment for a man who warned her against it. I am not the twisted creature, consumed by self-doubt and delusions of soul mates, who let an incapable man lead her astray. I am not the girl seeking the validation of a woman who refused to relinquish it. I am not the struggling actress, begging for roles I don't want.

I have been to hell and back, but I am stronger now. Forged by fires of my own making into steel and self-determination. Loved by a man who is made of light and hope and happiness. And, finally, able to love him back with every part of me, even the dark parts I feared, for so many years, to expose to the light.

"Go inside, please." Wyatt kisses the tip of my nose gently. "You're supposed to be resting."

"I'm *supposed* to be a lot of things," I remind him. "In labor, for one."

"You can't rush perfection." He touches my stomach again. "Don't you know by now, tiny dictators make their own rules?"

"Yeah, yeah, yeah," I grumble, grinning at him despite myself.

It feels strange sometimes, to be so full of life and joy and love, after what happened to Masters. After what happened with Harper.

The grin slides off my face.

I miss my best friend so much, sometimes, it levels me. I'm haunted by the last words I spoke to her.

"He wanted me to tell you that he loved you. He loved you so much, Harper."

I'm equally haunted by the words she spoke back to me.

"You made him leave early. You did this. You... You killed him."

Wyatt says she didn't mean it. That it was the grief, talking.

I try to believe him. Try to tell myself she doesn't hate me for taking away the man she loved, while I have everything I've ever wanted out of life.

...Except, of course, my best friend.

I haven't seen her in months. Not since she packed up her car and drove home to Iowa. I can't say I blame her. The heartbreak of being here, without him... it was too much to handle. Still, each time I reach a landmark moment in my life, I automatically look around for her, thinking she should be by my side. Thinking none of it really means anything at all, without her with me.

She may hate me, now, but that doesn't change anything. I want her back. I want her here. The more that happens in my life, the stronger the feeling gets.

So much has already changed, in the months since she left.

Getting released from the hospital.

The *Uncharted* premiere.

Wyatt re-publishing his book without the pseudonym.

Unofficially moving in with him.

And now, as of today... *officially* moving in with him.

Truth be told, I've been living here for months. I never went back home, after they discharged me from the hospital. Not really. Wyatt insisted on taking care of me, and I wasn't in any position to argue with him, with a bruised body and a broken spirit.

My Viking.

Strong enough for both of us.

Holding me together with his bare hands.

He brought me back, day by day, piece by piece, until I remembered the good things in the world. The smell of spring in the air, the taste of fresh blackberries on your tongue, the simple joy of a summer sunset, the feeling of strong arms around you.

I never would've survived, if not for him. And... I never want to be parted from him again. Not ever. Not even for a moment. I know now, better than anyone, that life is far too short to waste time when it comes to the people you love most.

So, I put my house in the Palisades on the market and I put my belongings into boxes. My favorite foods are stocked in his fridge. My toothbrush sits on his bathroom sink. My books are scattered on every surface of his meticulously organized study, driving him to distraction. And there is a beautifully decorated nursery down the hall from our bedroom, painted a gender-neutral shade of yellow.

Sunshine yellow.

I walk into the kitchen and pick up my phone to call Harper, like I do every single day around this time. She never answers, but I always leave a message anyway. I figure she must check them, because her mailbox is never full when I call.

I never say anything exceedingly important. Mostly, I tell her about my day. Stupid stuff — the things we used to laugh about over sushi and cocktails, a million years ago.

The phone rings twice, then kicks over to voicemail.

"Hey, Harper. It's me. Kat. Your stalker." I walk to the fridge, seeking a snack, and bend to pull an apple from the fruit drawer. "Not much happening here. The movers dropped off all the boxes today, so I guess this means I'm officially moved in. Wyatt's being insufferable, as usual, bossing me around about how carrying *one little box* is going to send me into labor." I munch a bite of the apple, shaking my head. "Which is totally ridiculous. I mean, I'm *fine* and—"

Something splashes against my shoes.

I look down and feel my eyes widen.

"Harper," I whisper into the phone. "I'm actually going to have to call you back." I set the apple on the counter with a dull thud. "Don't tell Wyatt I said this, but he may have been right about the boxes. Because... well, I'm pretty sure my water just broke."

I hang up the phone and stare at my soaked shoes. *Dammit.*

He's going to be absolutely unbearable, after this.

* * *

"She's perfect."

I nod, not taking my eyes off our daughter. She's got a cap of bronze hair and eyes like the bluest sky. I knew, the first moment I saw her, that she was Wyatt's. Not that it matters much — he would've loved her the same, regardless.

We've been standing over the crib, staring at her like lovesick idiots since we brought her home this morning. Neither of us can stop examining her tiny fingernails, leaning in to catch her every cooing noise. I'd actually be disgusted by our obsession, if I had any space at all in my heart for emotions besides pure joy.

The doorbell rings and we glance at each other, wondering who the hell is at our door at this hour.

"I'll get it." Wyatt kisses me on the cheek. "You stay here. If she does anything exciting, take a video."

I laugh, but don't argue with him. I don't even have the energy for a snappy comeback. Every bone in my body is so exhausted, I'd like nothing more than to sleep for the next hundred years. But, since I cannot seem to tear my eyes away from my daughter, sleep is going to have to wait.

Her tiny fingers are wrapped around my pointer when I hear Wyatt come back into the nursery. When I look up to ask who was at the door, I see he's not alone. My eyes fill with tears.

Her hair is a nondescript shade of mousey brown. If I had to guess, I'd say it's the hue she was born with, not an ounce of dye coloring the strands. Her face is completely free of makeup. She's thinner by about ten pounds and there are deep shadows etched beneath her eyes.

But she's here.

"You came." My voice cracks. "You're here."

"Of course I'm here," she says with a shadow of her old vitality. "That's my goddaughter. What kind of godmother would I be, if I didn't show up?"

Tears are filling my eyes, slowly tracking down my face as I stare at my best friend.

She stares back at me, her own eyes wet with unshed tears.

"Sorry," I say stupidly. "Postpartum hormones are no joke. I've been crying about everything, today."

264

She nods, attempting a smile. "Weepy cow."

"Emotionless mule," I whisper, crying harder.

Her smile widens a hair.

"Do you…" I take a breath, trying to get myself under control. "Do you want to hold her?"

"Yes, I— *Yes*." Harper crosses the room in slow strides.

I lift the infant and gently place her into Harper's arms. Wyatt steps up to the other side of the crib, so the three of us are flanking the newborn on all sides. A circle of love, surrounding this little life.

I stare from the man I adore to my best friend to my tiny dictator, and am filled with such irrepressible lightness, such indescribable love, I think I might burst from it.

"What's her name?" Harper asks after a while, looking up at me.

I hold her stare for a long time before I answer.

"Kent. Her name is Kent."

THE END

ACKNOWLEDGMENTS

Words are strange.

There never seem to be enough of them. At least, not when it comes to thanking you, my readers, for changing my life.

I am so unbelievably fortunate to wake up every morning and (after consuming at least two cups of coffee) spend my days doing the thing I love most — creating characters. Quirky, damaged, crazy, compelling, lovable, hatable, awful, wonderful characters.

Writing fiction truly is the job of my dreams.

Thank you for making it my reality. Thank you for leaving reviews. Thank you for telling your friends. Thank you for coming to signings. Thank you for making teasers and trailers. Thank you for your blog posts and personal messages that touch my heart. Thank you for all the little things you do to make my days brighter.

They do not go unnoticed.

I appreciate them more than words can ever express.

To my friends and family — I realize it's not easy being friends with a writer. We're mercurial, over-caffeinated, opinionated monsters. Thanks for putting up with me anyway.

To the girls of my reader group, the *Johnson Junkies* — you ladies always keep me smiling, even on the tough days! Thank you for your enthusiasm, your support, and your kindness.

To my dog Scout — you might not be Instagram-famous, but you're famous to me. I love you. Who's a good boy? (You are.)

Lastly, to **Katharine Motherfucking Firestone** — I know you're a figment of my imagination. Thank you anyway. Thank you for teaching me that it's okay to reinvent yourself. That it's all right to grow. That it's not the end, even when a boy burns you down to your most basic elements... so long as you rise, brush off the cinders, and fly into the future, a better, stronger, happier version of yourself.

* * *

I AM A GIRL OF ASHES AND EMBERS.
AND NOW... I WILL RISE.
A PHOENIX, REBORN INTO SOMETHING BETTER.
PERHAPS A LITTLE SADDER, BUT DEFINITELY A LOT STRONGER.

KAT FIRESTONE, *THE SOMEDAY GIRL*

ABOUT THE AUTHOR

JULIE JOHNSON is a twenty-something Boston native suffering from an extreme case of Peter Pan Syndrome. When she's not writing, Julie can most often be found adding stamps to her passport, drinking too much coffee, striving to conquer her Netflix queue, and Instagramming pictures of her dog. (Follow her: @authorjuliejohnson)

She published her debut novel LIKE GRAVITY in 2013, just before her senior year of college, and she's never looked back. Since, she has published six more novels, including the bestselling BOSTON LOVE STORY series. Her books have appeared on Kindle, B&N, and iTunes Bestseller lists around the world, as well as in AdWeek, Publishers Weekly, and USA Today.

Julie graduated cum laude from the University of Delaware in December 2013, one semester ahead of schedule, with two B.A. Honor's Degrees in Psychology and Mass Communications. She now hopes to put off the real world for as long as possible by writing full-time.

You can find Julie on Facebook, follow her on Instagram, or contact her by email at juliejohnsonbooks@gmail.com. Sometimes, when she can figure out how Twitter works, she tweets from @AuthorJulie.

For news and updates, be sure to subscribe to Julie's newsletter: http://eepurl.com/bnWtHH

269

ALSO BY JULIE JOHNSON

STANDALONE NOVELS:

LIKE GRAVITY
SAY THE WORD
ERASING FAITH

THE BOSTON LOVE STORIES:

NOT YOU IT'S ME
CROSS THE LINE
ONE GOOD REASON

THE GIRL DUET:

THE MONDAY GIRL
THE SOMEDAY GIRL

Made in the USA
San Bernardino, CA
14 February 2017